the playboy's proposal

a Sorensen Family novel

ASHLEE
MALLORY

Entangled Publishing, LLC
2614 South Timberline Road
Suite 109
Fort Collins, CO 80525
Visit our website at www.entangledpublishing.com.

Bliss is an imprint of Entangled Publishing, LLC. For more information on our titles, visit http://www.entangledpublishing.com/category/bliss

Edited by Alycia Tornetta
Cover design by Brittany Marczak
Cover art from Shutterstock and iStock

Manufactured in the United States of America

First Edition July 2016

Bliss
an Entangled imprint

To my own siblings: Jen, Piper, and Zach.
My lifelong supporters and tormentors.

Chapter One

The music's never-ending thrumming surrounded her. There was no escape, despite the bright pink plugs stuffed in her ears or the mountain of pillows stacked on her head. Her whole bed was now vibrating in sync to what sounded like Ariana Grande's latest release.

Unbelievable.

Benny Sorensen cracked her eyes open to stare at the clock on her nightstand. It was after one in the freaking morning.

That's it. This impossible, selfish cretin had to be stopped.

Red-hot rage surged through her as she tossed off the covers. It wasn't enough that she'd come home tonight to find someone had parked in her one designated parking spot, but then to have to park almost a block down the street thanks to the dozens of extra cars taking up the rest of the parking spaces in the visitor lot added insult to injury.

All because one extraordinarily selfish resident decided to throw a party. One of *four* in the past three weeks since she'd moved in.

She shoved her feet into the green dinosaur-foot slippers her nieces and nephew had given for her last birthday and stomped to the door as a new song began. Seriously?

Moving to this high-rise condo with the secured underground parking was supposed to have been a step up from her squalid little apartment with roaches and meth heads as neighbors. It was her reward for finishing her residency and getting the plum practitioner spot that had opened up at a prestigious pediatric clinic ten minutes from here.

Only Mr. Animal House from next door was determined to make what was supposed to be her sanctuary more like a sanitarium. She hadn't even met him, and she was already certain that there could not be a more selfish human being.

The sound intensified in the hallway as she strode furiously down it, stopping in front of the door before pounding. She waited, counting the seconds until she could lay into the guy.

Nothing.

She rang the doorbell three times, hoping to penetrate the unceasing sounds from inside.

Still no response.

Apparently they were all too busy doing God knew what to hear a simple doorbell. No matter. It wouldn't stop her if she had to rip the speakers from the walls with her own hands.

She tested the doorknob. Unlocked.

She pushed the door open, a little at first, almost afraid to look inside. The lighting was low compared to the glaring light in the hall, and it took a moment for her eyes to adjust. There were easily thirty people crammed inside. Didn't they have jobs? It was Monday night, for crying out loud.

No one seemed to notice her, even after she threw open the door and stood there for a good long minute taking it all in. The place was twice the size of her own modest one-bedroom unit, which she'd fallen in love with after her first look at the jaw-dropping view from the windows, the gleaming wooden floors, and the high-end appliances.

Her neighbor had the same wooded floors and appliances, and undoubtedly the same view, but that's where the similarities ended. Her place was cozy and classic and warm, while his was modern and sleek and opulent. His television alone was easily three times the size of hers…and the grand piano in the corner? Nothing short of pretentious. But what had she expected? The guy drove a flashy red Ferrari.

She shut the door behind her, hoping the sound would draw the owner's attention to the fact that he had a new guest.

Nothing.

Fine. If her neighbor wasn't going to be a courteous host and greet his new guest, then she was going to have to track him down herself. Even if she had only a vague recollection of his profile from the glimpse she caught last week when he whizzed by her in the parking garage in his Ferrari. If she had any doubt, she supposed she could just look for the guy with the horns and cloven feet.

Benny zeroed in on every face, every voice, trying to determine who was her target. A few people finally noticed her, if the widening of their eyes and the slight grins that crossed their faces before they diverted their gazes were any indication. She'd bet the ratio of women to men was close to three to one. Although "women" didn't quite describe the beautiful creatures flitting around in short dresses and cleavage cut down to there. "Goddesses" or "supermodels" might be more appropriate. Maybe he was running a high-end escort service. What else could explain the number of frogs to princesses in this place?

Over by the windows was a guy in his midthirties with short, dark blond hair, a sculpted, cleanly shaven jaw, and a harem of women hanging on his every word.

Yeah, that was definitely him.

She headed directly toward her neighbor, her rage from

earlier incensed at his entirely overconfident posture—and the amused smile that played on his lips when his brown eyes settled on her.

"Are you Henry Ellison?" Benny demanded, stopping in front of him.

"Yes," he said, looking her over, from the top of her hair to the slippers on her feet, before meeting her gaze. "I'm afraid you have me at a disadvantage, though."

Of course he wouldn't have bothered to learn her name. Although to be fair, the only reason she knew his was because she'd already had three other residents—female residents— ask her what it was like living next door to *the* Henry Ellison. A quick Google search had shown her all she needed to know about her new neighbor. The man was trouble. A rich, entitled playboy who had more press covering his escapades than Justin Bieber. Okay, maybe not more, but close enough.

"Benny Sorensen. Your next-door neighbor, who, for the past couple of hours, has been trying to sleep despite the insanely loud music pouring from *your* unit," she snapped. "Do you have any idea what time it is?"

"Sorry, I'm afraid I'm still a little jet-lagged. Just arrived from Paris this morning." He looked at his watch. "Or I should say last night. But I'm guessing you didn't drag yourself out of bed to come and ask me the time."

She gritted her teeth. He knew why she was here. But he seemed to enjoy toying with her. Something she might find amusing in the light of day, but when she had to be up in less than five hours, it only served to seriously piss her off.

Flying off the handle, however, would only serve to amuse him further. She'd have to reason with him, tactfully. "I'm afraid not. You see, I have an early morning tomorrow. Patients who will want me to be awake and reasonably alert when I treat them, you understand. So maybe you'd consider turning the volume down a few thousand decibels so I can get some sleep and not have to come and rain on your party like this again."

"Oh, believe me, honey, you're not raining on my parade. Quite the opposite. I like your T-shirt, by the way." His eyes lit with humor as he stared at her chest.

She looked down. He'd have to be blind not to see the outline of her boobs under her favorite—if threadbare—T-shirt. Especially when, thanks to the slight draft by the windows, she was on high alert. She crossed her arms before meeting his gaze again.

He was smiling smugly. Aware he'd thrown her off.

Her hands balled into fists. She wanted to punch him.

• • •

Henry Ellison knew he shouldn't be smiling at his neighbor's discomfort, but the situation was so bizarre he couldn't help himself.

It had been quite a shock to look up and see a woman with dark brown hair poking out in every direction and wearing a T-shirt and purple flannel pajama pants storming toward him. Particularly in those clunky green dinosaur slippers. But it was her blazing blue eyes that completely enraptured him, despite the fact that she looked like she might try and kill him.

How could he not bait her, just a little?

She might have hissed at him as she narrowed those dark lash-fringed baby blues. "I'm afraid my invite for the black-tie event went missing and I threw on what I had available when you practically shouted *come over* with that blaring music." She leaned forward. It was hard not to notice the bright pink earplug stuck in her hair, which served to take the bluster out of her caustic tone. "I'm going to ask you nicely this one time. Turn the music down. Next time it won't be me breaking up your little party."

He raised his brows. "Are you suggesting you'll call the police? What, are we in high school?"

"That's a question that I might ask." She didn't look away, meeting his gaze for a long minute. She was a fierce little thing, he'd give her that.

"All right, Ms. Sorensen. I'll be sure to turn the music down, and I'll remind the kids to stay off your lawn while I'm at it."

"Great."

Before he could make another comment, Benny Sorensen whirled around and stomped away. "Stomped" being the only appropriate term when she was wearing such awkward footwear.

He chuckled and took a sip of his almost forgotten drink. Tiffany or Tasha—he couldn't keep it straight—returned to his side, a sultry smile on her full red mouth. "Friend of yours, Henry?"

He ignored the question. "It's getting late. I should probably wind things down."

"You read my mind. I was just thinking we could use a little alone time." She licked her bottom lip—something that ordinarily should have been enticing to him, only now it seemed too practiced.

"Wish I could take you up on that, but I have an early morning. I'll have to take a rain check."

Tiffany-Tasha stuck her bottom lip out into a pout but, to his relief, didn't try to change his mind, instead slinking away with the grace of a cat. A much different departure than Benny Sorensen, in her flannel pants and crazy bedhead. Aside from her lack of taste in sleepwear and complete distaste for him, he had to admit his new neighbor was interesting, to say the least.

The start of another song blared over the speakers, which he'd only had installed last month. He briefly considered pushing the limit of Benny Sorensen's patience, to see if she'd really have the temerity to call the police on him—or, preferably, march back over here *sans* bra and lay into him again.

Maybe another time.

He noted the level of volume before turning it to a whisper. "That's it for tonight, folks. Thanks for coming."

• • •

It was close to nine the next morning when Henry reached his office. Marion, his assistant, was already leaning against his desk holding a cup of coffee in her hand.

"I was starting to wonder if you'd forgotten you worked here."

He took the cup and grinned at her. "You'd think after last week's announcement that Studio 180 is a finalist for the best ad campaign from a small agency I would earn a little slack from you."

"Not a chance." The woman smiled despite her words. "Becks was just here and wanted you to come by later today. Murdock also called and needs you to call him back ASAP and, in case you forgot, you're scheduled to meet with the department at ten on the Crombie account. Oh, and a Mrs. Davenport has called twice this morning. Says she's from your HOA. Seems kind of anxious to talk."

Good grief. Benny Sorensen hadn't taken long in making her complaint. "Thanks, Marion."

With coffee in hand, prepared just as he liked, Henry headed down the hall to Becks's office, returning well wishes and greetings from the half dozen people he passed. Outside her office, he paused long enough to make sure his boss wasn't on the phone or with someone before knocking. She waved him in, and he sauntered into the large corner office that was a smidge bigger than his own.

Becks gave him the same look of disapproval as his assistant when he walked in. "Glad to see you decided to come in today. What with the late nights you've been keeping and the high-profile guests you've been entertaining."

He didn't make any apologies, instead coming to stand casually in front of her desk. Becks, who managed to emanate authority and confidence but also cool beauty with her blond hair tucked back in a neat bun, didn't even look up, still staring at something on her computer screen.

Becks had taken him under her wing nine years ago, when he first came on the scene at the agency, and taught him what it took—once you had the talent, of course—to play the game in the advertising world. He'd risen in the ranks pretty fast with her help and his marketing finesse. He knew how to sell just about anything and it had been that talent that earned him the position of creative director two years ago. Although Becks was still his boss, she was also a good friend. A friend who didn't pull any punches.

"I figured that since I nailed the Crombie account I was due a little indulgence of a late night and even later morning." He took a drink of coffee, noticing she looked more high-strung than usual. "You and Stewart might want to try it some time." Stewart being her husband. "Might take the starch out of that shirt."

"I'll be sure to pass that on to him."

"I was referring to you."

"I know." She finally looked up from her computer. "Although I'd love nothing more than to spend the rest of the morning engaging in the usual bullshit, I do have something I need to talk with you about."

"You look so serious. Should I have a seat?"

"If you like."

He'd humor her. He leaned against the corner of her desk.

"We have a meeting this Friday with a prospective client. You may have heard of them...AirPro Athletics? They're an older, well-established company specializing in fitness wear based here in Salt Lake, but they also operate across the western United States. They want to overhaul their whole image. I have it on good authority they were in talks with Blaine Thomas but decided they wanted to go with a more locally based ad agency. It would be quite a coup for us to gain someone of their stature as a client."

"Sounds exactly like my kind of challenge. What's the problem?"

She leveled her gaze on him. "You. Or, I should say, you and the playboy image you've been fostering for far too long. It's finally catching up with you."

She turned the computer screen around so he could see it. It was a picture of him and a few scantily dressed women in a hotel room in Cannes taking shots. The photo was contrived to make it look like he was almost part of some orgy—never mind the fact he'd been there with three other guys from the office and their wives, unwinding after a long week of workshops, presentations, and networking.

"It was an after-party. The picture makes it look far worse than it was. Ask John and Ted. They were there. Where'd you get that? TMZ?"

"It doesn't matter where I got it or how innocent it all was, the point is how you've let yourself be represented these past few years as this immoral, partying playboy with no ties to family or community. And now it might be coming to bite you in the butt. These clients are looking for a firm that they believe shares the same vision of community, of family values, of moral integrity as they do, or at the very least, they want to know we understand that vision. Photos like this popping up aren't helping, nor was the latest gossip that you're throwing all-night ragers at your place that have the residents of the building wanting you out."

He froze. "Excuse me?"

"I'll let you read all about it later, but apparently you're one complaint away from being tossed out on your butt if you don't clean up your act."

Had his neighbor actually had the temerity to go to the press?

He'd thought her fiery before. Now he thought she was a menace.

Becks sat back and studied him. "You know, Henry, I've seen how hard you've worked all these years to prove yourself, prove your merit to me and the clients, to not stand on your family name to get where you are. You're good. Very good. Which is why I'd hate to see everything you've worked for—that *we've* worked for here at Studio 180—reach a plateau because of this public persona you've fostered. We need this account, Henry. Fix this. And for crying out loud, when we meet with these clients Friday to convince them we are the best agency to represent them, there had better not be any reports about the playboy heir getting kicked out of his condo for having too many damn parties."

He could stand there and argue all day that if the clients couldn't separate Henry's private life from the award-nominated work he was doing at the agency then they were shortsighted and narrow-minded. But it would be a stupid argument. In advertising, the client's needs and wants and opinions were all that mattered. If this group had any doubts that Henry and the agency would be able to encompass their vision because of tomorrow's headlines, then they'd go somewhere else. And he'd be royally screwed.

So instead, he nodded. "I understand." And he did. There was no point in being mad at Becks. She was just the messenger. "Thanks," he said and headed back out.

Marion didn't look up from her desk when he returned.

"Mrs. Davenport is holding for you on line one. Should I take another message?"

"No. Just give me a minute."

He shut the door to his office and went around to his desk, setting his now cold coffee on the corner before taking his seat, his conversation with Becks running through his head.

As blasé as he'd acted earlier about the agency's nomination for best ad campaign, he was secretly ecstatic over the accomplishment. An accomplishment that he and his team had achieved based on hard work and creative merit. Not because of who he was or who his family was—something that had hung over him since childhood. No, he'd busted his ass through college and for the past nine years to get this recognition.

This award nomination was for a campaign that he, not his predecessor, had fostered, which meant everything to him.

He grabbed the baseball from his desk and rolled it in his hand. The feel of the soft leather under his fingertips, the predictable weight and size in his hand, was familiar and welcome. A souvenir from the last game his dad had taken him to just before he'd passed.

His dad had always told him how important it was not to rely on his family's laurels and to make every achievement his own, through his own hard work. It would have been easy to rely on the Brighton name—a name belonging to his mother and her family. A name as renowned internationally in the jewelry business as its competitor Tiffany & Co. But witnessing the way his mother placed the business over Henry, his sister, and even his father had made him resentful of it—as well as her. Maybe that was why he'd practically thumbed his nose at her and the family business over the years, uncaring of how he was portrayed in the media if it meant sticking it to the oppressive Brighton name.

But with his mother's passing last fall, he was beginning

to wonder whom he was sticking it to after all this time. It had become rather tiring.

Up to now, he'd been able to keep that fake persona separate from his business reputation and his work for the agency. He knew that this award would be his. From his hard work. Nothing else. And he wouldn't let anything jeopardize that.

The phone buzzed, and Marion's voice chirped in. "That Mrs. Davenport is still holding."

He knew the woman, and that a few compliments and effusive apologies would go far and he'd be in the clear.

Benny Sorensen, on the other hand, was going to be harder to get off his back.

He'd clearly underestimated her. He wouldn't make that mistake again.

Despite himself, he smiled at the challenge.

Chapter Two

A grape Popsicle in hand, Benny was on her way back to finish up with her sixth patient of the day when the sound of a deep, masculine voice from inside the exam room slowed her step. Her pulse instantly quickened as she recognized the voice.

She stepped inside, pinning on her brightest smile. "Here you go, Chance," she said to her seven-year-old patient, pretending she didn't know there was a visitor. She stopped when she saw him. Her throat felt like it was constricting. "Dr. Seeley, I—I didn't expect to see you here," she said, but it came out so quietly and choked she didn't know if anyone even heard it.

He was sitting on the stool, his legs kicked out and crossed in front of him. He seemed to fill the whole room with his presence—which she supposed wasn't too difficult in the small, confining space. He turned his dreamy, greenish-gray eyes— eyes that even the glasses perched on his nose couldn't hide— on her and grinned before returning to Chance. "Couldn't miss a chance to see how one of my favorite patients was doing. Sorry I wasn't able to squeeze you in today, buddy, but

I assure you, you are in extremely competent hands."

"Aren't you the sweetest? It was a shame that we missed you, though," Chance's mother said in a fawning voice. Apparently Benny wasn't the only one awed by his presence. "But we'll see you in two months at his well visit."

"I look forward to it," Dr. Luke Seeley said, rising to his feet. He glanced down at Benny and winked. "Thanks, Dr. Sorensen."

She managed a quick nod but looked away under the intensity of that gaze. Why was it that speech seemed to escape her whenever she was in the presence of this man—or any man, for that matter, that she found remotely interesting?

She'd been working at the practice for almost two months now, and if she were to count the number of actual conversations she'd had with Luke Seeley, she would only need one hand. It was mortifying, really, her complete inability to function in his presence. She was sure every one of the other four pediatricians—and the office staff—had noted the fact.

"You have one of Dr. Barnett's patients waiting for you in room three," Roz said, her voice toneless.

"Thanks, Roz."

Roz was officially her RN, who took the preliminary information from the patients before Benny saw them. Roz had been Dr. Martin's nurse before Benny arrived, but for reasons unexplained, she was reassigned to Benny and Dr. Martin was assigned the more friendly and kindhearted Cindy. After having worked with the woman for two months, Benny had some suspicions about the reassignment. Her cool stare alone when Benny took too long with a patient could practically freeze water. But it wasn't like Benny was in the position to ask for a different nurse. She was the newbie. She only hoped that with time, the woman would thaw a little. Glacial would be an improvement.

Outside room three, Benny took the clipboard from the

door and read through Roz's notes.

"Thanks for helping me out with that one," Luke Seeley said from behind her. She froze. "Ms. Taylor can be a little more...thankful than I'm comfortable with sometimes."

She turned, reminding herself he was only human, not a god, and that it was okay to talk to him. "Sure—"

But she'd misjudged his proximity and the clipboard she'd been holding sailed to the floor. Crap.

She bent down to grab it a second after he had apparently made the same decision. Blinding pain shot through her face as her nose connected with his head. She stumbled back, only to have two hands steady her.

"Whoa. You okay?" He was looking into her eyes and she blinked, trying to focus. "You're bleeding. Hold on a minute." He let go of her and watched for a second, as if to make sure she wouldn't collapse, before walking the five feet to the counter area behind them to soak a paper towel. "Here, hold this to your nose and pinch. Lean forward."

"I think it's okay," she said, pressing the towel around her nose. She could imagine what she looked like standing there, red faced and holding a Brawny towel to her face. If she could, she'd hide her entire body behind it.

He smiled and handed her back the clipboard. "Good. Just make sure you watch out for walls, doors, and low-hanging cabinets."

"O-okay," she mumbled as he walked away.

Kill me now.

Instead, she turned the doorknob and walked into the exam room, shutting the door behind her. She didn't think she was going to leave it again. Ever.

Where was her usual quick wit and her ability to one-up any jibe, which she was famous for in her family? She was a basket case any time she got within ten feet of him.

The small scream from the five-year-old girl staring up at

her brought her back to reality. Benny looked down over the paper towel still pressed to her nose to see the unmistakable bright red splattered over the front of her white lab coat.

Great. Now she'd terrified a kindergartener.

Please let this day end soon.

· · ·

But the torture had really only begun when, after being sneezed on, hit in the face by a two-year-old who didn't like the tongue depressor in his mouth, and dropping a container of cotton swabs after she tried to reverse direction when she spied Dr. Seeley again, she arrived at her parents' home for her celebratory birthday dinner.

Not just any birthday, but the big 3-0.

She was officially old.

She walked into the kitchen where her mom and her sister, Daisy, were finishing preparations over the stove, and Kate, her sister-in-law, grated cheese. Kate was as helpless in the kitchen as Benny and was doing the task that Benny usually got stuck with. Arriving late had its benefits.

At seeing her daughter's arrival, her mom wiped her hands on a towel and rushed over. "*Feliz cumpleaños*! Happy birthday," she exclaimed, a sentiment echoed by Daisy and Kate before her mom kissed her and wrapped her small arms around her, squeezing tightly. "How's my doctor daughter?" her mom asked and stepped back, beaming at her.

Benny flushed at the phrase, but she knew it was only because her mother was so proud that she used it whenever she talked to someone about her. Her friends, her dentist, their priest, and the clerk at the grocery store. "Good, Mama. A little tired thanks to the Hugh Hefner wannabe next door."

Kate looked up from her task. "Uh-oh. Did your neighbor throw another party?" Kate had actually been over on one of the nights when Benny's walls felt like they'd fall in from the music next door.

"Of course." Benny slid onto the bar stool next to Kate and stuffed some of the cheese into her mouth. "He has no consideration for anyone but himself. I even had the luxury of meeting him last night." In short order, she described the previous night's events that led to her graceful exit. She didn't share how she'd stewed another hour over the horrible jerk and kicked herself for not at least throwing on a robe or running a brush through her coarse, frizzy hair—particularly after she'd caught a glimpse of herself in the bathroom mirror.

Daisy laughed then covered her mouth quickly. "Sorry, Ben, I just wish I'd been there to see you march through the party in that getup." She tossed her long, silky black hair over a shoulder, a vision as always in a white tank top and skinny jeans that clung to a slim figure—despite giving birth to three beautiful children. Daisy had always been a tough act to follow growing up. Especially when Benny had been the chubby tomboy without any of the style, grace, or prettiness of her older sister.

"Have you complained to the home owners' association yet?" Kate asked. "I imagine there must be something in the CCR about noise control."

"CCR?" Daisy asked.

"Covenants, codes, and restrictions," Kate clarified. Benny's sister-in-law also happened to be an attorney, something that had come in handy recently when Daisy was filing for divorce. "It's basically a set of rules that all tenants or owners have to abide by, and violating those could end up in a fine."

"I already called the board this morning," Benny said and sighed as she remembered the woman's indulgent tones when she mentioned Henry Ellison's name. "I got the distinct impression they were just humoring me. He probably has them all wrapped around his well-manicured finger."

"If you want, I can help you draw something up. Make them listen to you."

Benny considered the offer. Kate had already done enough by helping Daisy, and Benny hated to take up any more of her time. "I just met him last night, and for now, I'll give him the benefit of the doubt and hope things improve. But if not, I'll give you a call. Thanks, Kate." It was time to change subjects. Henry Ellison had already plagued too much of her time. "Has anyone heard from Cruz and Payton lately?" she asked, referring to her older brother and his new bride who were still on their honeymoon in Mexico.

It was like an epidemic, the way both of her brothers, single for so long, suddenly found the women of their dreams and married them in quick fashion. She wasn't jealous. Not really. How could she be when the women they married were so freaking fantastic and her brothers were so happy? She didn't want to throw herself off a bridge at all, even if it was going on six months since her last relationship tanked.

"I heard from Payton yesterday," Kate volunteered. Payton, coincidentally, was Kate's best friend and had been her maid of honor when she married Benny's other brother, Dominic, last spring in Puerto Vallarta. The maid of honor and best man had ended up traveling by car across Mexico and had somehow managed to fall in love and get married— not necessarily in that order. "They're heading to Guadalajara tomorrow and are expecting to be gone another week."

The sliding door to the deck opened, and Benny's dad, a tall, blond figure despite his approaching seventieth birthday stepped inside. Dominic, who had their mom's dark hair and complexion and their father's height and eye color, followed, carrying an oval platter filled with a large, seasoned flank steak that already had her mouth watering.

Her dad's usually stoic face broke into a smile when he

saw her. "Happy birthday," he said, before lifting her off the floor in a warm hug.

"I'd say let's have a game after dinner," Dominic said, "but I'm afraid that now that you've hit the big three-oh, you could break a hip or something. They say it's all downhill from here."

"You would know, dear brother. Isn't that gray? Right there?" she asked, touching just above her ears, hinting that his own dark hair had already started turning, which it hadn't.

"Aunt Benny!" two high-pitched voices called out at once, storming up the stairs from the basement. Her two nieces, recently turned ten Jenna and eight-year-old Natalie, reached her first, hugging her tightly.

Their younger brother, Paul, came last, his enthusiasm barely readable. "Hey, Aunt Benny."

"What's wrong with you, bud?" she asked, tousling his hair.

"Please don't start, Paul," Daisy interrupted. "I have gone over this a dozen times already. We are not getting a dog. I have a hard enough time keeping track of you three—I'm not throwing a pup into the mix."

Her older sister was finally getting back on her feet after her divorce, with a new promotion as assistant manager at a trendy neighborhood café and bakery as well as moving into Kate's old house with the kids. Benny couldn't blame her for not wanting any more chaos thrown into the mix.

"Why don't you come and take the tortillas to the table, Paul," their grandma said. "And girls, maybe you can set the table for us, please."

Jenna walked around the table setting plates down in front of each chair. "Since Uncle Cruz and Aunt Payton aren't here, can we sit with you guys tonight? Please?"

"It's a celebration, isn't it?" Benny asked, grabbing a tortilla from the stack and biting into it. "Of course."

At the news, they shouted their approval. The kids usually got stuck at the bar due to lack of seating around the table during family dinners, something they were good at voicing their opinion about.

Natalie finished counting silverware and went around the table, leaving them at each setting. "Aunt Benny?" the younger girl asked. "Are you ever going to get married?"

The once tasty soft flour tortilla turned to paste in her mouth. Benny took a glimpse at the other adults. They were all looking at her with amused faces. Dominic's eyebrow shot up, waiting for her answer.

"Maybe. One day," she said, trying to keep her voice upbeat.

"Don't you need a boyfriend first?" Paul asked. "You don't ever seem to have one of those."

Now Dominic was trying to choke back his laughter. She glared at him.

"Your aunt Benny is a busy doctor lady," her mom said, finally coming to the rescue. "She'll find the right guy when it's the right time."

"Well, she should probably hurry. I mean, thirty is pretty old," Paul added helpfully.

"That's enough, Paul," Daisy said. "Aunt Benny is younger than me, and she has plenty of time.

He looked dubious. "Yeah, but you've already been married and have three kids. She has…no one."

Ouch.

"Why don't we all sit down and eat," her dad said. "I'm starving. Your mom tells me that you three are starting soccer next week?"

At this, all three kids began talking at once.

Kate reached out and patted Benny's arm, a smile on her lips. "Welcome to thirty."

. . .

It was two hours later when Benny pulled into the parking garage and maneuvered her Mini Cooper around the corner and to her designated spot.

A spot that was currently occupied. This time by a silver Lexus SUV.

She'd take one guess as to where the owner of the vehicle was right now. The familiar boiling of her blood had her gripping the steering wheel. Fighting the urge to ram her car into the back of the offending vehicle, and the red Ferrari next to it, she drove away.

A couple minutes later, she pulled into one of the few visitor spots out front, relieved at not having to make another trek from down the block, and picked up her cell phone. Kate's voicemail answered. "Kate? It's Benny. About that complaint to the HOA? Let's do it. And I want to add some parking violations to the mix. I'll send you a copy over in the morning."

With satisfaction, she hung up. It was time Mr. Henry Ellison realized the whole world wasn't his playground and that he, like everyone else, had to follow the rules.

As she paused in the hallway outside his door, she rolled her eyes at the faint but distinctive sound of a John Mayer song playing softly.

What. A. Player.

Inside her own place, she poured herself a glass of wine and went to the couch. She kicked off her comfortable orthopedic sneakers and flipped the television on, bypassing changing into pajamas since her scrubs were just as comfortable.

Bonus. *Property Brothers* was running a marathon, and a new episode was just starting. She settled back to enjoy it, savoring her wine. Only halfway through the episode, she wasn't paying attention to the show at all. Her thoughts were still on her nephew's comment from earlier. About being alone.

As if hitting thirty hadn't been hard enough, having the people she cared about echoing the same thoughts she'd been trying to block out for months hadn't made it any easier. Usually she shrugged those comments off, excusing her single status as a necessity from her studies and then her work. But in recent months, seeing her brothers reach the level of happiness she'd only seen from her parents—and in fairy tales—she'd started realizing that something was missing from her life.

Not that she hadn't been in relationships. But she'd never thought for a second that the four months she'd spent with Chip—a twenty-four-year-old orderly with a sweet smile and nice butt but not much happening upstairs—had been anything more than a fling. And when Chip had talked about making it more, she'd ended it quickly, not wanting to lead him on. Because he wasn't the one. None of the guys she'd gone out with had been. They just happened to be the only ones she wasn't a complete dork with when she tried to talk to them.

The guys that really made her pulse race, her breath catch…they were never going to want her anyhow. She'd learned that a long time ago. It was women like Daisy, pretty and vivacious, and naturally gifted with social skills, who easily earned the attention of men like Luke Seeley. And Jeff Nausbam before him, and Scottie Hall before them. Benny had resigned herself to halfhearted relationships with tepid chemistry and ho-hum romance—until Kate and Payton came and turned Benny's brothers' worlds around. She'd be lying if she said she wasn't a little envious.

She threw back the rest of her wine and got up to get a refill before turning the television off and heading to her bathroom. She set her glass down and leaned forward, peering into the mirror. It wasn't that she was ugly. She knew that. Nor was she the same chubby-faced tomboy of her childhood.

But she did have a few more lines around the eyes than she once had. A chin hair that was growing more persistent and darker every year and would require pliers to remove soon, it was so stubborn. She leaned back. Her boobs, massive double Ds and once the bane of her pubescent existence, were only settling farther south.

Basically, everything was downhill from here.

And if she didn't do something more proactive, she was going to be alone for the rest of her life. She'd be the old, lonely spinster aunt who would be extended the pity invitations to every holiday event.

Something had to change. *She* had to change. And she wasn't talking about settling for anything second best. Not anymore.

If she wanted Luke Seeley to see her as more than the dorky new doctor who couldn't string a sentence together in his presence, she was going to have to do something different.

The question was…what?

Chapter Three

"Your sister's on the phone," Marion said just after three on Thursday afternoon.

This can't be good. She only called when she wanted something. Henry picked up the phone. "Hey, Morgan."

"Henry, I need a favor." Just as he'd thought. "I have to catch a flight tonight to Orlando and my nanny has a family emergency, so she can't stay with Ella. Can you take her? It would just be until Monday."

Until…Monday?

"I don't know…" It was one thing to have his niece for an overnight visit, but this was four *days*. Four nights. That was a lot of responsibility. "Don't you have a friend or someone she would feel more comfortable with?"

"Jess and her family are leaving for Yellowstone on Saturday. It's you or I'm going to have to cancel, which would be a logistical nightmare. Look, Ella is in a summer day camp on the weekdays until five thirty, meaning you'd only have the evenings and the weekend to keep her entertained. I wouldn't be asking this if there were any other options."

He didn't have to ask whether this had something to do with work. There was nothing else in his sister's life but her career as a motivational speaker and her four-year-old daughter, Ella. Sometimes he worried that despite having sworn to never become like their mother, she was getting awfully close to becoming a mirror image of Margaret Brighton.

He sighed, knowing that there was really only one answer here. "What time should I come get her?"

She gave him the details before ending the call to dash home to get Ella's things together. Henry didn't mind having his niece hang out with him and had actually enjoyed the time she'd slept over before—again, because Morgan was away somewhere for work. He'd even played a game of Candyland for the first time in his life.

He pressed his assistant's extension. "Marion? You're going to have to reschedule my four thirty meeting." He considered the current contents of his refrigerator, which, according to his memory, consisted of hummus, brie, caviar, and maybe a bag of carrots. He should probably head out early, get some kid-friendly options. Including Skittles, which Ella had thought the greatest junk food ever when he'd bought some last time, even if they had to keep it their little secret since his sister was trying to raise a sugar-free kid, or some such nonsense. "I'm actually going to cut out of here in another hour. If there are any emergencies, send them to my cell phone, otherwise I'll handle it tomorrow."

"No problem. And don't forget, you and Becks have that meeting with AirPro Athletics first thing in the morning."

As if he could forget. The clients who needed to believe that Henry was merely misrepresented in the media. That he was a man of strong moral fiber and responsibility. A man who understood their vision.

Hell, selling things was his expertise. He could sell this.

He could sell anything.

• • •

He had to be the worst uncle in the history of the world. Henry couldn't imagine what his sister was going to say when he talked to her later tonight. The only reason she didn't know where they were now was because she'd written the name of Ella's pediatrician and his phone number on the long list of contacts she'd left for him. Thank God Dr. Barnett's office had an after-hours clinic versus taking Ella to the ER.

A Skittle up the nose? Now he was really busted.

Ella didn't seem to be all that affected by the fact her nose was bulging on the left side thanks to the offending piece of candy, or by the more strenuous breathing sounds she made with the reduced air capacity.

It scared the crap out of Henry, though.

Where was the damned doctor? He looked at his phone. Twenty minutes past their appointment. There was a scuffling sound outside the room, like someone was flipping through pages, then the door opened.

"Hi, I'm Dr. Sorensen and I'll be—" But whatever words were going to follow stopped as the good doctor looked up.

The madwoman who strode into his place like Godzilla the other night was standing in the doorway. No slippers, at least. Her hair was combed and pulled back into an uninspiring ponytail this time. Her clothing wasn't much of an improvement from the pj's either. She wore light green scrubs that successfully hid any curves from the discerning eye, hideous white sneakers, and the usual white lab coat, probably thrown on to convince her patients she really was a bona fide doctor. From what he could tell, her face was devoid of any makeup, not even a hint of colored ChapStick on those full lips.

Was she allergic to wanting to look pretty?

Her overall packaging was completely unflattering—something he couldn't understand as a man whose whole career was putting forth the best package that consumers would clamor to get. Entirely unflattering...except for those dark-fringed, spectacular blue eyes that had widened in horror as she recognized him.

He grinned. "Dr. Sorensen."

She looked from his niece, spinning around on the doctor's stool, back to him, clearly confused. Then she seemed to snap out of her shock and came in, shutting the door behind her. "I didn't realize you were a father."

"Uncle. This is Ella, my niece, who's staying with me for a few days."

She bent down to peer into Ella's face. "Hi, Ella. I'm Dr. Sorensen. Let's have you sit up here so I can have a better look. Okay?"

Henry stood and without being asked, lifted Ella to the exam table. The woman didn't appear to see him, her attention now on her patient. "You know you're supposed to eat the candy, right?" she teased.

This earned a giggle from Ella. "I just wanted to see if it would fit."

"I can see that." She turned to look at Henry, with clear judgment in her eyes. "And you approved?"

He raised his hands as if helpless. "I was getting us root beer floats in the kitchen."

Her right brow shot up—in question, he was sure, at his diabetes-inspired diet—before turning back to her charge. "Well, I'm going to try a few different things to see if we can get that thing out of there. Okay?"

A few minutes later, however, the Skittle remained.

"Okay, Ella, I'm going to go get a couple of things that might help to get that out. I'll be right back."

When Benny returned with a small pair of tweezers and alarmingly large forceps, Ella turned to him in terror.

"I know they look scary and they may be a little uncomfortable, but I promise you're going to be okay," she said in assurance. "And I know with certainty I have a root beer-flavored Popsicle for you when we're all finished."

Ella shook her head, panicked. "I want my—my mom," she stuttered.

"Ella, honey, it's going to be okay." He grabbed the little girl's hand in his own and nodded as he met her eyes, now filled with tears. It was like a kick in the stomach to see her so distressed.

It took about thirty seconds to pull out the offending candy, but every second that he saw the fear on his niece's face felt like an hour. Was this what it was like? Having a kid? Being responsible for every little scratch and cut? It was… terrifying.

Benny held the purple Skittle up to Ella for a moment. "We got it. Great job." She walked to the garbage and dropped it inside. "I'm just going to do a quick check inside your nose again to make sure I have everything, Ella." She pulled a scope-looking thing from the wall and peered in both of Ella's nostrils and her ears. "Looks good. She might be sensitive for a few hours. If there seems to be excessive runniness or she complains of pain, give us a call. Otherwise, she should be fine." She turned her attention back to Ella. "Now you've got to promise me that you're not going to stick anything else up your nose, okay? That goes for the ears, too."

"Promise," Ella said with a burst of enthusiasm. "Can I have that Popsicle now?"

"I'll be back in a minute." Benny opened the door and headed down the hall.

"Are we going to tell mom about the Skittle?"

Henry looked at his niece, considering only briefly the

possibility of keeping this a secret. "I'm afraid so." In good time, anyhow.

Footsteps were returning, but before they reached the door, there was a startled yelp followed by a thud. In a few steps, he was at the door, looking out at what caused the commotion.

Benny Sorensen was sitting on the floor, still grasping the Popsicle in her hand. A guy in a white lab coat was trying to help her up. It was hard to miss the stain covering her front—coffee, if the mug tipped over on the floor next to her was any indication.

"Dr. Sorensen, are you okay?" the guy was asking her.

She nodded, barely giving him a glance. "Y-yes. Fine thanks."

"You were walking so fast around that corner I didn't have time to get out of the way," the guy said apologetically before chuckling as he looked down at her. "You're going to need to keep a few extra coats in the office if we keep running into each other."

Benny Sorensen was actually *blushing*? This was intriguing, and Henry leaned against the doorframe to watch the scene unfold.

Benny, however, didn't appear to realize she had an audience, her gaze on the guy's coat, which looked like it had suffered a little from the spill, too. "Oh, your jacket. I'm sorry." She reached out like she was going to blot it with her fingers but realized, hand in midair, what she was about to do and froze.

"It's fine. I'm done here tonight anyway. You have more patients?"

"Dr. Seeley?" interrupted the nasally voiced nurse who'd seen Henry and Ella when they first arrived. She'd come out of nowhere, and her brown eyes quickly assessed the situation, but she made no comment.

The doctor who'd taken out Benny Sorensen with his mug of coffee nodded at the nurse and waited for whatever message she had for him.

"Your friend is here. Should I send her back to your office?" There was a hint of disapproval in the nurse's tone.

"Sure, Roz. Thanks." Roz's face didn't show any reaction as she turned and headed back to the reception area. "Glad you're okay," Dr. Seeley said, returning his attention to Benny Sorensen. "I'll catch you tomorrow."

She just nodded, tongue-tied still, and Henry might have laughed if it wasn't all so tragic.

The guy smiled indulgently—if Benny had been a dog he might have even patted her head. "Okay, good night then."

Dr. Seeley went down the hall and stopped at a closed door at the end and opened it, flipping on a light.

"Luke!"

Dr. Seeley turned his head just as a tall woman with wavy blond hair and dressed in a slinky black dress reached him. She put her arms over his shoulder and practically sucked the guys face off with the determination of a Hoover vacuum.

Hot. She was definitely hot. Henry wouldn't mind if she sucked on his face a little bit, either.

Benny was still as a statue, the Popsicle gripped tightly in her hand as she watched the embrace, her own reaction momentarily unguarded. She looked devastated.

Man, she had it bad.

Before she could realize he'd witnessed the entire thing, he stepped back and returned to his seat.

Ordinarily, considering how much of a pain in the ass she'd been since he first laid eyes on her, he wouldn't give any further consideration to her obvious pain. But after the way she had taken care of Ella and made the whole experience so painless for them both, he felt more gratitude for her. Could even feel some sympathy toward her plight.

She clearly had no idea how to interact with the doctor other than colliding with him.

It made her seem almost…vulnerable. It couldn't be easy being hopelessly in love with a guy who, from the tolerant albeit friendly smile he gave her, saw her in more of a brotherly fashion than anything else.

Maybe Henry could cut her a little slack after all.

. . .

Benny could hear the woman's almost neighing laughter from where she was standing, even with the door closed. Could the woman be phonier? She'd bet those boobs were as real as the woman's hair color.

Then, just as quickly as those thoughts came, Benny forced herself to stop and shook her head. She was being ridiculous and petty. The woman hadn't done anything to her, and being catty—even only in her mind—wasn't going to change the fact that Dr. Luke Seeley preferred his women pretty and polished and…not like Benny.

To make matters worse, she was standing there soaked with coffee, and she still had to go back inside the examination room and see *that* man.

She took a breath. The sooner she got in there and sent them on their way, the sooner she could leave and shower away her humiliation. "Sorry about the wait. Here you are, Ella." She smiled and pulled the plastic off before handing her the Popsicle.

"You're all wet," Ella said matter-of-factly, sucking loudly on her treat and staring at Benny's chest. She pulled her coat around herself more tightly.

"We should go, Ella," Henry said. "Can you tell Dr. Sorensen thank you?"

Ella complied and, happy with her Popsicle, clambered

off the table. Benny finally met Henry's gaze, noting the odd look in his eyes, the slight twist of his mouth. "Thanks for the help, Dr. Sorensen. Have a good night."

Was that pity she saw? Had he heard what had happened in the hall?

Any guilt she'd felt when she first saw him tonight, knowing that she'd just sent such a nasty complaint against him to the HOA with Kate's help, evaporated. "You two have a nice evening," she said stiffly, trying to convince herself that he couldn't possibly have witnessed her humiliation with Luke. That would just be too much.

Henry, fortunately, had already grabbed his niece's hand and was leading her out the door. "We'll see you later, Dr. Sorensen."

Out in the hall, she heard Ella ask her uncle what he meant by *later,* but she didn't catch the answer. She continued to her office, intent on finishing up whatever paperwork was left so she could get out of here before she could cause more damage. Fortunately, Luke's office was on the opposite end of the hall to hers, so she didn't have to run the risk of hearing or seeing the two lovebirds again.

So much for her promise to herself to take more chances, to engage in at least one conversation with the doctor a day until it became like an old habit. She was not supposed to hear him coming and take off at full speed in the other direction— only to reverse right into him.

Graceful. Again.

She might have to start wearing a plastic raincoat. Her dry-cleaning bill was ridiculous.

Why, oh, why couldn't she have half the social skills as Daisy, who was born hardwired with the ability to flirt with anyone, anywhere, anytime? Such as the lifeguard at the neighborhood pool Benny had stared at from behind her book all summer when she was fourteen. Daisy, at a confident and head-turning eighteen, had walked right up to him and started a conversation. Daisy and Scottie had spent the rest of the summer attached at the hip until they both left for college that fall.

Daisy had always been able to do that.

And as much as Benny loved her sister and wanted only her happiness, she couldn't pretend she hadn't resented Daisy the tiniest bit growing up. She was only human.

But she couldn't continue to hate and resent every pretty woman who got the attention of the men that Benny was too tongue-tied to speak to herself. If only she could picture Luke as nonthreatening. Like her brothers. Or Chip the orderly. Or even the detestable Henry Ellison. Then she'd have no problem engaging him in actual dialogue, maybe even a few witty retorts.

Henry Ellison. He'd actually seemed almost likeable tonight with that cute niece who had the same golden-blond hair and brown eyes and that impish smile. Almost...human.

At least she had one thing going for her tonight. With his four-year-old niece in residence, Lover Boy wasn't likely going to be having late-night parties or playing music at record high levels.

Maybe she'd even get a good night's sleep before she returned to work tomorrow, ready for more inevitable humiliation.

Chapter Four

"Can we get McDonald's for breakfast again, Uncle Henry?"

It was six thirty in the morning. On a Saturday. Wasn't it a law that no one could be up this early?

Apparently, four-year-olds didn't care much if it was Saturday or any other day of the week. Ella was wide-awake and raring to do something, while Henry needed to pour a full carafe of coffee down his throat before he could consider going anywhere.

"Let's just have some cereal. We can go there for lunch."

A few minutes later, with Ella eating Captain Crunch in front of the television and a full cup of coffee flooding Henry's veins, he decided he was awake enough to get his mail and the package he was expecting.

Last night after he'd picked Ella up from day camp, the two of them had gone to dinner and a movie, arriving home after eight, when he'd had to carry the little girl, half asleep, to bed. Now that the kid was up and preoccupied for the time being, Henry felt better about leaving her alone for a couple of minutes.

The place was dead quiet, as he would expect on a Saturday at the death of dawn, and he was able to catch the elevator back up with no wait. While the floors ticked by, he looked through the mail, his package tucked under his arm.

The letter bearing the building HOA's name and address caught his eye. It looked awfully official. He ripped it open, barely glancing up when he stepped off the elevator.

Thirty seconds later, he was standing outside the madwoman's door. He pounded, not caring if she was still asleep.

She opened the door in under a minute, fully dressed in — what else — scrubs, light blue this time. Did she live in those things?

"Mr. Ellison?" She scrunched up her face at him in feigned confusion even though they both knew why he was here. "What can I do for you?"

"Ah, Dr. Sorensen. Terribly sorry to have pulled you out of bed, in pj's again, no less."

She narrowed her eyes. "They're scrubs."

"Yes, I see that." He looked behind her, as if expecting to see an operating table. "Are you scrubbing in for surgery in there?"

"What can I help you with," she managed between clenched teeth.

He held the letter up in front of her, noting the gleam of satisfaction that entered her eyes.

"I received an interesting letter this morning from our home owners' association. It seems there have been some *complaints*" — he emphasized the word, watching her face for any sign of guilt, but it was now carefully blank — "about me. Maybe I can read you a little bit of this so you know what I'm talking about. 'Tenant is in violation of section three, subsection (a), which requires all tenants to cease loud and excessive noise, including music, that interferes in another

tenant's quiet enjoyment of their property.' Let's see here...
Oh, another good one, 'tenant is required to park entirely
within the borders of the owner's space or be subject to fine.'"

"Sounds like you have a real problem there."

"Yes. You could call it a *problem*. According to this and
the monetary fine schedule for said violations, I'm on the
hook for six hundred dollars. Not to mention that if there
are further complaints, the fine goes up to twelve hundred,
followed by possible eviction proceedings. Evicting me from
my own home."

"That's rough," she said with feigned sympathy. "Maybe
you should save yourself the aggravation and just move out?"

"And give the coward who set this all in motion the
satisfaction? Not in a million years. I prefer to appeal the
decision and ask for a hearing with the board so I can confront
this coward face-to-face."

"Coward? Or perhaps they're smart enough to know
that if some ignoramus is too stupid to know they should
turn their blaring music off by one in the morning, or not take
someone else's parking spot, or not park so close to another
tenant's car they have to climb in from the passenger side,
then confronting said ignoramus becomes pointless. A waste
of their valuable time."

That's it. He'd tried to be nice. Tried to talk to her in a
calm, level, and somewhat respectful tone. "Is that right?
You think that playing games like siccing the HOA on me or
leaking this crap to online gossip rags is going to win you any
friends, lady?"

"I don't want to be friends, I want to be able to come
home and not wonder what my inconsiderate, egotistical
neighbor has in store for me," she said, her voice rising. "And
as for leaking 'this crap' to any gossip rags, I don't have the
slightest idea what you're talking about."

"Right. It's just a coincidence stories about my late-night

partying hit the web the very next morning after you crashed the party."

"I can't be the only one who finds your selfish antics immature and frustrating."

He studied her, trying to decide whether to believe her or not. Before he could push it farther, a soft, less certain voice broke in.

"Uncle Henry?"

Both of them turned to see the small girl in her bunny pajamas standing in the hall, staring at them with uncertainty and a little fear on her face. Holy hell. Now she was causing him to traumatize his young niece.

"Happy?" he hissed under his breath.

She gave him a scowl, then turned back to the little girl. "Ella? Your uncle and I are just having a little discussion. Nothing for you to worry about," she said in the familiar soft voice she'd used in her office. "How's your nose feeling?"

"It's fine. Are you and Uncle Henry going to yell at each other much longer? Because I need him to pour me more cereal."

"I'll be right there, honey," Henry said, not taking his eyes from Benny Sorensen. For a woman who couldn't put two words together the other night in the presence of Dr. Suck Face, she could be surprisingly verbal with him.

What the woman needed was a distraction. She needed something or some*one* to take her attention off every little thing he did. Someone who could fill her time with human companionship, dinners, and dates…

He stepped back and studied her.

She wasn't a bad-looking woman, not at all. If you could get past the lips pursed in disapproval, and the eyes that had their laser-beam quality burrowing a hole in his head. If she stopped pulling her hair back in that unflattering ponytail that left frizzy pieces flying all over her head, maybe tweezed those brows back a bit, and smiled once in a while, she could be actually pretty.

Okay, maybe he'd gone too far. She could be…less terrorizing.

In fact, her eyes were such a bright, iridescent blue that if she could stop glaring at everyone or, in the converse, dropping her gaze down whenever Dr. Suck Face looked her way, they could be almost…captivating.

"Why are you looking at me like that?" She peered uncertainly at him.

"No reason." He smiled. "I think I've just come up with a solution to our little problem, however. Would you like to hear it?"

She glanced at her watch and back. "If you can tell me in four minutes or less. I have early-morning hours at the clinic."

"You work on Saturdays?"

She shrugged. "We hold after-hour care on the weekends. We rotate so it comes to be about once a month. Today's my turn. You now have three and a half minutes."

"Okay. I have a little proposition for you. I couldn't help but notice the other night that you have a certain…affinity to that other doctor. The guy with the blonde attached to his mouth?"

Her eyes narrowed. "I knew you were spying on me. Well, for your information, Dr. Seeley is merely a colleague, and I have no interest in him other than profession—"

He raised his hand. "Save it. If it's one thing I know, it's how to read a person. To see what they want sometimes before they know it themselves. That's why I'm so good at my work. In advertising," he added when she didn't bite or look particularly impressed. "And I know that you have the hots for the good Dr. Seeley."

"Two minutes left," she said, her eyes narrowed to near slits now. But he also could see a faint blush on her face, making her forehead glow almost red. "I hope you have a point."

"I do. In exchange for you dropping this"—he waved the notice in front of her— "vendetta you have against me, and telling the HOA that you are withdrawing your complaint and any legal threats you made to them—since they sure as hell have never been this proactive in enforcing the rules in the three years I've lived here—I'll get you a date with the esteemed Dr. Seeley."

She snorted. "Yeah. Right. First, not that I'm admitting to having any feelings whatsoever for Lu—Dr. Seeley, but you must be crazy to think I'd drop anything on some tenuous promise that you couldn't possibly deliver."

Now it was his turn to gloat. "Try me. I can sell anything to anyone, and I can certainly sell you. Believe me, if anyone knows what a guy like Dr. Seeley—or any guy, for that matter—wants in a woman, it's me."

She nodded. "Oh, that's right. Because you're a man whore. Of course you know what all men want, in your diverse and vast experience. However, I'm afraid Dr. Seeley is on a different level than you."

He remembered the stocky blond guy who probably played quarterback in high school while running for school president and maintaining a 4.0 GPA. Your typical all-American high-school hero who'd grown up to become your all-American grown-up hero as a doctor—to children, no less. "Trust me. I know what that guy wants. What kind of woman he wants. And I know that with a little effort on your part—scratch that, a lot of effort—I can make you into that woman."

The last dig might have been too much, the way she puffed out her chest like she was going to launch herself at him. But whatever she'd been about to say got caught in her throat, and instead, something else crossed that face of hers. Something that told him maybe they might have a deal.

Hope.

• • •

She'd known the moment he knocked on her door she should just ignore him. Refuse to engage with him until he'd had the chance to cool down after reading the letter—a copy of which she'd seen yesterday. But there'd been curiosity, an almost masochistic instinct to see his anger at an inconvenience that, for once, *she'd* caused *him*.

And it had been entertaining, up until Ella had come out into the hall to see what was going on.

But now, with this so-called proposition of his, she was at a loss. Was he even serious? Or was this some cruel joke to string her along until she'd dropped her complaints?

She studied him, his smooth polish even at this absurd hour in the morning. He'd retired his expensive refined suit for more relaxed jeans and a T-shirt that, unfortunately, made him look impossibly more debonair, which, if she didn't hate him so much, would be disarming. But she loathed him with a deep and growing fire, the way he just thought he could smile that charming smile of his and get people to do his bidding. She'd seen the articles about him, the women, the parties that would inevitably follow him not just because of his professional success, but because of his standing as heir to Brighton Jewelers—one of the oldest and most reputable jewelry companies in the country.

But…she had to admit, he did make a convincing argument. He not only knew what men wanted, but he knew how to play people, to create the perfect package for whatever snake oil he was selling. Hadn't she just been commiserating over how she was going to be alone unless she made a change? He could be a guru of sorts—if she could learn to tolerate him.

"I'm not looking to be dressed as some bimbo Barbie. Slapping on makeup and prancing around the office isn't going to do anything but humiliate me."

"Lord, don't I know it."

She wanted to kick him. "Forget it." She should have known that even talking to him was a mistake. She stepped back, ready to slam the door in his face.

"Wait. Benny. Hear me out. I'm sorry, sometimes you just leave yourself open and I can't resist the opportunity. But I promise, I'll work on that—and keeping the music down to a respectable level and giving you access to your parking spot. Look, I know better than anyone that a decent hairstyle and a little lipstick aren't going to make any difference if you can't say two words without falling down in a faint, or running into a wall or whatever you do when he speaks to you. I'm going to give you the whole Henry Ellison treatment. When I'm done, you'll be able to not only slay Dr. Seeley with your wit and unbounding charm, but you're going to have him wrapped around your little finger after I verse you in the fine art of flirting."

"You're promising me a lot. But you have to be crazy if you think I'm going to drop my complaint now that I actually have your attention."

"I'm so certain of my prowess, that I guarantee you'll have a date with the good doctor by"—he scanned the contents of the letter—"August Twenty-Ninth. The day of the HOA hearing. That's a little over a month away. If I can't make you the walking dream this guy wants by then, then I'll agree to pay whatever fees the board rules on at that hearing, and I won't fight you any longer. But if I do prevail, then you're going to march in there and tell them you made it all up. Do we have a deal?"

Five weeks. Five weeks where she could pick his brain, learn the subtle art and skill of not just flirting, but socially engaging any man and not dissolving into Jell-O at his feet. That was, if she could stomach being in the same room with this guy without killing him.

It was a lofty promise. But what did she have to lose? As things were going now, Luke Seeley was never going to see her as a woman. A woman he wanted. Not a cute, nerdy klutz good for a little laugh every now and then. A woman to love.

"And you'll keep the music down and let me use my parking spot?" He nodded. "All right. Deal."

He raised his hand toward her. He actually wanted to shake on it? She accepted it begrudgingly. "So. What do we do first?"

He dropped his gaze down her body, skimming over the loose but comfy scrubs and down to her favorite worn sneakers. "First you need to stop dressing like a seventeen-year-old tomboy. What time are you off work today?"

Chapter Five

This was a bad idea.

Never in a million years would she have gone into this store. This was the place where women like Payton and Kate, her beautiful sisters-in-law, would shop. Where Daisy would shop. Benny much preferred the low-stress ambience of Target. They had designer clothes, too, right?

She looked at the tall brunette that was hanging on every word Henry uttered. If she pushed her breasts out any farther she was bound to pop him in the eye with those things. Not that he'd be complaining.

"I don't understand why we're even here," she said when Henry returned, taking a perch on the back of the chair where Ella was playing Angry Birds on Henry's monster-size smartphone.

"Because I'm betting that your wardrobe consists of twenty shades of scrubs and more of those hideous sneakers you're partial to. You don't have to go glamour girl, but it wouldn't hurt for you to look more feminine every once in a while. When was the last time you wore jeans?" She just stared at him. "You do own a pair of jeans, right?"

"Yes." She'd bought some just two years ago. But she hated the way they kept sliding down her butt and she had to hitch them up every ten minutes. The elastic waist and draw ties of the scrubs were infinitely more comfortable and didn't threaten to fall down.

"The first thing you need to realize is that you're a woman. This shapeless, amorphous look of yours is fine. If you're trying to disappear in a crowd. But you want to stand out. And clothes that actually fit is a good place to start."

The saleswoman returned with stacks of clothes in her arms and went to hang them up in the dressing room. "How did she even know what size to get?"

"We took a guess. Now stop complaining and get inside. We're not leaving until you have two pairs of slacks, a pair of jeans, at least three tops, and one dress." He stopped, eyeing her cleavage. "A new bra couldn't hurt, either. I know you've got breasts under there, but you make it almost impossible to tell."

The urge to kick him was almost too powerful but she managed to restrain herself and gave him a withering glare instead, then and turned to follow the saleswoman back to the dressing room.

The door shut behind her, she stared at the clothes hung neatly on hangers and stacked on the bench next to her. A particularly pretty green wrap dress caught her eye, something she would never have chosen for herself in a million years. But it was pretty.

She glanced at the price tag, and her eyes bugged out. She could buy lattes for a month with what it would cost her for this one dress. No, probably a year. Not that she couldn't afford it now, with her new salary, but not living frugally was a new thing for her after scrimping the past few years.

The next dress with a cutout in the back had her cringing.

How would she even wear a bra in that thing?

She wiped her forehead, which was damp with sweat from her barely repressed panic attack. *Is it hot in here?*

She was so out of her element.

Benny had always felt like she was trying—and failing— at playing dress up when she wore dresses, only wearing them under protest, like at Kate's wedding last spring. It might have something to do with the fact that most dresses she wore as a kid had been Daisy's castoffs. Castoffs had made up the majority of her wardrobe growing up as the youngest of four kids. Unfortunately, when Benny hit her teens and puberty, the pounds just seemed to pack on, and she found it near impossible to fit in any of Daisy's clothes without her belly hanging over the top of the pants, so she would have to leave the zipper not all the way done up. The feeling of her legs squished into Daisy's old pants, the tightness of the shirt when Benny doubled her bra size in one summer, was a distant but distasteful memory.

When her dad's construction company started to take off by the time she was sixteen, thanks to his growing sons' help, the family was finally able to afford a lot more things, including a firsthand wardrobe for Benny. But by then, all she wanted was the biggest and loosest things she could find. To hide the rolls and bulges. To hide swelling breasts that the boys snickered at and the girls looked at in disgust. And even though she'd lost most of that baby fat—although there were some curves that just weren't going to go away, the curse of being a Latina woman—the inclination to want to hide herself was hard to suppress.

And now this guy wanted her to dump the baggy for tight and formfitting? It was enough to give her hives.

She pulled off her pants and kicked them to the corner and held up a pair of jeans. They looked like someone had already worn them, with crease marks on the sides by the pockets, the scuffing along the leg. This was stylish?

"How's it coming in there?" Henry called out just as she finished zipping up the jeans.

"You do know I'm a pediatrician, right? I don't think the kids are going to care about what I'm wearing before they throw up on me."

"But *you'll* know. You'll care. And so will Dr. Seeley. He is the person we're here for, right?"

She didn't bother to respond, instead tugging the first shirt off the hanger and pulling it over her head. "Shouldn't we be working on conversation? What to talk about? You know, the real stuff?"

"You're not going to feel capable of talking to him until you feel confident about yourself. When you know you look good, when you're at your best, you'd be surprised how much easier it is to hold a conversation with a person you might not otherwise."

She made a fake gagging noise. "Thank you, Dr. Phil."

"Trust me on this. In one week's time, you're going to feel like a different person."

"I like the person I am."

He sighed. "I'm sure you're a terrific person." She could hear the sarcasm in his tone. "But you're trying to get Dr. Luke Seeley to see you as a woman. Not the goofy new kid in the office who would sooner run into a wall than make eye contact."

He might have a point.

She stared at herself in the reflection, still unable to feel anything but ridiculous. The shirt was pink and hideous. Not helped by the way the buttons puckered around chest level, trying not to burst.

The jeans though… She turned around and lifted the shirt up. Hmm. Her butt didn't look too bad. Actually, almost kind of decent. She turned back and studied the front.

Okay. So these didn't make her legs feel like summer sausage, stuffed in thick, uncomfortable casings.

This shirt, though, had to go.

She threw it off and grabbed another one. It was a soft blue that she was kind of curious to see on.

Another minute later and she studied herself. Not bad, even if she might hate the slight constriction around the chest.

"Are you going to show me anything? I am something of an expert and might be able to give you a qualified opinion."

What was she waiting for?

She opened the door and stepped out to the waiting room to find Ella seated on Henry's lap, her little legs dangling in front of him, Henry's phone tight in their hands as they played a game together. The sight of the philandering playboy with the preschooler in such an unguarded and sweet moment sent an unwanted rippling of something hot down to her belly... and beyond. Henry sensed her presence and looked up at her, unaware of the reaction she was having to the scene.

Henry tilted his head and nodded. "Other than the eye rolling when you came out here, I would say you already feel a little different. The jeans look great on you. And the shirt—" He studied her again. "Great color." His eyes dropped to her chest. "But that bra isn't really helping. You know, bras were invented to lift you up, to be supportive. I'm not exactly sure what kind of action is going on here."

The saleswoman, who had been standing to the side waiting for Henry's slightest command, nodded and came toward her with a measuring tape in hand. "Let's get you measured."

Benny raised her arms to her chest almost defensively, and the saleswoman actually smiled. "Let's go to the dressing room. I promise you'll thank me for it."

With another glare thrown in Henry's direction, who already had his eyes back on the phone screen as Ella giggled, she followed the woman back to be groped.

• • •

Henry looked at his watch, wondering what was taking Benny so long this time. She defied everything he understood of the opposite sex—he'd thought clothes shopping was naturally built into their DNA.

And it wasn't like she didn't have a surprisingly decent shape once you got rid of those damned scrubs. Thanks to the pair of jeans she'd begrudgingly put on, he was hard-pressed not to notice the curves the woman had in all the right places. It had been, frankly, something of a surprise.

The door of the dressing room creaked open and he prepared himself for whatever scowl or objections she was going to lay on him. But the soft-looking, sexy woman standing in front of him barefoot in a snug green dress that wrapped around her voluptuous body was not what he'd expected. He swallowed, telling himself not to overreact.

She was watching him uncertainly, he realized, and he studied those nervous blue eyes. Even without a trace of makeup, they were captivating.

He smiled, hoping he didn't look as lecherous as he felt.

"Pretty. Like a princess," Ella volunteered, glancing up for a moment from her game.

"Now *that* is exactly what you want to wear to capture the attention of the good doctor." He tore his gaze from hers—harder than he'd have expected—to follow along the lines of her body.

The bra the saleswoman had found for her was nothing short of genius. Why had she been hiding those things? He smiled and glanced up to find her eyes narrowed, as if she knew exactly where he'd been looking.

This was not being overly pervy. He had a task to do. That

was all. He grinned again, without apology.

"I feel like I'm trying too hard. It's not too much?" she asked, wrapping her arms around her waist as if trying to hide from inspection.

The dress was actually conservative by many women's standards. Even though it clung to her body, it wasn't overly tight, or too short, hitting just at her knees, and the neckline stopped in a V that revealed an enticing amount of skin, but no real cleavage.

"I think this is exactly what you need. It's classy but also sexy. And Dr. Seeley won't know what hit him. I promise. Now I think all we need is a few pairs of nice, tailored slacks that you can wear at the office and maybe a pair of shoes that don't say, 'geriatric grandma,' and you'll be set."

A little over an hour later, Benny had just paid for her clothes when Ella pulled on Henry's arm. "I'm hungry. Can we stop at the place with the funny hats and get corn dogs?"

It was about that time, he supposed. Henry, however, hadn't had a corn dog in God knew how many years, and he wasn't sure he wanted to break that record just yet. "We definitely should eat. But is a corn dog really what you want? The Cheesecake Factory is right around the corner and—"

Ella scrunched up her pert nose. "It always stinks in there, and it takes forever to get our food. Please, Uncle Henry? I just want a corn dog." The kid's voice had taken on a high, whiny tone that was drawing a few heads turned their way.

Benny took the receipt and dropped it in the bag. "Seriously? Are corn dogs beneath Henry Ellison? Ella, for being such a good sport, how about I take you to the food court and buy us each a corn dog while your uncle goes and waits for a table for one at the restaurant."

"Yes!" the little girl shouted. "And can I have an Orange Julius, too?"

"Don't push your luck, Ella," Henry interrupted. "But I

can see I've been outvoted. To the food court we go."

Ella apparently knew the way and skipped ahead. Benny followed, dressed in a new pair of jeans and a pretty white blouse with some embroidery along the neckline. He took a moment to appreciate the wider hips and backside she'd been hiding away under bulky cotton fabric before he caught what he was doing and settled on the back of her neck and that darn scruffy ponytail.

Over corn dogs and too-sweet lemonade, Ella chattered away about her excitement at starting school next month and the friend she'd already made. "Will my mom be there my first day?" she asked wistfully and peered up at him.

Benny shot him a curious look but didn't say anything, just sipped from her straw. "I'm sure she'll try her hardest."

"Yeah." But Ella didn't sound like she believed it, the sadness almost heartbreaking. He really needed to have a long-overdue talk with his sister. Soon.

"And if for some reason she can't be, how would you feel if I took you myself?" he offered. "Would that make you feel better?"

She smiled, her baby teeth shining back at him. "Of course, Uncle Henry."

Ah, she could really tug at his emotions. He glanced up to find Benny still sucking her drink through her straw, but this time her eyes as she looked at him were curious and... almost soft.

Before he said anything else to embarrass himself, he bit into the greasy corn dog, and looked away.

• • •

Benny had been home about two hours, all her new purchases hung or folded nicely and a glass of wine in hand, when someone knocked on her front door.

She glanced down, realizing that for once, the soft fabric of the jeans hadn't bothered her enough to require that she tear them off and slide into her usual pajamas or scrubs, and that she was still in them. And presentable.

"Wow. Can't get enough of me, huh?" she asked when she opened the door to Henry's handsome face. "I'm kind of too beat to go over the fine art of flirting with you tonight."

"It's Ella," he said, and she instantly dropped the teasing and went on alert. "She was only asleep for maybe an hour and woke up screaming. She wants her mom, and no amount of talking with her has calmed her down."

"Have you tried calling her mom?" Benny asked, already pulling the door behind her, making sure it was left unlocked, and followed barefoot down the hall.

"No answer," he said tightly. "Then she wanted you."

How could Benny's heart not twinge just a little at that?

They entered his place, and the first thing she noticed was the soft lighting and Dean Martin playing through the speakers. Then she heard the faint sound of crying. Henry led the way, and she realized as they passed his decked-out kitchen—and she'd thought hers was nice—and two closed bedroom doors that his place was much bigger than she'd thought. Enormous, actually, compared to her one bedroom. Which wasn't surprising if she considered the fact that other than hers, there were no other units on this end of the tenth floor. His took up almost half the floor.

Ellie sat up when she appeared, and Benny barely processed the navy and taupe décor of the room—nice but not particularly homey or comfortable for a child—before rushing to the little girl's side. She gave Ella a big hug before leaning back to tuck some hair away from the girl's damp and flushed face. "Maybe while your uncle gets you a glass of milk, I can tell you a story. Would you like that?"

Ella nodded and clung to Benny's hand before snuggling

farther back in bed.

Since Benny's own nieces and nephew had moved back permanently nearly a year ago thanks to their dad skipping out on Daisy, Benny'd had to brush up on her storytelling skills, and after reading one particular book dozens of times—kids really liked repetition—she figured she could probably remember the gist of the tale about the bunny and her first day of school.

By the time Henry returned with the glass of milk, Ella had already nodded off. Holding her finger to her mouth to stop him from speaking and waking his niece up, Benny tucked the covers around Ella's small shoulders and turned off the light. Henry waited outside the door, still holding the glass of milk.

"That's it? You already got her back to sleep?"

"What can I say? I'm good."

She headed back down the hall and into his living room, where another bluesy jazz song was now playing.

"Would you mind sticking around for a few more minutes? Just to be sure she's asleep?"

She imagined that angelic face waking up in terror again and nodded. "Yeah. I guess."

"I'm having a drink. Can I get you something? I have red wine, if that's your preference." He smiled, and she wondered how he knew what she liked when she remembered the open bottle still on her kitchen counter and the glass waiting for her at home that he must have seen.

"Sure."

She took a seat on a leather sofa and brought her bare feet up to tuck underneath her. With the lights dimmed like this, she was able to see the downtown skyline and the city before them. No wonder he was so popular with the ladies. All he needed was to plop himself down in front of that piano and hit a few keys and the women would be tossing their panties at him.

She was dang close herself.

"What's with the piano? Do you actually play?"

He didn't even look at the instrument, just carried the two glasses of wine over. "Not anymore," he said vaguely and handed her a glass before sitting opposite her. "Thanks for your help tonight. I was at my wits' end, and when her mother didn't pick up, I was seriously considering giving her some of the Benadryl packed in her bag just to try and get her back to sleep."

For someone who had apparently been at his wits' end, Henry looked alarmingly suave and sexy, not a hair of that sleek and perfect blond coif out of place. His white linen shirt still crisp, and the way he sat back, so casual but poised reminded her of some commercial for men's cologne.

"It's fine, really. But what's going on with her mother? Anything serious?" She didn't want to be intrusive—maybe the woman was sick and was in the hospital, for all Benny knew—but she was curious for Ella's sake.

Henry shook his head and took a drink of whatever was in his glass, something dark and caramel in color. "No. Other than forgetting what it's like to grow up with an absent mother whose first and only loyalty was to her career, she's just fine."

Huh. Benny didn't really know too much about Henry Ellison other than he was likely worth millions alone because of his family's company, he held late-night parties, and he was pretty good at his job at an ad agency. But it sounded like maybe growing up, his life wasn't as charmed as she'd have thought.

"Before you think you know my life," he interrupted, as if reading her thoughts, "why don't we stick to what we've joined forces to accomplish. Getting you the date with Mr. Right and getting you out of my hair." He took another sip. "What can you tell me about this guy? Other than the fact you can't string together a sentence longer than two words in his presence. It might help us figure out the best way to approach him. Work into his good graces."

She took her own drink, enjoying the heady flavor of the wine that was clearly triple the quality—and price—of her own choice at home. "He went to school in Portland, graduated with top honors, has been working at the practice for six years. Thirty-six years old, and as far as I know, never married. No kids."

"I need more. How about sports? Music? Do you know what team he roots for? Does he prefer the symphony to rock concerts? That sort of thing."

She thought about that one for a minute. "Oh. His car. There's a sticker in the back window about the PGA Tour. I think he likes golf."

"Okay, that's an in. How are your golf skills?"

"Golf? Are you kidding? Trekking outside in the hot sun trying to get a little ball into a hole does not sound like my idea of fun. I'd rather skin my right arm with my teeth."

He actually chuckled. "If this man that you think walks on water is a huge golf fanatic, how do you think he's going to react when he hears your feelings about his favorite sport? You know, if you want, I could take you out for a few lessons. Maybe you'll find it's not as painful as you think."

"Only if I'm desperate enough."

"Don't sweet-talk me, now," he said wryly. "What else have you got? Any favorite foods or restaurants? Bars he hangs out at?"

She honestly didn't know. And that realization was really depressing. Other than being perfectly perfect, with those sweet, smiling eyes and a voice like butter—and the details of his life appropriate for a résumé—she didn't know much more about her crush.

Henry must have understood from her silence that she

had nothing. "Why don't you spend the next few days at work finding out whatever you can about the good doctor? Take a look around his office if you can—there's got to be some insight."

It made sense. Even if it felt a little weird to have to spy on her own colleague.

"The other possibility is you could actually hold a conversation with the man. See what he did over the weekend. In fact, why don't I set you up with one little task to do first thing Monday." She looked up to see him appraising her. "You're going to hold an actual bona fide conversation with the man. And initiate it if you have to."

Her stomach roiled at the prospect. What if she couldn't even squeeze a word out and ended up hyperventilating and passing out?

Henry was smiling. "Here's what you're going to do."

Chapter Six

Henry was not in a good mood when at nine o'clock Monday morning his sister finally called him back to assure him she was in town and would be picking up her daughter from day camp.

"Henry. I already told you how much I appreciate you helping me out of that jam. Are you wanting blood, too?" Morgan quipped when he answered.

"Funny. How'd your trip go?" he asked, wanting to ease into the discussion.

"Fantastic, actually. Not only did the seminar sell out, but I unloaded close to two thousand copies of my books."

"Great to hear, Morgan." He really was happy for her success. Like him, his sister hadn't wanted to rest on their family's laurels when she set out. She'd wanted to do it on her own, and from all accounts was doing it well. It wasn't her career, however, he was worried about. "Ella's just fine, in case you were wondering."

She paused just for a moment. "Yes, I'm sure she is, Henry. I knew that she'd be more than fine in your capable hands.

Are you seriously about to give me attitude because I trusted her care to you this weekend? Knew you'd have everything under control?"

"No, but I am giving you shit because Ella missed you. And from what I've learned from her, she's barely seen you more than I have over the past month. She needs you, Morgan."

"I love Ella more than anything on this earth," she said quietly, but the anger was there. "Everything I'm doing—these tours, these seminars and speaking engagements—is for her. For us. It might be a little rocky right now, but that's because I need to create my platform. Once I have a steady fan base, name recognition that will sell my next book, then things will quiet down and I'll be around a lot more. But really, Henry? You are the last person who should be dishing out advice about anyone's personal life."

He sighed. "I am only saying this because I love Ella and don't want to see you repeat mistakes that...*she* made." He didn't have to say whom he meant. They both knew. No matter how long it might be, how grown-up they were, their mother and the pain their childhood caused would always be something they'd remember. "Don't take for granted the best thing you have in your life."

"I know you mean well, Henry. I do. But I've got this. I know what I'm doing. Is there anything else?"

"Nah. Glad you're home."

He hung up and stared out the window for a minute, a memory niggling at the back of his mind. He'd been eleven, having just returned to his mother's stately home after his dad died. He was scared and heartbroken but determined not to show it, instead trying to pretend he didn't care. Didn't care about the life he'd lost, his father, or that his own mother looked at him like she barely remembered his name. And he certainly didn't care for or even like the four-year-old blond

girl in pigtails who tagged around after him, so excited to have someone else around the house she could try to connect with. At least, that's what he'd told himself.

But Morgan had been persistent, and soon enough he found himself a guest at her tea parties, sitting opposite her as they drank from empty teacups and nibbled on broken-up Pop-Tarts. And liking it. Liking *her*, even though he'd tried to fight it.

She'd given him something to love again. An adoring little sister who thought the sun rose and set behind him. But somewhere in the past few years, life had become busier, and the closeness they'd once had as kids became a distant memory.

How had he let that happen?

But this weekend, he'd had the most fulfilling few days he'd had in a while. Spending time with his niece, sharing little moments like bedtime stories and singing songs in the car on the way to her day camp. Holding her on his lap as she giggled when he fumbled over her silly Angry Birds game while Benny tried on clothes. Holding her hand when Benny pried the Skittle from her nose. It had been nice.

Then there was Benny.

A woman who both frustrated and amused him at the same time. She was definitely unlike any woman he'd ever been around. Women usually flirted with and teased him, looking for some angle to get their hooks into him. Benny Sorensen barely tolerated him. The woman was crazy and outspoken and stubborn.

But she was also bighearted, rushing to help Ella not because she felt an obligation as a doctor, but because she genuinely cared. And she made him laugh. Made him actually look forward to their next meeting.

In fact, tonight, he might have to stop by her place just to see how today went.

See if she'd managed some face time with Dr. Seeley without physically maiming someone.

. . .

Benny stood outside Luke's office, a Starbucks cup in each hand.

You can do this. It's like Henry said. Pretend Luke is just another colleague, a friend. Pretend he's your last boyfriend, Chip. And, if worst comes to worst, pretend he's Henry. That should quell any nervousness she had at speaking to him.

Taking a breath, she stepped inside the doorway. Luke's head was bent down over his desk as he wrote notes on a chart. Apparently he hadn't heard her arrive.

She cleared her throat nervously, only it sounded a lot worse than she would have liked and she nearly choked on the phlegm she'd rattled up. Lovely.

He glanced up and broke into a smile. "Dr. Sorensen. Benny. Good to see you."

Okay. Just the start she was hoping for. She held up one of the cups. "Thought I'd bring you a fresh coffee this morning. Payback for the last cup that I cost you." It had sounded really good in her head, but somehow, all the oxygen had squeezed out of her lungs and, as she'd tried to speak, her voice sounded alarmingly like one of the Chipmunks. She took in a breath, trying not to appear as winded as she felt.

"Coffee sounds pretty good. Thanks." He waited, and she realized she was supposed to bring him his cup.

Careful. You don't want to trip and send this coffee sailing into his lap.

Even though the shoes Henry had picked out were stylish slip-ons without even a heel, she felt unsteady outside of her reliable sneakers with the orthopedic inserts. But she had to admit, they did pull together the look of her black ankle-length pants and the blue shirt she'd liked so much. She had even brushed her hair out and loosened her ponytail. The effect, with the small gold hoop earrings Henry had made her buy, softened her features a bit. Not bad.

He took the cup from her. "Thanks." His eyes seemed to pause on her, taking in her face—for possibly the first time—and a quick once-over down to her shoes as he took a drink. Was that a flicker of surprise in his eyes?

She took a sip of her own drink, steadying the excitement creeping over her. Maybe there had been some truth in Henry's assessment. She felt a little more confident today. More feminine as she'd stood in front of the mirror, noticing the way the formfitting clothes gave her an hourglass appearance. Was Luke picking up on that?

Silence followed. Now what? Oh, the weekend. Details. She'd heard people turn the phrase often enough, and she'd done it herself a time or two. But not when it came to Luke Seeley.

"So, how was your weekend?" she forced herself to say. Above Luke's head was an autographed photo of a golf pro she didn't recognize, unsurprisingly. Inspiration struck. "It was a beautiful weekend for golf, right?"

His light hazel eyes shined. "It was amazing. I spent practically the whole weekend on the greens. I shot an eighty-three on Saturday and eighty-four on Sunday. My driver and long clubs were spot-on, and I hit one of my best games. Do you play?" he asked and took a drink from his cup.

She didn't see much choice here. "I do. Love it. Nothing better than being out there. On the green. Um, shooting." That sounded pathetic, but he didn't seem to notice.

"Really? What's your best game?"

"I, uh..." He'd said eighty-four. So she should probably stay in that ballpark. But...higher or lower? She took a gamble. "Ninety-three?"

"Not bad. Maybe you should join us one of these mornings. Dr. Albert and I usually play with a couple of thoracic surgeons from two floors down."

"That would be great," she said, her voice a little high. "Let me know."

Okay. She'd met her objective. Made actual interface with Luke, and so far, hadn't done anything to embarrass herself.

Time to make a graceful exit.

"Guess I'd better go. Don't want to leave the patients waiting." She turned, narrowly missing the chair that she'd forgotten about.

Outside in the hallway, she wanted to leap up into the air, do a jig, something to celebrate the moment.

She'd made contact.

And was still pretty much intact.

· · ·

The rest of Benny's day after her chat with Luke had gone remarkably well; she'd managed not only to avoid colliding with any nonmoving objects the next time she caught him in the hall, but she'd also made eye contact with him for several seconds before ducking into the examining room. Progress.

So she'd thought nothing was going to sour what was left of the day when she pulled into her open parking spot, ready to dive into the bag of Thai food she'd picked up to celebrate her win. And with four minutes to spare, she might even catch the opening of *Suits*. Hoisting the bag into her arms, she pushed the car door shut with her hip and headed to the elevator. The faint dinging of the elevator told her that if she hoofed it she could make it and not have to wait the decade it usually took for it to return. She rounded the corner just as a stunning, leggy brunette stepped inside.

"Hold the door," Benny called out, relieved she'd made

it in time.

Only the woman—who Benny was absolutely certain had not only heard her, but seen her as well—stepped farther back into the elevator. Not even pretending to hold it for her.

Hurrying, Benny surged forward, determined to make it onto that elevator, her hand in front of her to push that call button before it could leave without her.

The doors sealed a second before she pressed it.

The woman had completely ignored her.

A second later, the bottom of the takeout bag, not reinforced for running, gave out and her container of red curry exploded on her feet. "Mother of—"

Muttering a string of curses at the woman Benny blamed for her predicament, she leaned down and grabbed the pile of napkins that had fallen along with her food and wiped the tops of her new shoes off.

"Am I interrupting something?"

Benny looked up from her squatting position to see Henry staring down at her, amusement in his eyes.

Figured.

• • •

Henry had heard the woman talking to herself in Spanish before he turned the corner, and from the frustration in her tone, he sensed her ramblings weren't PG rated. He'd watched her probably a minute too long before he'd made himself known, his attention riveted to the opening at the front of her shirt as she tried to wipe the soupy mess from her feet.

She didn't bother to respond to his quip as he leaned down and took the empty Styrofoam bowl and lid and tossed it into the garbage as she grabbed the only two containers still intact.

"Thanks," she said, and straightened up.

It was hard to miss the anger shining in her bright eyes, or the flush on her face, and for a first, he hadn't been the one to cause it. "Bad day at work? Did things between you and the good doctor not go according to plan?"

She blew at the strand of hair that had fallen across her face, but with her hands filled, she couldn't wipe it away. Other than fleetingly blowing it off her face, it returned, and settled across her lips.

"Here." He moved his hand and tucked the hair back, touching her cheek just for a moment. She sucked in her breath and glared at him.

The contact was simple, but he couldn't deny the fact that standing so near the woman didn't have some appeal. She smelled like vanilla. And curry.

"I'm sure it couldn't have been that bad," he tried again.

She took in a breath and exhaled. "It went fine. Sorry. Just had a bad moment. It actually went better than I thought. We talked about golf. I think he even might have invited me to join him."

"A date? Already?"

"Not exactly. He suggested I join him and his golf buddies some time. But that's progress, right?"

Not good. Not if the guy was going to see her in a more romantic way. "Okay. The important thing is you talked and you didn't throw up on him. You didn't, right?" he teased.

"Ha-ha. I thought you'd be more excited about this. Maybe I should go out and hit a few holes with you or whatever. Get in some practice."

"Unless he's asking you to join him—and him alone—I wouldn't be celebrating just yet. What you have to be careful of is venturing into the friend zone. Once you're there, there is no going back."

"That's so not true. There are loads of people who started out as friends and went on to become more."

"Really? What, in movies? Books? Look, you want me to be honest? If a guy sees a woman and he has any interest whatsoever in her—"

"Meaning he wants to sleep with her."

"If he finds her attractive and wants to sleep with her," he conceded before continuing, "he might *pretend* he just wants to be friends until he can find the right opportunity to make his move. A man either wants to have sex with you or he doesn't. You have to make sure Luke Seeley sees you as someone he wants to sleep with, not become golf buddies with."

"The other day you were telling me I needed to learn golf," she said, frustration in her voice.

"Learning golf is still a good idea, but you want to make sure it's because he's doing it to spend time with you, not to fill an empty spot on his golf game. See what I'm saying?"

The elevator doors finally crept open, and they stepped inside. "I guess so. But it was hard enough just to talk to him. What would you have me do? Push my boobs together and bat my eyes at him?"

He glanced pointedly down at said boobs, which looked remarkably perfect in that formfitting top, and smiled. "Yeah. Go ahead. Try it. I want to see that."

She rolled her eyes. "You know what I mean."

"You've opened the lines of communication. That's a start. Now you need to make him see you as a woman. You've seen the kind of woman he likes," he said, referring to the supermodel from the other night. "Now you have to *be* that woman."

"I don't think minidresses are something that will blend in well at my pediatric practice."

"I'm not saying you have to wear four-inch heels and slinky dresses, but there's got to be more." He looked her over, nodding in approval.

She was wearing an outfit they'd chosen the other day that made her appear chic and sophisticated. Her ponytail was lower and looser, already making her seem softer, more approachable. In fact, that hair he'd just tucked away had come loose again and was curling below that full bottom lip. Subtle but sexy. If you looked hard enough. Because other than that, she looked like a kindergarten teacher.

She was going to need more if she wanted to catch the attention of an eternal bachelor like Luke Seeley.

"You look nice—for holding little kids' hands, blowing their noses, and putting that little scope into their ears like you do. Nice. Nonthreatening. But you're going to need to step it up if you want Luke to want *you*. Try wearing your hair down. It's true. Men really do like long hair." He looked at her face, bright and young, cheekbones that were there but barely discernible. "Get some layers in your hair. And do you know what a mascara wand is for?"

She crooked up her lips into a smile. "Do you?"

"I've dated my share of women, so I know a thing or two about what they wear. Lipstick, base, eyeliner. Just go easy on it, okay? You want to enhance what you've already got. I know someone who will get us started."

"I'm not saying I'm doing any of this, but let's say for argument's sake that I did try a little makeup, maybe get a haircut. And let's say I have Luke's attention, he's smiling at me in that way he smiled the other night at the glamazon creature. But then what?"

He glanced at his watch. He was meeting that cute barista for drinks at ten. He had time. "What are you doing now?"

Half an hour later, the two were stretched out on his couch, eating what was left of Benny's takeout.

"Get him talking about something he likes. Check. Nod and smile, look as if I'm hanging on his every word. Check. Giggle and laugh at everything he says because my brain is too soft and empty to have anything more to do than engage him. Check."

He smiled at the annoyance in Benny's voice. The disgruntled look on her face. "Oh, and don't forget to lean forward as much as you can, preferably in a low-neckline top with a lacy bra underneath."

"Should I baby talk, too? Maybe ask him if I can massage his feet?"

"If you think it might help." Her brows drew together in vexation again, and he chuckled. "Okay, I'm not saying you have to do all this. But—I'm not proud to admit this—all men, even the best of us, are still little boys underneath. We want to be assured that a woman likes us. Finds us irresistible. But it's a fine line. You want to be interested but not an easy conquest."

"I've lost half my brain cells just listening to all of this." She set her plate down.

"Just give it a try. Also, lick your lips a lot. You have great lips. You want to draw his attention to them. Make him want to kiss you."

"All those years in medical school, and now I'm resigned to licking my lips to elicit his interest. Great."

"You're forgetting the bigger picture. These are just little tricks, small steps you can take to initially capture his interest. His attention. Once Luke's looking at you with more than clinical interest and more actual bona fide sexual interest, then it's up to you to keep his attention. Engage him in any debate or whatever burning medical question you two might want. Just be sure that when it's all over he still wants to slip his tongue down your throat."

She wadded up her napkin and threw it at him. "You're disgusting."

He grinned. "But I know what I'm talking about."

She studied him now, picking up her wineglass. "Yeah,

because you're kind of a slut. I've seen the women parading in and out of your place. Always a different woman for a different night. Don't you ever want more? You know, something actually long lasting?"

"Why?"

"Why? Because that's what we're built for. Humans. To forge relationships, find that person you want to spend forever with."

"You really believe that forever is possible? Well, look at you," he said, settling back in his chair, kicking his legs up on the coffee table between them. "I had you pegged as a cynic, not a closet romantic."

"I'm hardly a romantic, but I do think—no, I know—that you can find someone and make it work. Make something wonderful together."

"I'll have to take your word for that." He thought about his mother, who had been on husband number seven when she died. He didn't remember his dad really being with anyone after the divorce. And his sister? She'd been in and out of relationships since she was in high school, barely taking the time to marry Ella's dad before they both called it quits and moved on. He knew from experience that as much as people like Benny wanted to believe in forever, it just wasn't realistic.

"You're forgetting what I do. I know people. I base my career on tantalizing the average consumer, who thinks they're happy with what they have, into wanting the newest and brightest. People who think they're content with that reliable and even still attractive 2015 SUV, until they see the newest model, with the newest bells and whistles. Then they're trading that SUV in and moving up. Same with cell phones, furniture, even a favorite coffee flavor. Anyone can be hooked by something new. Trust me."

"You're even worse than I thought. But you're wrong. I've seen it myself. My parents have been happily married for nearly forty years. And they're not together because they're used to each other or they're afraid to be alone, like you're probably about to argue. They're together because they love each other and are devoted to each other and know the only one who can make them happy is the other. My brothers are the same way. Both are married to amazing women, and I can assure you, they're not looking to trade up. They have the only one they'll ever want."

It was cute how naive she was.

But to each his own. He shrugged. "If you say so. But for me, I don't have any expectations going into anything. I'll enjoy someone's company, their attention for as long as it lasts, knowing that eventually we'll both be ready to move on. No hurt feelings. No unreasonable expectations."

"And on that note, I'm heading home. I have an early morning." She stood up and headed for the door.

Henry suppressed the tiniest twinge of disappointment at losing her company, even if he was probably ten minutes past the time he should have left to meet the barista. But it had been fun to rile Benny up, to see her eyes flare with disgust and disbelief.

"I'll reach out to my hairdresser and see if we can get you in tomorrow." She looked like she was about to argue, and he held his hands up. "I know you think everything I've told you is a bunch of BS, but as you agreed, we'll try things my way. See if I know what I'm talking about."

"I can't wait."

"I know." He smiled and watched her walk down the hallway, still shaking her head and probably muttering a few more choice words at the superficiality of it all.

And he'd agree. It was superficial. But people were superficial. He should know.

Chapter Seven

Benny thought of a million excuses to get out of tonight's torture as she drove to the address Henry had texted her earlier today.

An actual freaking makeover? The last time she'd succumbed to anything similar she'd been in junior high, and Daisy had bribed her to sit still while she practiced her hand at applying eyeliner, thinking for about two weeks that she wanted to go into cosmetology before the next great career prospect popped into her mind.

It was a good thing Daisy had found something else to work toward, because a cosmetologist she was not. When Benny had looked at herself, her eyebrows plucked to near slivers, black eyeliner that made her look like a raccoon rather than a woman—let alone an attractive woman—and the brightest orangeish lipstick her sister could find, an actual scream had ripped from her throat.

Needless to say, tweezers had never passed within a foot of Benny's face since that day.

The women leaving the salon looked like they'd posed

for the cover of some fashion magazine, their hair swishing around them. Benny's own hair was too thick and coarse to swish, and she'd accepted that long ago.

She sat in her car another minute, deciding whether a date with Luke Seeley was worth the agony she was bound to endure over the next hour. Then she thought of Henry's smug smile, knowing that she'd been too afraid to go through with it.

Pull on your big-girl panties and get inside.

Cool and fragrant air greeted her as she stepped inside, a relief from the sweltering nineties outside. The earthy scent was actually somewhat calming, but not enough to still the rapid beating of her heart as anxiety took hold.

What if it was seventh grade all over again and she was resigned to spending the next few months praying that her eyebrows finally returned?

She spotted Henry flirting, as usual, with an attractive woman with short but sleek burgundy hair. He waved her over when he spotted her.

"Katrina, this is Dr. Benny Sorensen. Benny, this is Katrina, my good friend." *Yeah, I'll just bet.* "She's going to take care of you today. Believe me, you're in the hands of a pro."

She bit off the witty retort she had ready about the woman's "pro" hands, realizing she didn't want to risk offending the woman Benny was entrusting herself to for the next hour.

"Benny? That's an interesting name. Is it short for anything?" the woman asked her and guided her to a salon chair where she proceeded to clasp a cape around Benny's neck.

"It is." Benny slipped a sideways glance at Henry, who was watching them both. Damn. Why did the woman have to start with such prying questions? "It's short for"—she cleared her throat—"Bernadette." A name more appropriate for a saint than a former tomboy who'd grown up hating the old-fashioned moniker.

Henry's eyebrows lifted at that. But he fortunately remained silent. Probably knowing he'd risk bodily harm if he dared utter anything.

"Bernadette, huh? Pretty name." The woman pulled the elastic from Benny's hair and spread the mass around her shoulders and back. "Wow. That's a lot of hair."

No one said anything, and the silence felt oppressive to Benny, squirming under both of their gazes. They'd probably already decided it was a lost cause.

Katrina's eyes narrowed, and she nodded, almost to herself.

"Let's get you washed, and then we'll get started. Henry, weren't you saying you had to be somewhere?"

Huh. The lady was growing on Benny. Dismissing Henry like that.

"As a matter of fact, I do." He looked at Benny again, his eyes speculative. "You'll be fine. Try and enjoy it. I'll catch you a little later. Katrina, thanks again. I'll have those tickets sent over tomorrow for you and Sherry."

Then he was gone.

Probably for the best. Because when Katrina held the gleaming scissors in front of her a few minutes later, Benny might have wanted to cry. Just a little.

It was absolutely silly, really. The way this transformation instantly made her feel like a whole new person. Benny stood at the counter while Katrina tallied up her purchases, trying not to stare at herself in the mirror ahead of her.

A good four inches of her hair was back on the floor

around Katrina's chair, and even though Katrina had assured her there was still enough length to pull it back into a ponytail if she needed to, it felt a lot shorter. Lighter. Then there was the fringe of bangs that grazed the top of her eyebrows. The last time she had bangs she'd been seven. But Benny had to admit, they actually looked…not bad.

Katrina kept smiling—actually, more like gloating—every time she glanced at Benny. "You like it?" she asked.

"It's definitely going to take getting used to." That was about as much as Benny would give. For now. She still needed to go home and plant herself in front of the mirror and analyze herself at every angle to make the final judgment.

But her head did feel a million times lighter. Her face, even with the layer of products, somehow felt smoother and more polished. Curious.

Her phone chirped, and she looked down to see a text from Daisy asking if Benny wanted to stop by. Her sister was settled into her place, and the kids were thriving, but even with their aunt Glenda next door, Benny knew she got lonely.

Well, there was no reason to let this little makeover go to waste, now was there? She needed to hear accolades—and with Henry taking off early and not seeing the final creation, she had to get someone's opinion. Who knew how competent she'd be in the morning when it was time to duplicate it.

I'm on my way, she texted back.

Thanking Katrina, she took her bag and headed outside. The fading sun was still warm, and the air was cloying, but Benny felt lighter as she headed to her car.

The sound of her nieces and nephew shouting and laughing around the back of Daisy's place greeted her a few minutes later when she pulled up into the driveway. It was good to hear, considering how shattered their world had been over the past year after their dad walked out.

Her nieces, Jenna and Natalie, were pumping their legs

trying to get higher than the other on the swing set that everyone had helped chip in to buy last spring—ignoring any arguments from Daisy, who hated taking anything that she might view as charity. Paul was digging a hole, for some unknown reason, while Daisy sat on the back step, a tall glass of iced tea next to her.

"Hi, guys," Benny yelled loud enough to be heard over the girls.

"Hi, Aunt Be—" the two girls started in unison but when they saw her, they both stopped, stunned.

Daisy glanced over, a ready smile on her face for her sister, but her eyes nearly bugged out when she caught sight of Benny. "Wow. Look at you." She came to her feet and met Benny halfway on the lawn, stopping to stare at her hair and then face. "You look…great."

Well, that didn't sound as enthusiastic as Benny had expected.

"Great?" Her hands went to her hair, now doubting the cut and style and everything she'd put herself through the past couple of hours.

"Sorry, Ben, you just took me by surprise. It's…different. I didn't expect it. You almost don't look like…you."

"Different." Benny blinked, trying not to let the deflating feeling show in her face. "Different is painting my face green and shaving my head. That's not exactly a resounding compliment."

Her nieces had reached her now and were staring at her wide-eyed. "Aunt Benny, you look so…"

Benny held her breath, waiting for another hit. Eight-year-old Natalie touched her arm, as though almost unsure she was real.

"Beautiful. Like a princess or something."

Jenna, a more sophisticated ten-year-old, disagreed. "No, dummy. Not a princess. More like a movie star. Mom, can I have my hair cut like Aunt Benny's?"

Benny swallowed a lump. That was better. Kids didn't lie, right? She glanced back at Daisy, who was studying her again, nodding. Then smiling. "They're right. You look gorgeous, the hair, the clothes, the makeup. It's all so glamorous and chic I almost didn't recognize you." Daisy grabbed her and hugged her. "I'm sorry. You look beautiful. Really."

Somewhat appeased, Benny nodded. She had thought the makeup was a bit heavier than she'd like. The lip color a little more dramatic than she was used to. *She* was still getting used to it, and she knew it was there. She couldn't blame her sister for being thrown off.

"You hungry?" Daisy asked and flipped Benny's hair. "We ordered pizza. I was tired and it's too darned hot to cook."

"Starved." Benny glanced back to see the girls back on the swing and Paul still digging the hole. "What's with Paul?"

Daisy sighed and shut the door. "He's still set on getting a dog. He's digging a hole to show he's responsible." Benny raised her brows, unsure of the connection. Daisy expanded. "He's showing me his scooping skills to prove he won't balk when it's time to clean up the dog poop."

"You've got to give the kid credit for creativity."

"Don't start."

Daisy grabbed a plate and handed it to Benny, who grabbed a couple of pieces and sat at the kitchen table, where they had a view of the kids playing outside.

Daisy joined her, setting out glasses of tea for them both. "So, I've been bugging you since, oh, about, birth, to let me do your hair, and you've never let me prevail. What inspired this new look suddenly?"

Benny hadn't shared with Daisy the fact that her new coworker was adorably cute, smart, and overall wonderful and was meant to be the father of her children. She still wasn't sure she wanted to. It had been a hard lesson that summer when Daisy had scooped up the dreamy lifeguard Benny had been certain was her soul mate. Truth was, ever since that moment, seeing her sister on the arm of the guy she had been so desperately in love with, she'd realized she would never be able to compete with Daisy. Couldn't trust that whomever she liked wouldn't fall at Daisy's feet.

Not that Benny was going to be competing with Daisy for Luke Seeley's attention. She knew that. On some level. But it didn't mean she could just ignore old habits of pretending disinterest when it came to some of the hotter men the two had met. No sense setting herself up for the inevitable crushing blow when the guy went for Daisy. It was too humiliating, and her sister would only feel sorry for her. Which was *not* acceptable.

So she fibbed.

"I just figured that I needed to overhaul my general professional appearance. I spend half of each visit just convincing the parents that, yes indeed, I did go to medical school, and yes, I am a bona fide doctor."

"Yeah. I guess I can see that." Daisy took another sip of her tea and wiped the lipstick from the glass with her thumb. "I wanted to apologize to you for what the kids said at your birthday party the other night. I know that you acted like it didn't bother you, but being reminded that you're single can't be easy. Believe me, I've been fielding a few invasive questions from moms at the kids' summer camp. I can see the judgment flash in their eyes that quickly disappear behind smiles as they rush their kids on their way. Like my single status is going to rub off on them or something."

"Don't let them bother you, Daisy. You wouldn't want to be friends with someone like that anyway."

"I suppose not. Sorry. Pity party for me. I'll adjust."

"You will. You're a great mom. Look at them. They're

lucky to have a mom like you." Benny nodded outside to where Paul had given up on the hole digging and was chasing his sisters around the yard with a water gun.

Daisy smiled. "No, I'm lucky to have them. They're my bright rays of sunshine. But enough about me." She turned a sly smile to Benny. "Since I'm not really ready to be back in the dating game—Lord knows if I ever will—I have to rely on you to live vicariously through. So, are you seeing anyone?"

Benny rolled her eyes. "What was that whole bit earlier where you apologized because everyone was scrutinizing my single status?"

Daisy waved dismissively. "That's different. I'm your sister. I get to ask the prying, embarrassing questions. So spill. At least tell me what this hot playboy bachelor who lives next to you is like. I've seen his pictures, you know. Does he have a revolving door of women coming in and out of his place? Are any of them supermodels? I heard he used to date that British supermodel, Kyra something or other."

"Henry is…Henry. Handsome, rich, used to getting what he wants." Although she wasn't sure if that was as true as she'd thought. And even though he had his own motive for helping her get a date with Luke, he had been more than cooperative. Helpful, even. "He's not all bad, though. Has a darling little niece he helps out with."

Benny explained Henry and Ella's unexpected arrival in her examining room the other night—purposefully withholding the meatier details about their deal and his help with this makeover, since she didn't know how she'd even tackle explaining why she'd asked his advice in the first place. She could see Daisy melt a little at hearing how sweet he'd been with Ella. Then Daisy's eyes turned more speculative as she looked at her sister. Her smile widened. "Sounds like maybe he has some deeper layers than you thought, huh?"

"Don't look at me like that. I am not, one hundred

percent *not*, interested in Henry Ellison. He goes through women faster than your household goes through a roll of toilet paper." Which, with three kids, Benny knew was fast. They'd spent one afternoon at her place and gone through an entire roll. "I am not looking to be another notch on his bedpost. Can you imagine how awful it would be to have to continue seeing him after a breakup? Talk about awkward."

Plus there was the fact that he'd taken off earlier with particular urgency, not even interested in seeing how the whole haircut and makeup thing went. It was like he'd said—a man either wanted to sleep with you or he didn't and was content to be friends. Men like Henry would only peg Benny in the friendship camp. Which was fine. She could always use more friends.

"You seem to have already done a great deal of thinking about this prospect already," Daisy teased, breaking into Benny's thoughts.

"Shut up. And if you don't stop, I'm going to start asking all my single dads if they'd like your phone number," she threatened back, even as Daisy laughed.

The back door swung open, and Natalie came running in, her face soaked and tears in her eyes. Conversation over, Daisy rounded the kids up and started their baths while Benny enjoyed her pizza and thought about more reasons why Henry was someone she would never be interested in in a hundred years.

• • •

Henry wasn't sure what he was expecting when he headed down the hallway to Benny's door later that night. He'd only known that when she first arrived at the salon, even without her hair fashionably styled or her face touched by an iota of makeup, she'd caught his attention the moment she'd walked in. Which had kind of irked him, since he had a date with Ursula, one of the models from the last ad campaign they'd done for that fitness wear company, who should have been occupying all of his attention. But instead of eyeing the door, eager to meet the sultry platinum blonde, he'd actually been reluctant to depart, wanting to see what Benny Sorensen would look like after Katrina got ahold of her.

The fact that he was home unconscionably early, having begged off after dinner with Ursula pleading an early morning, had nothing at all to do with seeing how things had gone with his pesky neighbor. He was really and truly tired, and he did have an early call at eight.

But…while he was home at a respectable hour, it wouldn't hurt to see how things had come along.

From the blaring television coming from the other side of her door, he guessed she was still up. It was only nine.

"Coming," he heard her say inside before the door whipped open.

He lifted his brows as he stared at her.

She was back in pajamas, this time blue plaid pants and a hoodie sweatshirt. Her hair in a ponytail, of course, and her face freshly washed and clean.

For some reason, he actually chuckled, not entirely surprised. "Really? This is the big reveal?"

"It's after nine. What did you think, I was going to sleep in that stuff?"

"Good point. How did it go, though? Did Katrina do a good job? Do you like it?"

She shrugged. "It was okay, I guess."

"Okay? You guess? You're killing me, you know that."

She had the temerity to smile. "Okay. It was more than just okay. Although I don't know if I'll be able to repeat the magic in the morning, I'll give it my best try."

He studied her closer, noting that even though she was

makeup-free and her hair was drawn back, there were still subtle changes. Like the fringe of bangs that made her blue eyes nearly pop from her face.

There was something else about her eyes, though… "You have two distinguishable brows now. I'll take that as a victory either way."

She slugged him, and he rubbed his arm at the surprising strength in the small woman's punch. "Ouch."

"Serves you right. Besides, I had good reason for being leery before about tweezers and plucked brows. You didn't see the infamous makeover fiasco of '98."

"So I am not the first one to attempt it, I see. Well, it's getting late and I should let you get back to whatever dire and serious programming you're watching." He glanced behind her to the television screen that was now paused.

"It's *Property Brothers*. Haven't you ever watched it before?"

"Can't say that I have."

"This is one of the best episodes. The homeowner is totally OCD and it's hilarious. You've got to watch it at least once. Come on, you're not going to bed straight away. I can tell you all about the horrors of overplucked eyebrows and blue eye shadow."

Even though he'd begged off early from his date because of fatigue, he had to admit he wasn't all that tired anymore. He supposed he could use the company. "All right. But only if you have pictures of this '98 fiasco to prove it."

"Don't push your luck, buddy." But she was smiling, her eyes glinting mischievously as she opened the door wider for him.

He stepped inside, curious to see what kind of decorating minimalist Benny Sorensen would have. Her hardwood floors were maple honey in tone, like his, but there was a cozier feel to her place that was due only in part to the fact that it was a fraction of the size of his own place. She definitely liked color, which was thrown in small amounts through the kitchen and front room thanks to a few pillows and pieces of art on the walls. And, of course, that bright cherry-red couch centered in front of her television and the floral-upholstered chair next to it.

Interesting.

She took her seat at the corner of the couch, and he joined her on the opposite end, declining the flowery chair.

"Sorry, did you want something to drink? I have wine and soda. Water?"

"I'm good." He crossed his leg, hooking his ankle over his knee and looked around again. Next to him on the end table was a photo that he picked up.

"That was taken this past spring at my brother Dominic's wedding in Puerto Vallarta," she explained as he studied it.

He'd spotted the bride and groom right away, of course, the couple striking with his dark hair and her long red locks. An older couple he assumed were Benny's parents stood on one side of them, as well as another taller guy with an overly serious face. Three kids were sprinkled in the front, while Benny and two other women stood on the other side of the couple, one a sister, he guessed, from the long dark hair and dark eyes similar to their mother, and the other a reddish blonde with a beaming grin.

But it was Benny he was studying now. Dressed in a formfitting turquoise dress that, even from the camera's distance, enhanced the prettiness of her eyes, she was one of the shortest in the pictures, along with her mother. Her hair was pulled back, of course, and aside from a flush of excitement on her face, it was bare of any enhancement.

She looked…happy. It made him want to know what she'd been thinking in that moment, what happened just after that photo was taken. Had she danced with any particular person?

Laughed and let herself enjoy the moment?

"Interestingly enough," she continued, "the tall brooding guy there? My oldest brother, Cruz, had just the night before gotten secretly married to the maid of honor, the strawberry blonde. Of course it wasn't legal, but at the time, he didn't know that." She nodded to another photo on the other side of the couch by her. "In fact, they made it official just a few weeks ago and are now enjoying their honeymoon on a repeat road trip across Mexico."

"And here I thought you were allergic to things like heels and slinky dresses."

She groaned. "I wasn't really given much choice. Don't get me wrong, Kate was hardly a bridezilla or anything, but my mother and my sister, Daisy, pretty much forced me to dress up at threat of personal harm."

He put the photo back, the image of her sexy figure burned permanently in his brain. He cleared his throat and nodded back to the television. "So what is the idea of the show?"

Benny explained the concept, and soon enough, the homeowner demonstrated his OCD qualities and sent the guy, in the course of a week, about thirty emails detailing what he wanted done, not to mention daily inspections. Henry knew clients like that, but fortunately, they were few and far between, leaving the creative side of things to him and the team. He told Benny about the one who'd insisted his team have at least four storyboards to show them at their first meeting compared to the usual one or two.

"I don't know how you do it. I wouldn't be able to play nice. Thank heavens four-year-olds are easily appeased with Popsicles."

The show picked up again, and they watched it with little quips here and there, both enjoying a good laugh when the homeowner discovered a nest of rats in the walls. It was close to eleven when Henry finally stood.

"Thanks for the enlightened evening. But I have an early morning, so I should go. You're going to have to give me a reveal of the complete look some time soon. And let me know how it goes with Dr. Seeley tomorrow."

But as he walked back to his place, the thought of Dr. Seeley sitting on Benny's couch, talking renovations, and sharing worst-patients-of-the-day stories kind of annoyed him. Which was pretty ridiculous. He and Benny had become…friends. And this was the whole reason they'd set this all in place.

Good friends. At that thought, he smiled. Already looking forward to their next encounter.

Chapter Eight

Benny was outside an examining room the next morning reading the chart of her fourth patient when she heard the low timbre of Luke's voice coming from around the corner. Normally, she'd hightail it the other way, but this time she made herself take a deep breath and wait.

After all, she'd spent an extra torturous hour this morning blowing out her hair and applying makeup as Katrina had instructed, to look her best for this moment. Nervously, she smoothed one hand down over the cloying white top and short, flirty skirt she'd taken another half hour agonizing over, determined not to embarrass herself today.

Okay. All good. Game time.

Benny looked back down at the chart, pretending to be absorbed in reading about her patient's reported arm rash when she saw Luke arriving from the corner of her eye.

"Dr. Sorensen?" he asked, sounding uncertain, and she looked up, feigning surprise. As if she hadn't known he was coming.

Only Luke's light hazel eyes hadn't yet met her own, his

gaze still perusing her from her toes up, and she tamped down the nausea and terror she felt. It wasn't as if she was wearing anything overly revealing, but the skirt was short enough to show off her legs and the blouse tight enough to show what she'd been hiding under oversize shirts and jackets for so long—breasts.

"Wow. You look so…different. I mean—great. Not that—I mean. How are you doing?" he finished lamely and this time met her eyes, looking the tiniest bit flustered.

That was different, and she felt suddenly a little more confident in the face of his own uncertainty. Was this what Henry had meant?

"I'm great, thanks. How are you?" she said, trying for casual.

"Good. Good. Thanks." His confusion was easing away, and a slight smile was turning his mouth up in an adorable way.

She smiled back, feeling suddenly empowered. "Well, I'd better get in there. See you later."

Before he could form a reply, she knocked on the door and swept inside the small room even as her heart raced The three kids climbing on the examining table despite the harping of the weary-looking mother seated on the bench did nothing to bring down Benny's excitement.

Luke Seeley had definitely noticed her today. And it felt good. No, great.

She thought about pulling her phone from her pocket and shooting Henry a quick text, but the sight of the smallest kid about to leap off the exam table brought her quickly back to reality.

Later. Definitely later.

• • •

The next day, Benny arrived at the office wearing another skirt and top that she'd picked up last night on the way home. She found that the array of clothes didn't fluster or horrify her as much as they had before. She was more familiar with what styles flattered her and had a good idea of what she wanted. That in itself was miraculous.

She'd spotted Luke a few more times yesterday after their first conversation, and she'd definitely seen his face light up when he saw her, a warm smile crossing his face as he greeted her or nodded, so something had to be working.

A yawn pulled from her mouth now, and she stretched her arms in front of her. She and Henry had spent another late night watching two episodes of *Property Brothers*, and she'd shared her victory at not having bumped into any door, wall, or cabinet the entire day.

She considered Henry's advice, imparted on his way out the door. "Keep in mind, when he asks you out—" A statement she'd interrupted when she snorted and started to object, but he'd pressed two fingers to her lips, effectively cutting her off.

"*When* he asks you out," he continued, "you can't be too available. Remember, you have to make him work for it. He has to know that you're not just sitting home pining away, waiting for him to ask you out, and that you have other... options. You're going to have to turn him down."

She'd almost laughed then. "Turn down a date with Luke Seeley? Are you insane? That's what we want—what I want. What we're doing all of this for."

"Do you want to just be one of the many women the guy sees once before moving on, or do you want to be someone he's really interested in? Someone he has to work to see, a prize in itself? Guys like a challenge. And that's what you need to give the good doctor. You have to trust me on this. Say yes too soon, and that's all it's going to be. Think long-term."

Even now the thought of declining a date from Luke seemed ludicrous. Not that she was in imminent danger of his asking her out, since it was Thursday and he was bound to have plans already set for the weekend.

So it was something of a shock when five minutes later someone knocked on her door and, instead of Roz's long face, she looked into the warm gaze of Luke Seeley.

Holding two cups of coffee in his hands.

"Thought it was only fitting that I returned the favor and brought you some coffee today. I didn't know what you liked, so I got a skinny vanilla latte. Hope that's okay—it just seemed to be a popular drink of the women ahead of me."

"It's perfect, thank you." Even if she hated the flavor of vanilla in her coffee and preferred whole milk to skim, thanks to the richer texture it gave. But she smiled and took the cup from his hand.

"Not a problem." He stood there another second, staring at the floor as he considered something. "Actually, maybe you can help me out with something. Dr. Albert has to cover the clinic this Saturday, so it's thrown a little hitch into my golf plans."

He was going to ask if she'd mind covering for Dr. Albert. She'd been asked a couple of times before to cover by other doctors, and being the newbie, she didn't want to risk making enemies. She waited now for the appeal, resigned to having her hard-earned Saturday off taken away.

"So…since you play and all, I wondered if you'd consider being my partner."

She couldn't have heard him right. He was asking her to play with him? This Saturday?

Her head seemed to be spinning at the possibility, and she forced herself not to jump up and bounce around the office. Best to be sure. "Sorry?"

He smiled, confident and certain. "Saturday? Golf? With

me?"

Yeah. She'd heard him right. She opened her mouth, ready to say, "Of course," and ask what time should she be ready, but then she remembered what Henry had said.

To make him work for it. To…tell him no.

"I—I think that sounds like fun, only…I kind of already have weekend plans."

"Come on, I'm sure you can manage to pull yourself out of bed by seven no matter how hard your partying is the night before." If possible, he was smiling even brighter, sure he could charm her into coming.

Well, she'd acted so freaking infatuated around him the past couple of months, she couldn't blame him. It helped firm up her resolve.

She smiled and, like a pro, she licked her bottom lip— even though she felt like an idiot doing it. Only…

Luke was staring at her mouth. Hmm.

"No, I'm afraid we have plans the whole weekend." She played it coy, not elaborating more.

He seemed to finally realize the implications, and his smile cracked a little. "Oh, I'm sorry. I didn't know you were involved with anyone."

Her mouth went dry, her mind working to try and keep up with the pretense. What would Henry suggest she say? "Nothing serious."

Luke's smile brightened back up. "Another time, then? Maybe we can even go for dinner soon."

"Maybe."

He pushed his glasses back up on his nose in a boyish fashion, still grinning widely. "I'll let you know. In the meantime, enjoy your coffee."

"I will. Thanks."

Luke turned around and—in a surprising turn of events— *he* ran into the edge of the open door. She smothered a giggle, but when he glanced back at her, she pretended to already be caught up in her files.

Sure, it wasn't like he was asking her out for an intimate dinner alone, just the two of them. But he'd asked her to be his golf partner, which was as close to a date with him as she'd ever had.

With the door closed firmly behind him, Benny hopped to her feet for a quick celebratory jig, her arms pumping the air in victory.

Henry would never believe this.

Grabbing her phone from the desk, she sent him a text.

*Guess who just told Luke Seeley she was busy Saturday and couldn't play golf with him? ME!! That's right. *dancing**

His response was almost immediate.

Didn't I tell you? What did you tell him? ~H

No. Just like you said. That I had plans the entire weekend.

Attagirl. Congrats. Dinner's on me tonight. Chinese or pizza? ~H

Chinese. And Henry? Can I still take you up on that golf lesson?

Chapter Nine

"It has to be a sign of lunacy that people actually get up early—on a weekend, no less—to do this," Benny whined as she stepped out of the passenger seat bright and early Sunday morning in front of Henry's country club.

He had agreed to give her a lesson in golf in case Luke Seeley asked her to join him for golf again—or wanted to engage in some sort of discussion about the sport. She needed to be prepared. And although he usually spent his Sundays in a more leisurely fashion—preferably in bed with some delectable beauty—an unforeseen client crisis that mandated he spend Saturday at work had left Sunday the only day available. Although, to be honest, last night's date had ended early anyhow, as he just hadn't had the energy do the usual club thing. And he'd wanted to be fresh and awake for this interesting day.

Benny followed him to the trunk, where he pulled out his golf clubs along with an extra set he'd borrowed from Morgan. Henry had almost been afraid that when Benny opened her door that morning she'd be dressed in more scrubs or possibly that hoodie sweatshirt she'd worn the other night, even if it was expected to reach close to one hundred by midafternoon. But she seemed to have caught on to the idea of casual wear that didn't involve flexible waistbands and was wearing a white short-sleeved polo and a pair of slim green capris that showed the generous curve of her backside. Neither of which were items they'd shopped for on their first foray to the mall, leading him to conclude she'd supplemented her wardrobe on her own—and fairly successfully.

He wondered what else she might have purchased that he still had yet to see.

Her hair was pulled back into a ponytail again, but he couldn't begrudge her that, since she'd want to keep it up and away while they played. And with the fringe bangs Katrina had given her, the boring ponytail had infinitely more sex appeal, especially combined with the artful way she'd pulled some strands down to frame her face and the hoop earrings that swayed when she moved. But it was the light, berry-toned gloss on her lips that had him most hypnotized. Even now, his gaze kept dropping to their full softness, and he wondered if the gloss tasted as good as it looked.

Easy there.

"No one is making you do this, you realize," he said, trying to regain his sanity. He had *not* been just thinking about his neighbor's lips. He slung the golf bags over each shoulder before slamming the trunk. He handed the valet his car keys and headed inside the club. "If you hadn't pretended to actually know how to play golf, you could have used the opportunity to ask Luke to take you for your first lesson."

She arched an eyebrow at him. "You couldn't have thought to tell me this before?" She glanced around the club, looking a little less certain all of a sudden. "What time are we scheduled to start teeing off—is that what you call it?"

"We have an hour."

"*What?*" Her eyes widened. "You pulled me up out of bed and we still have an hour? If you wanted company for breakfast, we could have stopped at McDonalds's drive-through and given me an hour more of sleep."

"McDonalds? You sound like Ella. Are you sure you're not four? No, we're here early because we're going to go to the driving range to spend a little time working on your swing. There's more to it than just closing your eyes and hoping you make contact."

"Henry," someone called from one of the tables, and he looked over to see Mark and Jonathan, two club members he'd played golf with on occasion, now standing up and heading their way.

"Good to see you. Jonathan and I were just wondering if we were going to catch you this weekend since we missed you last week," Mark said as they reached him.

"Had some family stuff to attend to, but thought I'd get some time in today." Both men, however, weren't really listening to what he'd said and were instead staring at his golf buddy. "Mark, Jonathan, this is my friend Dr. Benny Sorensen."

Each man offered his hand, smiling a little too widely at Benny, who was smiling back just as readily, unaware of these guys' track records.

"Are you two playing in pairs today?" Mark asked. "Because it's just the two of us, if you wanted to make it a foursome."

"Sorry, fellows. Benny is something of a novice. I'm going to show her a little more about the game before we actually tee off."

"I'm afraid it's true. I'm what you might call a golf virgin," Benny said in a playful tone that had Henry's mouth dropping open. "Never even held an iron—is that the right word?—before."

"You know," Jonathan said, eyes still on Benny, "if you're trying to pick up the game, you could do a lot better than taking tips from Ellison here."

"I probably could. But you know how Henry is. His fragile ego needs to be built up a bit at times."

"Ah, yes. That's me. Needing to hear the endless cries of gratitude and appreciation that you, for one, are so quick to give."

Benny grinned back at him, and for a moment they stared at each other, his mind reeling at how the stodgy, reserved doctor had suddenly become so adept at flirting.

And doing it well.

And he wasn't sure he liked it. At least not when it was trained on someone other than *him*.

· · ·

"Well, we tee off in an hour if you two decide to have a go at it," said the shorter brown-haired guy, whom Henry had introduced as Mark.

Benny had almost forgotten they were both there for a minute, caught up in staring into Henry's eyes. Which was pure insanity.

She did a mental headshake and was about to respond when Henry cut in, a little more curt than necessary. "We'll certainly keep that in mind."

Sure to smile, she waved good-bye and followed Henry outside the clubhouse.

Minutes before, on entering the fancy clubhouse already teeming with people—particularly women, who were eyeing Henry like he was the only glass of water on a hot summer day—Benny'd felt out of place and expected someone to ask her for proof of why she was even there. Spending the day at a country club, let alone on a golf course, was the last thing she'd ever seen herself doing.

The county pool and community center were more her thing.

But Henry's friends had helped ease that discomfort. She had almost surprised herself with the flirty, sexually tinged comments that spewed so easily from her mouth. Comments she thought would have earned more amusement and encouragement from Henry. Instead he'd looked stunned and then…annoyed.

They reached the driving range, and she took a moment to take in the million-dollar view of the Wasatch Mountains, the clubhouse and pool, and the tranquil pond in the distance. The air felt unnaturally clear and sharp this morning, crisp in anticipation of the heat to come.

Henry pulled out a club from the smaller bag, handed it to her, and took another club from his own bag. "You're going to want to hold the club like this." He held his hands in front of them then curled one hand around the end of the club, waiting for her to repeat it, before gripping the other side. Then he raised it and did a practice swing, the air swooshing as he brought the club through.

Man, she hated golf, but the artful way Henry swung that thing was…kind of hot.

"Try it," he said, thankfully ignorant of her less-than-chaste thoughts.

Pulling her tongue back into her mouth, she tried the same swing in what felt like exactly the same motion. By the tugging of Henry's lips, she was going to assume she hadn't quite duplicated the movement. Henry repeated his instruction and directed her to make some adjustments in the grip before he swung again.

She greedily eyed his form while he was preoccupied. *Marvelous.*

When she realized he was waiting for her, she repeated

his motion.

"Maybe we should practice with the ball." He grabbed a couple and placed them on the tees in front of them before winding back again, the swooshing hypnotic, this time followed by the short cracking sound of the iron hitting the ball as it sailed up into the air and landed on the stretch of grass ahead of them.

At least, she was certain it had landed somewhere over there, since she was still watching Henry, his torso turned to the side and his arms flexed as he gripped the club, making it hard to miss the bulge of his biceps. His profile clean and striking, his lips parted as he watched the landing.

How did he get his hair to stay like that yet still look so touchably soft?

He turned toward her, and Benny tried to divert her eyes so he wouldn't know she'd been slobbering over him. She reminded herself that Henry Ellison was a self-absorbed ladies' man who was only helping her out to help himself—nothing more.

But when he smiled, telling her to give it a shot, that reminder went out the window.

She looked down at the end of her club as he continued to coach her. "Practice swinging, feeling the back-and-forth in your hips before you try and connect. The key is, when you're about to hit the ball, keep your eye on the spot where you want it to go."

Blah, blah, blah.

She practiced swinging, feeling silly as she did so, knowing Henry had to be watching her ginormous hips move back and forth as instructed.

"Good. Now, find your target and…"

She swung and waited to hear the same crack as the club connected with the ball. Only her swing continued forward, no cracking sound followed, and she nearly lost her balance, having to take a step forward to catch herself.

She'd completely missed.

Heat filled her face, and she cast an embarrassed glance at Henry. "Not bad. I have yet to see a beginner ever connect on the first try. Let's go again."

Only nine swings later, other than hitting and tearing up the grassy area *around* the ball, she'd been unsuccessful. She shot him a frustrated look, blowing back a strand of hair that kept falling to her mouth. "I suck at this."

"The problem is in your lineup. Here." Henry walked behind her, and before she could even catch her breath, she felt his hands on her hips. She nearly shot out of her skin from his touch. "Easy," he said somewhere near her ear before his arms went around her and his hands rested over hers on the golf club. "I'm just trying to show you the motion, the way you want your body to flow as you hit."

Her body was flowing, all right. Her whole freaking body was buzzing from having him so near her, surrounding her. He smelled…good. Clean. Masculine. Goose bumps prickled along her arms.

Was this even appropriate in public? She looked up, her eyes wild, to see if everyone was staring at them in horror, but no one was even glancing their way.

Steady there, Benny. He's just showing you a swing. Nothing more.

Do not turn around, though, whatever you do.

She exhaled slowly and worked to take in another breath.

It was unnaturally quiet, and she realized that Henry was no longer talking or trying to move. Birds chirped from somewhere overhead, but she was paralyzed from moving or looking up.

Henry cleared his throat and shifted behind her, his arms dropping away from her. "Okay, let's try again."

She raised the club, her heart beating a trillion beats a

second and brought it down, swinging through just as Henry taught her. Like before, she missed the ball and stumbled forward, trying to save herself on the follow through. Only this time, she did make contact with something.

From the *oomph* from behind her and the ball still perched on the tee at her feet, she knew it wasn't the contact she'd wanted.

She turned around to find Henry holding his head, his face in a grimace.

She'd clobbered him.

"Oh my gosh, Henry! I am so sorry!" She dropped the club and rushed forward, horrified by her actions. "Please. Let me look at it."

"It's nothing. Just a bump on the head," he said, trying to assure her and took a step back, only his footing was unsteady and he stumbled. Before he could fall, she jumped toward him and anchored his weight against her, wrapping her arm around his waist.

"You're not all right. You could have a concussion. We need to get you inside so I can examine you."

He smiled a little too widely. "If you wanted to see me naked, Doc, all you had to do was ask."

She laughed, unable to resist. "Try to keep it PG, big guy. I think I hit you harder than I realized."

While they walked back across the grass toward the clubhouse, Benny tried to ignore the fact that Henry's upper torso was toned and deliciously sculpted as she supported him, not an ounce of flab or anything extra to hold onto. Just sinewy strength. Combined with the heady aroma of eau d'Henry, it took every bit of her resistance not to attack him right there.

He was injured, for crying out loud. She was a doctor. And she was head over heels in love with Luke Seeley. She had to get a hold of herself.

Back in the clubhouse, she sat him down on a chair and knelt down in front of him to try and get a better idea of his injury. A guy in a green polo with the clubhouse name on it was there in a flash. "Mr. Ellison, is everything all right?"

"Fine, Nate. Just a bump on the head, I think. Nothing serious."

She might beg to differ with him. "You might have a concussion, Henry. Let me just check you out." She looked up at Nate, who she assumed was some kind of manager at the club. "I'm afraid we left our golf bags back at the driving range. Do you think—"

"Of course. I'll have someone retrieve them right away and have them placed in Mr. Ellison's car for him." The man hurried away.

Wow, that was easier than she would have thought. Money did have its privileges.

She turned to Henry again. His brows were scrunched up, and he was looking a little dazed now. "I'm sorry. Have we met before?"

Her stomach sank. It was much worse than she thought.

She was a menace. That was all there was to it.

She placed her hand over his and lifted his hair up from his forehead to look at the damage. No laceration, but there was swelling and a red mark from where the club had hit him.

"You really don't remember? I'm Benny. Your neighbor." She bit her lip, unsure how to proceed as she stared into his brown eyes.

The pupils were even, no dilation. That was good. In fact, his eyes were shining a little too brightly. Henry's lips trembled then, almost like he was trying not to—

"You jerk." She slugged him just as a chortle shot from his mouth.

"The look on your face was priceless," he said and rubbed his arm. "But you do carry quite a punch, so take it easy, slugger."

"Serves you right. But I am serious about the concussion. Here." She held her hand out. "Take it. I need to test your strength. Okay. Squeeze. Next hand."

Ten minutes later, she was somewhat mollified that Henry wasn't suffering severe brain damage, but from his stumble and his concession that he did have a mild headache, she hadn't ruled out the possibility of a concussion.

"We should get you to the ER to be examined, just in case," she said as he swallowed the two Tylenol the club had provided at her request.

"Absolutely not. What would they tell me that you can't confirm yourself? I know a little something about concussions. I may have suffered one or two back in my Little League days. All they'd suggest is that I take it easy, not do anything too strenuous over the next few days, and if I feel any sort of confusion, dizziness, increased headache, that sort of thing, to get myself more thoroughly examined. All of which I can do without going to the hospital."

He stood up, and two seconds later, sat back down. "No. That was nothing. Just a little head rush from coming to my feet too fast."

She sighed. "Well, we should get you home, at any rate. But you should know, for the next twelve hours, I'm not letting you out of my sight. You shouldn't be left alone in case your symptoms worsen."

"I'll be fine. I don't need a nursemaid."

"Sure. And when I come by in the morning to see how you're doing and find you either comatose or dead, having suffered massive brain swelling or bleeding, that will be of some comfort to me. To Ella."

He quirked up a brow, probably about to deliver some zinger about not knowing that she cared, but his effect was diminished when he flinched and raised his hand to touch the growing goose egg.

She couldn't resist a tiny smirk. "See?" She came to her feet and held her hand out to him to offer assistance. "In fact, I think it only makes sense, considering your dizziness and lack of equilibrium, that I drive us home."

"You think you're up to it? That's a lot of power."

"I went to medical school. How hard can it be?"

Chapter Ten

Okay. So up to now, had anyone asked Benny whether she thought the bloated prices that people paid for flashy sports cars like Ferraris were insane, she'd have agreed and added it was a ridiculous display of money and conceit for those who might be compensating for...*something*.

At least up until they reached the freeway and the slightest touch of the gas had her cruising at a dangerously heart-stopping speed—for Benny, anyway. Her adrenaline was pumping, and she had the crazy notion to throw back her head and laugh maniacally, even as the wind was making fast work of messing up her tidy ponytail.

"You do realize what the actual posted speed limit is," Henry said from the passenger seat.

She pulled a piece of hair from her mouth. "Yeah. Guess I should take it down a notch." Only...wow. The way the car rode was so smooth that the temptation to take it higher was intoxicating.

But common sense prevailed, and she eased up on the gas a smidge. She grinned a little wildly over at Henry. "Had

I known driving this thing could be this much fun, I might be the proud owner of a shiny new Ferrari. Even if I would have to curl up in the front seat in a sleeping bag every night since I couldn't afford to live anywhere else. How much does something like this actually set you back? Wait. No. I don't want to know."

"If you're really enjoying it that much, why don't we take it for a longer spin? Maybe to Vegas? We could be there in five hours. Four at the rate you're going now."

"The idea is tantalizing..." She imagined the purring motor as they cruised at a steady one hundred miles per hour on the freeway, or driving down the Las Vegas Strip with the top down and feeling like a million bucks, like she owned the world, maybe having a turn at the slots or taking in a show. But... "Unfortunately, I have work bright and early in the morning, so taking off like that isn't an option. It is Sunday."

As soon as she said the words, she cringed. Crap. She'd nearly forgotten.

"Actually"—she risked a sideway glance at him—"I should mention that I have a standing dinner invitation this evening, and since I am not letting you out of my sight"—she had nearly killed him, after all—"I'm afraid you better get used to the idea that you're coming along."

"Standing dinner plans? That does sound intriguing. Where are we going?"

"My parents'. For Sunday dinner. It's tradition."

"Seriously? People actually do that? I thought that only existed in television shows like *The Waltons* and *Parenthood*. How...quaint."

Quaint? Good Lord, this was going to be a disaster.

Henry Ellison in her family home while her brothers played their usual head games like they had with all of her— okay, mostly Daisy's—dates. *Not that this is a date!*

Any other Sunday dinner, under these circumstances

of playing Henry Ellison's nursemaid, she'd beg off. But her older brother and his new wife had just returned from their Mexican honeymoon, so everyone was going to be there to welcome them home.

Bailing just wasn't an option.

"Whatever you do, let's not mention to anyone the role you're playing in my little scheme. Not a word about makeovers or Luke Seeley. Got it?"

He glanced at her, the picture of a saint. Then he grinned widely, his eyes twinkling in anticipation, and she fought a nervous dread compounded by something a little more... excited.

"Let's just see if you're still grinning when this night is over."

. . .

Despite the dozen or so girls that Henry had dated in high school, he didn't have a lot of experience when it came to meeting parents and brothers and sisters and all that might constitute a family. Up until he left his mother's house at eighteen, the girls he'd dated had usually—not to brag—come to him. Showed up at his house because they were curious to see where he lived and what it was like to step foot in the massive mausoleum, maybe even catch a glimpse of the mysterious Margaret Brighton. Those rare dates when he did pick someone up, they came running out the door before he'd stepped out of his car.

So he wasn't exactly sure what was in store for him when they pulled up to Benny's parents' modest ranch-style home, where a driveway of cars told him most—if not all—of her family was already inside.

"Don't be nervous, everything will be fine," Benny told him, her voice barely a whisper as she hopped out of the car.

"Should I be?" he asked, joining her on the sidewalk. He eyed the sexy white capris she'd changed into, the sleeveless navy blouse with more pretty embroidery around the neck, and the black heeled sandals. She had really gotten the hang of this fashion thing. And a few other things.

All while keeping her sass.

He smiled and waited for her response.

The slight smile and furrow of her brows gave him the distinct impression she was looking on him with sympathy, which immediately made him curious. Before he could question it, the front door was thrown open and two young girls with long dark brown hair and bright smiles looked at them expectantly. He wasn't an expert, but he'd guess they were probably a handful of years older than his own niece.

"Everyone was here ages ago, Aunt Benny," the older one said. "We have Twister set up in the family room, but no one will play with us. Uncle Dominic said to ask you."

"I'll bet he did," Benny said and stepped inside.

But the younger little girl hadn't stopped looking at him, and her smile had now widened into a grin. "Are you my aunt Benny's boyfriend?"

The clatter from the back of the house he'd heard when they first stepped inside had suddenly gone suspiciously quiet.

Before he could articulate a response, Benny hurried in, her voice loud and clear. "Of course not, Natalie. This is Mr. Ellison. He lives next door to me and he might be suffering a minor concussion from earlier today, so I insisted he have dinner with us."

Something told him that this statement had been less for the young girls and more for whoever might be waiting for them in the other room.

"Henry, these are my two minions—I mean nieces, Jenna and Natalie," she added in a more conversational tone.

"I'm Natalie," the youngest and clearly most outspoken

of the two said. She reminded him of someone…

"Hi, Natalie. It's nice to meet you, and please. Call me Henry," he said and held his hand out to the girl, who now seemed to be looking at him a little more…affectionately. She shook it with aplomb. He did the same with the older girl. Jenna took it, her face solemn although her eyes studied him with curiosity.

"What your aunt isn't telling you is that she whacked me over the head with a golf club earlier and now feels guilty for nearly killing me."

Natalie covered her mouth with her other hand and giggled.

"One could wonder, however," Benny said and walked down the hall, with them following, "why a man who claims to be an expert would have let himself stand in the range of said club."

"I think I was so in awe of how truly atrocious your golf swing was that the club heading for my head took me completely off guard."

More giggles, and then they were in a bigger open room. To the left was a large kitchen with several people already working; to the right was a family room with a decent-size television and the aforementioned Twister game already spread out on the floor. Separating the two living spaces was a long dining table and French patio doors that led out onto a deck. The place felt airy and friendly.

The expressions of the people in the room were another question, and from the hush that followed he gathered they'd all been whispering just moments before.

"Hi, everyone. This is Henry Ellison," Benny said, repeating the introduction he knew everyone had already heard. "As I explained to Mom, he's going to be having dinner with us."

A petite woman with dark brown hair came over. "Hello,

Henry. I'm Benny's mom, Elena," she said with a faint accent that told him she wasn't a native speaker. She smiled at him warmly, though, the same curious gleam in those brown eyes as her granddaughters had shown him. "We've heard a lot about you."

Of course they had. He wouldn't bet on it being particularly flattering. But he'd used his charm and sparkling wit to get out of tough spots before. This wasn't impossible. "Nice to meet you, Mrs. Sorensen. Your home is lovely. And I appreciate your letting me crash your family dinner."

"Please, it's Elena. You are more than welcome in our home," she added and he was certain it wasn't necessarily meant just for him. "Let me make the introductions while Benny gets you two something to drink." Benny lifted her brows briefly and went into the kitchen, grabbing a couple of glasses from the cupboard.

Over by the sink, a tall redhead was watching him, suspicion in her gray eyes as she washed a bowl of tomatoes. The even taller hulk standing next to her with dark hair and blue eyes looked at him with less suspicion and more outright dislike as he gripped a butcher knife. From the cutting board and half tomato already diced, Henry assured himself the guy wasn't holding it to stab him.

"Henry, this is my son Dominic and his beautiful new wife, Kate." He recognized the couple from Benny's photograph.

"A pleasure," Henry said, offering his hand first to Kate, who quickly dried hers on a towel and took his firmly, smiling politely. He turned to Dominic.

"So you're the player next door to my little sister, huh? Partying at all times of the night like you're running a frat house." He hesitated but took Henry's hand, his shake solid and a great deal stronger than necessary.

"Yes, well, I'm a businessman, and often have clients over. We try to keep the toga parties reserved for special occasions, though."

Dominic didn't break into a smile. "Why were you giving my little sister golf lessons again?"

Tough crowd.

"Well, the truth is that it wasn't my idea. You see—"

"Henry, did you want beer, wine, water, or iced tea?" Benny interjected.

"Water is fine."

Benny handed a bottle to him and warned him with the flash of her blue eyes not to say another word.

"You haven't met my sister, Daisy, yet," she said and nodded toward the stunning brunette with dark eyes and long hair who was chopping at another counter.

"Hi, Henry," the woman said in a singsong voice and waved. "Nice to finally meet you. Benny, you didn't tell me you wanted to take up golf," Daisy added, not ready to let her sister off the hook.

"I didn't? It's not a big deal, I just thought it might be a good idea, you know, if, um…"

"Some of the doctors at her practice invited her to play next weekend, and rather than decline, she thought she'd take some lessons. Try to learn a few things."

"Learn a few things? We're just talking golf now, right?" Dominic challenged.

Henry didn't look away, steadily meeting the guy's gaze before breaking into a smile. "Yes. Just golf."

It was all rather cute the way they rallied to protect Benny like this. Didn't they know the woman could probably take them all on? One-handed?

"Oh, knock it off, Dom," his wife said and laughed. "Lay off Mr. Ellison at least until after dinner."

Benny took Henry's hand and dragged him through the dining area to the open French doors. "Let's introduce you to the rest of the bunch."

A tall man with light blond hair who Henry knew was Benny's father manned the grill, a small boy of six or seven standing next to him. Another couple was seated and had stopped speaking at their arrival. Henry recognized the other brother, the oldest of the siblings, with his arm around a pretty reddish-blond woman. The honeymooners, if he wasn't mistaken.

"Everyone, this is my neighbor *and friend*, Henry Ellison," Benny said this time with emphasis on the "friend" part. "Henry, this is my dad, Petter Sorensen"—Henry took the older man's hand, blue eyes steady on him but not necessarily unfriendly, despite the lack of movement of his facial muscles—"and this is my nephew, Paul, my brother Cruz, and his wife, Payton."

Dutifully, Henry walked around and greeted them all, noticing that Cruz's handshake was no less forceful than his brother's. "Nice to meet you. Hope you don't mind me crashing your dinner."

Cruz, like his father, didn't say much, but Payton and Paul were more effusive in their greetings. Paul in particular, when he ran over and grabbed both of their hands, tugging them into the house. "Twister time!" he shouted.

"Buddy, why don't you and your sisters just play—" Benny started.

"Not a chance, Benny," Daisy said, hearing her trying to beg off. "You bought the game for them. I think the least you can do is play with them as well." She smiled like the Cheshire cat.

Now all three kids were jumping up and down, shouting to get started, and Benny gave him a helpless smile. "You up for it?"

"Twister? I'd love to. Just don't let your aunt get too close to me," he said to the kids. "I wouldn't want to risk the loss of a limb or another smack to the head."

"No promises," she said, but she was smiling.

At least until five minutes in, when Jenna, who'd decided to sit out the first round on the couch in between her aunts Payton and Kate, called out the next move.

Right hand to blue.

Which placed Benny Sorensen practically underneath him while he tried to balance precariously with his body contorted in ways he'd never known possible. Not just beneath him, but her backside pressed dangerously close to his left hip and her hand nearly on his own. Something he probably would have enjoyed any other time, with the woman's intoxicating warm vanilla smell surrounding him.

But not when her entire family was looking on. Her brothers still seemed like they were waiting for a reason to tackle him.

Benny raised her luminous eyes to his then, and for just a moment, he was able to block out the dozens of eyes trained on them. Enjoy the flush on her face that had it pink and bright, her lips parted as she took in their close proximity.

And he realized.

Benny Sorensen was the most beautiful woman who'd ever been under him. And it took every ounce of strength he had not to lean toward her and kiss those delectable lips.

Something flickered in her eyes, and whatever had been holding her up slipped and she was suddenly falling, upending his left hand, and bringing him tumbling down on top of her.

• • •

"…and Cruz stood there, not even flinching while two busboys trapped the man-size cockroach and swept it out the terrace doors," Payton was telling everyone over dinner, her voice filled with laughter that matched her exuberant expression. Glowing, naturally.

Benny and everyone glanced to her ever-stoic older brother, who sat stone-faced, but there was a gleam in his brown eyes as he watched his wife tell the tale, his adoration clear. "Someone had to retain some level of calmness. Payton was standing on her chair and shrieking like the place was on fire."

"I wouldn't say...shrieking. But when a cockroach big enough to physically carry me out the door nudges my foot, I think my reaction was absolutely reasonable." But she was laughing along with everyone else.

Benny sneaked a glance at Henry, who was chuckling, looking the picture of relaxation with his natural debonair charm and one of her nieces on each side of him—clearly besotted from the way they both fought to sit next to him. Despite the humiliating moment before dinner when she'd been pinned underneath him, the weight of his body on hers not entirely uncomfortable, Henry had taken everything in stride. Even her brothers' attempts to drill him on his sports facts, which she'd been surprised to find were remarkably keen, hadn't broken so much as a sweat on his too-handsome face.

Now he sat back, his entire plate of fish tacos devoured, looking for all purposes like he belonged here among her family. She got the feeling that Henry naturally fit in any place he went, with his easy and teasing smile, his quiet confidence and way of making everyone like him.

Well, almost everyone. Cruz and Dominic had barely thawed, but no surprise there. Always overprotective.

Dominic was studying her now, his face perplexed. "What have you done? You look...different."

Of course that drew everyone's gaze to her, and she felt her face flush uncomfortably under the attention. "What do you mean? I haven't really done anything different."

Payton was staring at her with more careful scrutiny.

"He's right. You look great, but I can't quite put my finger on what it is…"

Benny hadn't wanted to do the whole glamour girl style that she'd been doing at work for family dinner, wanting to avoid this exact scrutiny. But she also enjoyed how she felt and looked when she took twenty extra minutes to brush her hair to a shine before drawing it back to a loose ponytail and slipping in silver hoop earrings, applying a touch of makeup to her eyes and lips so her face felt brighter and more…polished.

She'd never realized before how just taking a few moments could make her feel so much more confident. Not that she'd ever have Payton's stunning prettiness, Kate's strong and beautiful features, or her own sister's natural dark beauty. But Benny was a strong finisher now, and she knew that people noticed her more—men particularly. And she didn't…hate it.

"I like it," Kate said firmly.

"Are you wearing…makeup?" Cruz asked incredulous. "What was wrong with how you looked before? Who are you trying to impress? Did someone make you feel like you weren't good enough as you were?" His gaze, though, was on Henry, and he looked like he wanted to challenge him.

"Enough, everyone. Leave Benny alone," her mom intervened. "She's a professional. A doctor lady now, and she can't stay eighteen forever. She looks like…a pretty doctor." Her mother smiled and nodded toward her.

"Thanks, Mama." Benny glanced again at Henry, who was studying her with his own strange glint in his brown eyes. "The tilapia was seasoned perfectly," she said to distract everyone from her face, and motioned toward the last bite of her fish taco on her plate.

"Lime zest," her mom said, nodding. "You just need a hint of zest and salt."

"Hey, don't I get any credit for grilling the fish?" her dad asked, a faint smile around the edges of his mouth. He winked at her before taking another taco from the platter.

Well, the worst was over. No one was telling her she looked ridiculous. No one said she was trying too hard to be someone she wasn't. And the thing was, right now, with her family surrounding her, the strange swirl of excitement in her belly growing as Henry continued to watch her, she felt exactly like who she was meant to be.

"Okay," she said and tossed her napkin on the table. "I think it's time Henry and I took on the two geriatric brothers in a little game out back. You up for it, Henry?"

"I think I can hold my own."

"We'll see," Cruz and Dominic said at the same time.

Chapter Eleven

"How's your head?" Benny asked and threw a glance over to Henry.

She was back in the driver's seat of his car, a few minutes from home. It was a fair question, considering the possible mild concussion she'd caused earlier that day, but far more pertinent now after the "accidental" elbow to his head when he'd attempted a jump shot during their scrimmage earlier. Cruz and Dominic were denying accountability.

"Not too bad." He opened the visor and lifted the front of his hair to look at the darkening bruise near his hairline.

"You probably should take a couple more Tylenol before bed—just avoid ibuprofen. Sorry about what happened. My brothers tend to turn into complete idiots whenever Daisy or I bring guys home. But I think Kate and Payton have mellowed them a bit—or age. You actually got off easy compared to many who've gone before you."

"Good to know. I feel much better." But he smiled, not looking particularly concerned. "Believe it or not, I liked them. They kind of grow on you. All of your family, actually.

They were all so…kind."

"I'm afraid you came away with a little fan club tonight," she said, remembering the way Jenna and Natalie had cheered them—and by them, she meant Henry—on from the sidelines. They were adorable, fawning over him like they had. "Something I'm sure you're used to."

But he didn't seem to notice her teasing. In a quiet voice, he said, "You're very lucky to have them."

And she was reminded again of what he'd said earlier about living in his mother's house, vying for attention but failing. "Tell me about your family. Is it just you and your sister? Is your dad still in the picture?"

"My dad died a long time ago."

"Oh. I'm sorry."

"Yeah, well, you get on. You have to." He was quiet again, and she thought he was done with the topic when he added quietly, "He was a good dad, so I'm glad we got the time together that we did. My parents divorced when I was five, and for a while it was just the two of us. He loved baseball, was a huge Giants fan. The two of us would go to a couple of games a year in San Francisco. After he died, I moved back in with my mother."

"How old were you?"

"Eleven."

"And your sister? Where does she fit in all this?"

"My mother wasn't really much for making a commitment to anyone. Men were always coming in and out of her life. Part of why my dad left—he had already resigned himself to sharing her with her job, but he wasn't about to share her with another man. Or men, as the case might be."

She didn't have words to communicate how sad she thought it all was. A parent should be someone to set an example, or at least try. Someone to hug you and tell you how much he or she loved you each and every day. She was certain

Henry hadn't been so lucky.

Without thinking, she rested her hand on top of his and turned to meet his gaze. But she didn't say anything, words seeming unnecessary through this brief connection. And then it was over and she pulled her hand away and back to the steering wheel.

"Anyway," Henry continued, "after my dad and I left, she remarried two more times, and Morgan was a result of one such union. Like me, she'd been growing up in that huge mausoleum with our distant mother for company, although unlike me, she didn't have the comfort and love of her father. He took off before the ink was dry on the divorce papers. Needless to say, she was starved for affection when I arrived. She was my shadow for so long, so in many ways, as heartbroken as I was losing my dad, in moving back, her attention and need helped fill the void of my dad's absence. I found someone who needed me. We needed each other."

"And your mother? Do you see her?"

"She passed last fall," he said with no inflection.

Benny risked another glance at him. That had to be rough. As much as he had reason to dislike his mother, in death, there was no room for any kind of reconciliation. Or forgiveness. She held her tongue, though, sensing he didn't seek her sympathy.

They'd arrived at the garage, and she punched in her code and waited for the door to open before pulling in.

"Sorry we didn't make it very far in your lessons today. Maybe we can try again next Sunday. You know, if you still want to try and learn a few things."

She nodded as they reached his parking space and pulled in next to her Mini. "I'd like that." Because even if her morning at the club hadn't endeared her to the sport any more than before, the prospect of spending more time in Henry's company had some appeal. Okay, a lot of appeal.

But it was only because he was so irreverent and funny and easy on the eyes. "And since I don't think I've said it before... thanks, Henry. For your help."

She reached over to grab her bag, and before she could open the door, Henry was there, already holding it for her. She'd be lying if she didn't admit it was terribly flattering and sent her heart skipping a beat or two.

They walked toward the elevator, neither of them speaking, when the familiar ding of its arrival sounded. Looking over, Benny caught a glimpse of long black hair on a statuesque woman stepping into the elevator.

Lord. That horrible woman again. This time Benny didn't even bother to call out to ask her to hold the elevator. Not only because she knew the beast wouldn't, and there was no reason to give her the satisfaction of ignoring the request, but because she was enjoying the peace that had fallen between her and Henry.

Henry, however, wasn't aware of the woman's predilection toward deafness and shouted, "Hold the door."

And in an act that initially surprised Benny, the woman... did.

The wide smile the woman shot Henry a minute later disavowed Benny of the possibility the woman was maybe not as bad as she'd thought. Which she confirmed when the woman only gave a barely concealed disdainful look at Benny before leaning in toward Henry as they stepped into the elevator.

"Thank you," Henry said congenially. "You'd think with the prices we pay to live here they'd at least have an elevator that didn't run on weights and pulleys. I'd have aged another decade before it returned for us."

The woman opened her mouth wider and laughed. Benny managed not to roll her eyes and watched as Henry pushed the button for their floor.

"You're Henry Ellison, aren't you?" the woman asked with unbridled interest in her dark, almond-shaped eyes.

"In the flesh."

"I thought so. I was reading about you the other day. Your firm was just nominated for an award in the small agency category. Best digital campaign, wasn't it?"

Henry nodded modestly. "True."

"And if I'm not mistaken, at next week's Salt Lake conference, you're rumored to be finalists for taking the gold for best small agency of the year in the West."

How the heck had the woman known that?

As if anticipating Benny's thoughts, the woman added, "I'm in PR. I follow these things. I'm Lela." She held her hand out to Henry, who took it artfully. The woman, however, had ceased to recognize that Benny was there and drew her hand back, her attention only on Henry. "That's quite an accomplishment."

"I can't take all the credit. It's a team effort."

"Oh, I'm sure it is."

As if suddenly realizing Benny was still there, Henry smiled at her. "Lela, correct? This is Dr. Benny Sorensen."

The woman nodded—barely—and reached inside her purse and pulled out a card to hand to Henry. "Maybe you might be interested in having lunch sometime? Or going for drinks? I would love to bend your ear about how you've accomplished so much. Maybe you can offer me some guidance...from a PR standpoint, of course."

Guidance, Benny's ass. The woman was totally hitting on Henry and not even concerned with the possibility that Benny and Henry might be on a date. Or something. But considering she recognized Henry on sight, Benny wouldn't put it past the woman to have done research into Henry's background and to know his reputation as a proverbial playboy.

Henry slipped the card in his back pocket. "Maybe I

will," he said. "I haven't seen you before. Are you new to the building?"

"My brother lives here, but he's abroad for the moment, so he's letting me crash at his place until I find my own. I was working for a PR firm in Chicago until recently."

"Ah, yes. The Windy City. How's our little city holding up in comparison?"

"I'm quickly seeing its potential."

Good grief.

The elevator stopped, and the doors opened before any more of the cutting-edge wit could continue.

"This is me," Lela said and reluctantly stepped off. "It was such a pleasure to meet you, Henry. Don't be afraid to stop by sometime. I'm in 907. I'm afraid being new in the city I don't really know anyone or what to do with myself."

"Something that will have to be remedied," Henry said as Lela gave a final smile and the elevator door shut.

Benny didn't try to suppress her groan.

"What?" Henry asked, looking truly baffled.

"Sorry, I'm not used to witnessing such disgusting displays of desperation." Benny paused and gave an imitation of the woman's sultry laugh. "Oh, Henry. You're so wise and smart and little old me is just helpless and lost and I need you to help guide me." She batted her lashes for good measure and licked her lips.

Henry chuckled as the door opened and they headed down the hall to their respective places. "Yes, Benny, there is a certain artifice in all flirting, but it's part of the game. Lela wasn't afraid to go for what she wanted. She showed her interest and left the door open for further communication. If you want a date with Luke, you're going to have to take a page out of that playbook and put yourself out there."

Right. Luke. The reason she was doing all of this in the first place. She nodded. "Okay. I see your point." They reached his door first, and she looked at the time. Nearly nine. "So you think you'll be okay on your own? Your head is doing okay?"

"I know my name, the year, and the name of the current president if that's what you're wondering. You know, Dr. Sorensen, if you're worried about me, there's more than enough room in my bed to fit the two of us. I wouldn't want you to spend a long, sleepless night thinking about me," he said with a smile and gleam in those dark eyes.

"Does that really work on women?"

"You'd be surprised."

"Good night, Henry," she said and walked down the hall.

"'Night, Benny."

She just prayed that Henry hadn't noticed the flush that crept in her cheeks at the prospect of sharing his bed—joke or not. Of lying next to him, watching him sleep, watching him do maybe a few other things...

Then she remembered Henry's easy, casual flirting on the elevator. What was she thinking? A night with Henry would be setting herself up for heartache, since he'd just move on to the next woman the next night.

No. Henry didn't want any of the same things she did. Didn't want forever, just...for now.

Good thing they were totally incompatible.

• • •

Henry watched as Benny Sorensen headed into her place. He'd be lying if for a brief moment he hadn't entertained the idea of feigning some confusion or a sudden pounding headache that would obligate the good doctor to stay by his side. But then reality set in and he realized...he was nuts.

Benny Sorensen was feisty, opinionated, and surly. Definitely not his type.

But hell, she could really make him laugh.

He headed into his place and walked over to the stereo, in the mood for a little Frank Sinatra. He poured a splash of bourbon into a glass and took a seat in his leather recliner that looked over the city.

Today had not gone at all like he'd planned. But he didn't know the last time he'd ever enjoyed himself more, starting the moment Benny Sorensen opened her front door, tired and grumpy about the early hour but still a refreshing change from all the women who'd practically flip handsprings to please him.

She was intriguing.

And despite her spastic interactions with Luke Seeley, she'd handled his buddies at the club with aplomb, had them eating out of her hand. Something that had kind of irked him, the banter that flowed between them, the easy way she'd flirted with them. Fast learner, he supposed.

If Luke Seeley knew what was good for him, he wouldn't take no for an answer from Benny Sorensen the next time, diving in there before some other lucky guy usurped his place in Benny's heart.

Henry had meant what he'd said earlier about liking her family. Even the brothers who hadn't just slugged him in the head but had sabotaged him the entire game. Something he knew and was well aware *they knew* he knew. He took it as a sort of hazing ritual. What brothers and sisters did to protect each other.

Speaking of sisters, it had been too long since he and Morgan had shared space, let alone a meal. And he missed his niece.

Pulling his cell phone from his pocket, he dialed the number and waited for her answer. "Morgan? Hey, it's me."

"Oh, no. You've called to lecture me. What have I done wrong now? Did I forget your birthday?" But he heard the smile in her voice.

"I was thinking that maybe if you're in town, we might all have dinner together next week. Just the three of us."

There was silence. "Sorry, Henry—you're asking me to have dinner with you? Are you sick? Is there something I should know?"

"Very funny. It's just that having Ella with me last weekend made me realize how much I miss you guys and like hanging out with you. Something we haven't done a lot of lately. So I thought I'd try and fix that. How about it?"

"Okay. I—I'd like that. And Ella would, too. In fact... she mentioned something interesting to me the other day. Something about Skittles and the nice lady doctor who pulled one out of her nose—"

"Wow. Look at the time, I should let you go. I'll call you later this week to finalize the details."

She laughed. "Okay, I'll let it go this time. Good night, Henry."

"'Night, Morgan."

He hung up and returned the phone to his pocket, finding the card of the beautiful woman from earlier. Lela, was it?

He stared at the card, remembering the interaction on the elevator. Yes, she was beautiful, but it wasn't Lela he was thinking of. He smiled as he recalled the look of disgust Benny had shot the two of them, particularly Lela.

Any other time, he'd probably have accepted Lela's offer for company right then, having a long night of solitude ahead for himself anyhow. But for some reason, hanging out with the woman, no matter how beautiful she was, had no appeal. She would inevitably ply him with questions, lay the compliments on thick, and probably have him in her bed before they could finish the first bottle of wine.

It was...predictable.

Something that he certainly couldn't say about spending time with Benny Sorensen.

With panache, he tossed the card like a Frisbee, scoring a point as it hit and fell into the wastebasket. He felt lighter already, although why wasn't something he was ready to analyze.

Instead, he savored his bourbon, the music, the view before him, and the memory of someone's unbridled and joyful laugh as the wind whipped her hair while they'd cruised down the interstate.

Chapter Twelve

"That's the fourth case of hand, foot, and mouth I've seen this week," Benny said to Roz the following morning, watching two twin boys sucking on Popsicles follow their mother out of the office. "Once it takes hold at a place like a day care or summer camp, it just spreads like crazy."

"You have an ear infection in exam room four and well checks and vaccinations with the three Johnson kids in two."

Benny nodded and finished noting the chart as Roz left to get the vaccinations ordered and prepared.

"Good morning, Dr. Sorensen." Her heart skipped a beat as she glanced to her right to see none other than Luke Seeley bearing down on her, an easy smile on his face. "How did your weekend go?"

Right. The weekend with the mystery man who was not anyone serious. Although the mystery man might have been invented, the time with Henry was not. And that had been, strangely enough…fun.

She returned his smile. "Pretty well. Can't complain," she said vaguely, noticing the way he studied her with certain interest. "And yours?"

"To tell you the truth, I was kind of thinking of you. Enough so that I thought if you weren't doing anything, maybe you'd like to catch dinner with me tonight. There's a new sushi restaurant I heard about that I thought we might check out."

A date?

Benny clenched her fists at her side to stop the near overpowering impulse to fist bump the air or wave them around in victory.

Wait. Sushi? An image of cold, raw, gelatinous fish passing her mouth brought a wave of nausea. Sure, there were an infinite variety of choices of sushi and sashimi that were available and she'd tried many of them, but it seemed pointless to go somewhere where the only way she could consume such concoctions was by slathering them in soy sauce and wasabi until her nasal passages burned so she couldn't taste it in the first place.

Fortunately, she was supposed to play coy here, if Henry were to be believed. And he'd been right so far…

She looked down at her chart, pretending to consider it before answering apologetically. "I'm afraid I can't tonight."

"Okay. What about Wednesday? And before you decline, I know for a fact that Wednesdays you usually pick up a pizza from around the corner and head home."

"Really? Are you stalking me, Dr. Seeley?"

"Just paying attention."

And he was right. Wednesdays the restaurant offered free cheesy bread with any size pizza and Benny always grabbed a pepperoni-and-olive pizza and sat in for a night alone of television and gluttony. Kind of like every night, actually. Although of late, she'd been less alone than usual, thanks to the company of her neighbor, whose witty banter and observations were remarkably…enjoyable.

She pretended to consider it again before slowly nodding. "Okay. I think I'm open."

His smile widened, and he backed away. "Good. I'm going to hold you to it, and in the meantime, I'll get out of your way before you remember you have other plans."

He turned and headed down the hall, and for a minute, Benny fought the outrageous giggle that wanted to burst out.

She'd done it.

No tee time on the greens with Luke and his golf buddies. No, she had a real, honest-to-goodness date with Luke Seeley.

Dinner. Dim light, raw fish—no, she pushed that image away, and instead imagined the two of them laughing and talking in hushed whispers, of him taking her hand in his or maybe even dropping his hand to her knee as a shiver of excitement ran through her. Of Luke leaning forward until she could feel his breath on her face, the touch of his lips—

"Dr. Sorensen?" Roz's gravelly voice pulled her out of her daydream. "Ear infection exam room four?" she reminded her.

"Right, Roz. Thanks." Biting her lip to stop the ridiculous smile that wanted to burst out, she hurried to the exam room, determined to push away thoughts of kisses and hand-holding—at least until she was in the privacy of her office.

Henry was not going to believe it.

. . .

"You know, you've been in there for ten minutes already. If you want my opinion, you're going to have to come out at some point." It was after eight on Tuesday night, the night before the big date, and at Benny's request, Henry had stopped by to help her decide what to wear.

"I know, I know. I'll be out in a minute. Just remember, we're only going to dinner, so I don't want to look like

I'm trying too hard, but at the same time, I want to look… unforgettable."

"Understood," he said patiently. When Benny had texted him yesterday afternoon with the news that she'd scored an actual dinner date with Luke, he couldn't say he'd necessarily been surprised. Not after he'd seen her in action himself at the country club on Sunday. And from what Benny had reported, the good doctor had been showing definite interest in her, bringing her coffee and seeking her out for conversation, so it was only a matter of time.

Yet despite not being surprised by the invitation, Henry was feeling a bit out of sorts the past couple of days, and he couldn't exactly place why. This was the goal, the reason he was helping his pesky neighbor. To get her out and dating Luke Seeley so she'd get off his back and drop her complaint with the HOA. And it looked like not only were they accomplishing that goal, but in a surprising turn of events, he'd also made a new friend.

So why did the fact that things were coming together make him so damn…annoyed?

He returned his attention to the television where Benny had put on some legal show that starred that woman from ER. The episode was actually more interesting than he'd like to admit and he turned it up as he waited for Benny to get the guts to come out of her bedroom.

"So?" she asked finally, just as the jury was coming back with their verdict.

He paused the show, ready to give her his complete attention, determined to say whatever was necessary to give her the confidence she'd need to make the night a success.

Instead he was struck silent, stunned by the way the wispy blue dress patterned with bright red flowers settled so softly and enticingly around her curvy figure. The way the sexy red-heeled sandals enhanced her strong, shapely calves and legs, and the colors opened up her already pretty face, barely touched by makeup and a cranberry color to her lips. Her hair was down, the first time he'd seen it that way, and it was dark and thick and would make any man want to run his fingers through the wavy mass. Her eyes—framed so perfectly under the fringe of bangs—glowed as she watched his reaction, in equal parts excitement and nervousness.

He cleared his throat. "You've nailed it. Luke won't be able to take his eyes off you." Henry knew *he* couldn't. Not with the shy, sexy appeal that Benny exuded.

She looked down, frowning as she did so. "You don't think it's a little too low cut? I don't want to be shoving these things in his face."

Luke would only be so lucky, but Henry managed a smile. There was only a delectable hint of cleavage, nothing Pamela Anderson-ish, but for Benny—who, now that he thought about it, preferred higher necklines and minimal cleavage— it might seem immodest. Even if it was far from it. He did a mental headshake as he stopped any further thoughts of Benny's breasts. Which was harder than he expected.

She walked to the kitchen, the hem of the skirt flipping as she did, and uncorked a bottle of red. "Did you want a glass?"

He shook his head. Best to keep all his faculties about him. "I'm good."

She nodded and filled her own and came over to sit on the couch next to him. From his angle, he was seeing a lot more of that cleavage than he'd first observed, and he realized that Luke Seeley was going to have the same view tomorrow night—something that irritated Henry.

"You think you might want to go change? Wouldn't want you spill anything on it before you even make it to your date."

"No. I think I need to get used to showing this much skin. It might make me less self-conscious tomorrow."

Great. It took every ounce of his self-control to pull his gaze from Benny and back to the television. He unpaused it, hoping for any distraction. "I'm surprised you're into legal dramas. I would think you'd be watching medical shows like *Grey's Anatomy*."

She grimaced. "Only if I want to end up slamming my head against a wall or yelling rabidly at the television screen before counting every medical error and calling Daisy to vent. She's pretty much forbidden me from ever watching them again, or at least from calling her after."

He chuckled. "I can't blame you there. Television and movies never depict an ad agency correctly, either. Don't even get me started on *Bewitched*. My head will spin."

"I love that show."

"I'm sure you do. Let's just say their depiction of the guy's job was as fictional as the wife who only twitches her nose to practice magic."

She laughed, a nice, unabashed sound. "I'll keep that in mind next time I catch an episode. Congratulations, by the way. I looked up your agency the other night."

She had looked him up? He glanced back at her, keeping his attention on those blue eyes. Not trusting himself to look farther south. "Now who's stalking me?"

"What that woman said in the elevator the other night, about your firm and the awards it's received, made me curious. All your bragging about being able to sell anything, spin anything, wasn't too far off the mark, I see. You're…good. I can personally attest to that," she said, making a sweeping motion toward herself.

"You didn't need as much spin as you think. And thank you."

His job and the work he did there was a source of great pride for him. At one point in his life, he hadn't thought he'd ever be able to shake the family moniker and he'd go down as one of those spoiled rich kids who rested on their family laurels rather than ever accomplishing anything for themselves. He had been the Brighton heir for so long and it had taken him all of his adult life to finally gain recognition for anything outside that.

Getting that nomination was the consummation of that goal.

"She mentioned that your agency was nominated for best campaign?"

He nodded. "They announced the finalists a couple of weeks ago, the winners will be announced at the end of the annual conference at a big awards dinner. But even if we don't take the number-one spot, just being nominated is a huge honor."

"You've done well for yourself, Henry. And...I owe you an apology. When I first moved in, I made presumptions about you. That you were a shallow, spoiled, entitled playboy who had no true ambition."

"You wouldn't be the first," he said wryly.

"Well, I was wrong. You've surprised me. You're a whole lot more than I expected." She looked at him in earnest, her eyes wide and sincere. The effect of that gaze shaking him more than he liked. "So...I'm sorry."

"Apology accepted. What about you? What made you want to go into medicine?"

She took a sip of her wine and smiled at some memory. "When I was a kid, they showed these pictures in school from Doctors Without Borders about all these children in third-world countries who were born with physical deformities, like cleft palates. They talked about how these poor kids didn't have basic medical care, let alone the medical technology to correct these often life-threatening things. I came home crying, and with my mom's help, held a yard sale that same week, earning a whopping seventy-eight dollars that I then donated to the cause. Daisy still hasn't forgiven me for selling her new Easy-Bake Oven."

"Naturally," he said and chuckled at the image of a determined young Benny trying to save the world, even then.

"I knew then that I wanted to be able to do something as brave and meaningful. By the time I was in medical school, though, I realized surgery didn't have the same appeal as much as the day-to-day care of those patients, of being a caring face and voice to keep kids safe and healthy. I still plan on doing a stint in Doctors Without Borders, though. In five years. I just need to get on top of my student loans, and then I'm going to take a year off and try to give a little back."

A bleeding heart was what she was. But Henry couldn't help but admire her ambition and philanthropic spirit. "And how do you think this will fit in with your plan to date and—I imagine—marry the great Luke Seeley? Wouldn't a year apart be kind of difficult, especially if you two had any…kids." He nearly choked saying it out loud. Not because he had a problem with kids, but because the thought of Benny having them with Luke didn't sit well.

"I imagine, should the two of us be so entwined in the future," she said coyly, swirling the wine in her glass, "that he'll be perfectly fine coming with me. He actually served two years in Sudan with Doctors Without Borders."

Of course he did. Saint freaking Luke Seeley.

The episode ended, and Benny grabbed the remote sitting between them and flipped the television off before setting her wine on the coffee table. She reached down to undo the clasp on her shoes, giving him a dangerous glimpse of her full breasts pushed up against the delicate fabric of her dress.

Good God. This was too much.

He jumped to his feet. "I think I'll have a glass of that wine after all."

"Help yourself," Benny said, preoccupied with the other shoe now.

By the time he'd returned, both shoes were resting on the floor and Benny's feet were tucked beneath her while she sipped from her glass. "Here," he offered, topping off her drink, having brought the bottle with him. He took a seat on the other end of the couch, needing to ensure the maximum amount of space between them.

Benny seemed to be mulling over something as she stared into her glass. "Henry? Can I ask you something?"

He took a taste of the wine, nodding at her to continue.

"And I need you to be one hundred percent honest with me—no holding back. How much attention do men give to a woman's...experience? In bed, I mean."

He nearly spewed his mouthful of wine out. Henry hadn't known what question Benny had been about to ask him, but a discussion about sex was the absolute last thing he'd expected.

"What are we talking about here, Benny? Are you meaning...sex?" Good God almighty. She wasn't saying she was a virgin, was she? Trying to keep the shock from his tone, he asked her, "You've had sex before, haven't you?"

This was the twenty-first century, for crying out loud. Girls were having sex before they had their driver's license these days. He didn't even want to think about the appallingly young age he'd been his first time, but Candy Leland had been sixteen and curious and—

Back on track, Henry.

Benny's face was a furious red, a depth of red he hadn't thought possible. "Of course I've had sex before."

He took a breath in again, as he hadn't been sure if he could handle a discussion about the first time with anyone—least of all Benny Sorensen.

"It's just that...well. I would never bring this up in a million years, but I'm a little nervous. And here you are, a man with a *lot* of experience when it comes to women and knowing what men prefer."

Hell, she made him sound like some kind of gigolo or something. "I wouldn't say a lot of experience. It's not like my place is a Motel 6 or something."

She rolled her eyes at him. "I just mean that you know a thing or two about women. About…intimacy. And I wonder if someone's knowledge, or lack of knowledge, has ever been sort of a turnoff."

"I don't think I understand, Benny. Because, men? We're beasts. Sex with any woman is great; sex with a beautiful woman is fantastic. I don't think we give it much thought beyond that. Where's this coming from?"

She studied her fingernails now. "Nowhere. Forget I said anything."

"Not likely. Come on. You can tell me."

"I don't know. I think sometimes I waited so long to finally…do it that I might have lost some of the natural excitement that one has for the whole thing. You know? That whole young ineptitude that probably goes unnoticed when you're sixteen and with an equally horny sixteen-year-old. You learn stuff then. Get better. But I didn't really date much in high school."

Now he was beyond curious. "How old were you when you were…deflowered?" he asked in a teasing tone.

"Twenty-two." She still hadn't looked up at him, instead reaching over to top off her glass.

He let that sink in for a moment. She'd gone twenty-two years of her life without sex. It seemed…impossible.

"Jake was nice, he was in my organic chemistry class, and we'd been study partners all year."

"Jake was…nice? Benny, did you even like the guy?"

She shrugged. "Yeah, he was a really good friend. And since I'd been carrying this V card around for so long to the point I felt like I was a freak, I decided it was time to do something about it. Jake was more than happy to relieve me of that."

"How...romantic. So tell me, how was it?"

She shrugged again. "Painful, awkward. And the whole time I was wondering how long until it was over. We hung out for another month before I called it off."

"I'm assuming you've had sex with other men since then." He couldn't believe he was having this conversation with her. He tossed back the rest of the wine in his glass and refilled.

"What do you think, that I'm a prude or something? There was Steve and Jake. Then, of course, Chip."

"Did it get any better?"

"Sure. It's really...nice." Only she didn't sound particularly convincing. What was wrong with these men? Didn't they know how to properly make love to a woman? Especially a vivacious woman like Benny?

Not that it was his business.

"Okay, so you've had 'nice' sex with three or four men, so it sounds like you have some idea how things are done. So why are we having this conversation again?"

She tucked her hair behind her ear and lifted her gaze to him again. "I guess because I'm just worried. Worried that a guy like Luke, who's been with so many gorgeous women, is going to know just by one kiss how absolutely clueless I am to the finer points of seduction...in the bedroom."

His head was hurting. He had thought imagining Benny just walking out the door with Luke on her arm was going to be strange enough. The fact that she was asking Henry for coaching tips on seducing the guy was a million times worse.

He stared into her eyes, still watching him with embarrassment.

She was afraid Luke wouldn't find her enough.

Which was absolutely ridiculous. And even if it might be the last thing he wanted to do, she needed to know the truth. "Benny, if and when you take that step with Luke Seeley—

and I hope I don't have to go into why sleeping with him on the first date in the long-term is absolutely the wrong call—"

"No, don't worry, I don't intend to do that," she hurried in.

"If you take that step," he continued, feeling more relieved by her proclamation than he should, "Luke is going to be absolutely thrilled and excited at the prospect of just touching you, your skin, your lips, the silkiness of your hair—and I imagine the same will hold true for you. So, well, nothing else is going to matter. But if it gets to that point where you're still struggling to relax and be in that moment, then I think you should be up front with him. Tell him your experience has been limited and you're nervous. It will make him out of his mind with wanting you even more. Believe me."

Seriously, believe him. Was that a bead of perspiration on his forehead?

He sucked in some air, deciding that it was way too warm in here, and put his empty wineglass on the coffee table.

Only Benny was chewing her full bottom lip in contemplation.

"I just want everything to be perfect. I want—I *need*—to know that when he kisses me, he's not going to draw away in horror. That he'll be enticed to want…more."

A growing realization was coming over Henry, and he wiped at his forehead. No. It wasn't possible. She wasn't about to ask him—

"Would you be willing to, maybe, kiss me? Just for a minute? You've been so honest up to now, and I trust that you'll tell me if kissing me is like kissing a twelve-year-old—"

"I'm afraid I wouldn't have any recent experience there."

"You know what I mean. You said you can create the whole package, and what I need from you right now is assurance. Assurance and maybe a few…tips. What I'm doing wrong, what I'm doing right…" She trailed off, her eyes pleading with him.

This was too much.

Benny was actually sitting there, sexy as hell, asking him to kiss her, something he'd been fighting himself from doing since she first sat on this couch. Maybe even before that. She was asking him to feel what those full lips would be like under his and manage to keep his head enough to give her pointers, for God's sake.

"Benny, I'm not sure this is a good idea."

"Oh. Okay, I understand." A certain glimmer of humor entered her eyes. "You're afraid that I've made you into this guru in the fine art of kissing and lovemaking, that now that you're on the spot, you won't be able to hold up your end of it. It's a performance thing."

"The hell it is." He sounded angrier than he'd intended. He tried again, making himself sound levelheaded. "Believe me, I know what I'm doing. That's not the problem."

"Prove it."

The woman was positively deranged.

"Fine. If that's what you want. But when I tell you what you're doing wrong, I don't want you to try and physically maim me." He couldn't believe he was going to do this.

Kiss a woman he'd been thinking of more times than he probably should the past week. Kiss a woman whom he'd been wanting to kiss long before then.

He smiled a little wider now. Well, if it was what she wanted…

Chapter Thirteen

Benny couldn't quite believe that she'd voiced the request, a request she'd been toying with asking for two days. She wanted to knock Luke's socks off when they finally took that step, and who best to tell her—no, *show* her—than Lothario here? A man who knew women and probably had more than enough practice in this department before he'd even graduated junior high.

This was purely an experiment. A lesson.

But why was it that, now that it was going to happen, her belly was fluttering and swirling and she was having a hard time getting enough air in her lungs?

It was only Henry.

Henry.

She just wished he'd stop looking at her with that new glint in his eyes. A glint filled with mischief and something else…desire?

No. Definitely far from that.

"First, you're going to have to get a lot closer to me than that," he drawled, clearly enjoying this more than he should.

Of course. Why was she still sitting there like a slug?

She slipped her feet from under her and crossed the three feet to the spot where he was sitting. He patted the space next to him and, after drawing in another breath, she sank to the cushion, her shoulder pressed against his arm.

"You're sure about this?" he asked. "Because you're acting like you're about to be sent to the guillotine. You need to relax."

Sure. She could relax. She threw back the last of the wine and set her glass next to his empty one before making herself more comfortable, with one leg tucked beneath her and the other anchoring her to the floor.

She turned toward him, trying to ignore his subtle masculine scent, and the fact that she was sitting so close to him that she could see the slight stubble that covered his jaw. That his brown eyes were more caramel than almond colored, with flecks of green she hadn't noticed before.

Everything seemed to have slowed down—or maybe that was the two glasses of wine—as Henry's hand moved toward her face, brushing off a wisp of hair that had fallen, before his hand cupped it, strong and certain.

And then his lips.

Holy Hannah. They were opening and moving toward her now and he looked so determined—

Call it nervousness or the fact she was about to jump from her skin, but she dropped her head as a nervous laugh burst from her lips, then the laugh shook her belly and she was holding her stomach. "I'm sorry. It just hit me what we were about to do and I couldn't stop—"

"Get it out of your system. Because nothing cools a guy's ardor faster than being laughed at." His voice was monotone and slightly irritated.

She looked at his face. Had she offended him? "No. I'm sorry. I got it all out. Let's try again."

"I don't know. I'm only doing this as a favor, and if you're going to act like you're ten then maybe this isn't a good—"

Once again, she had no freaking idea what was coming over her as the humor of the situation fled and now…now she only wanted to finish what they'd started…

But on her terms.

So before he could finish his sentence, Benny lifted her face and stopped him with her own lips. He froze, and for a moment they were stuck like that, two sets of lips, immobile.

But then the funniest thing happened. She could taste the wine on his mouth, smell the subtle clean scent of his aftershave, and suddenly she realized she wanted…more.

More of him.

At the same moment, his own lips moved and parted hers, his mouth unexpectedly hot and sensual. Her head was swooshing, and the blood was suddenly racing through her as she followed his own movements, her lips somehow finding their own way as she savored the heat and the heavenly feeling of just being kissed.

His hand lifted again to cup her face, and she melted farther into him as her hand reached up to his shoulder and she braced herself against him. He'd moved forward now, and the pressure of the cushions against her back increased. Henry had settled his hips between her legs, the hem of the dress higher, exposing her skin.

Both of his hands slid down her waist and rested on her hips, his fingers digging in but not unpleasantly as he pressed her closer to him. Her legs wrapped around him, holding him to her deliciously.

She didn't want the moment to ever end.

Wait. Moment?

What on earth was she doing?

The same realization seemed to hit Henry, and he froze. She opened her eyes to stare into his, dark and filled with desire. His hands dropped away as he sat back, and her mouth, once so hot and connected to him, felt cool, almost...lonely. Self-consciously, she covered it with her hand.

What just happened?

Henry came to his feet. "I think that we can safely assume that you know what you're doing, at least in the kissing department. I don't think there's really anything more I can offer you."

He sounded so...awkward. Uncertain. Not the sure, confident Henry she was used to, and she looked up at him with a slight smile as he nearly stumbled back in his haste to gain more distance. "I almost forgot, I'm meeting someone for drinks in a few minutes, so I should probably be going."

She came to her feet, uncertain if they'd hold her, but she managed to stay upright and follow him to the door. "I'm sorry, Henry. Did I do something wrong?"

He paused and shook his head, his gaze finally meeting hers again for a minute. "Not at all. You have nothing to worry about. Go out on your date with Luke tomorrow and know that he's a very lucky guy."

Then he turned and opened the door and was gone before she could say anything more.

What the heck just happened?

She leaned against the door, bemused and still tingling from the effects of that kiss.

In all her life she had never felt the power of a kiss. She had kissed men before, of course. But nice, pleasant kisses that gradually grew more impassioned until things naturally moved to the next level.

But this kiss. This one had been like a powder keg. The lust and desire that rushed through her so instantaneous it still had her reeling.

From a kiss with *Henry*.

Her fingers touched her lips again. If that was what

kissing Henry was like for every woman, no wonder he had such a female following.

Well, he did have a *lot* of experience.

She shook her head. That was it, of course. And now he was off to kiss another woman senseless and probably bring her back to his place for a night of more kissing and pressing their bodies together like—

No. Stop.

She had what she wanted—assurance that kissing her wasn't the kiss of death. She was more confident now, having seen that Henry, who could barely even stand her before, had clearly enjoyed their kiss as much as she had.

She needed to push thoughts of Henry and his kisses out of her mind once and for all.

Tomorrow night she'd be with Luke. It would be *Luke's* lips she'd be kissing, his hands that would wrap around her waist.

That was what this was all for. Wasn't it?

• • •

It was after nine the next night, and Henry was on his second beer at one of his favorite bars, trying to pay attention to the game that was on. He told himself that he was there for the atmosphere, the sheer entertainment value of watching the occupants vie for the attention of whoever caught their eye. Including him sometimes.

But really it was a distraction, and he knew it.

He was there instead of entertaining the usual small group of clients and coworkers at his place because he didn't want to be around when Luke Seeley picked up Benny for their big date. Didn't think he could stand to see her look as enticing as she had last night, only instead of smiling and shining those brilliant eyes at Henry, she'd be flashing them at Luke. Would

Luke try to taste those same lips that Henry had claimed just hours before?

The thought made him want to smash his fist into the good doctor's face.

Lord. Henry ran a hand through his hair as he remembered that kiss. It had taken every ounce of restraint to pull away from those soft lips, leave that welcoming embrace, and get the hell out of there before he did something they'd both regret. Something he was equal parts relieved and frustrated with once the door shut at his own place and he could still taste the remnants of that kiss, smell Benny's warm vanilla scent, feel the softness of her skin and the smooth silkiness of her dark hair.

He was treading in dangerous waters, he realized, getting so close to the woman. Feeling idiotic things he shouldn't even be considering with anyone, let alone a woman in love with someone else.

"Henry, you've really got to come over and join us." He glanced to his side, where Valerie was holding her Cosmopolitan in her well-manicured hand and eyeing him with unbridled interest.

Valerie was new to the firm's research division and had recently worked on the Kettlebaum account with him. She was funny and lovely and definitely interested. The only reason he hadn't hooked up with her before was because she'd been dating someone. But she had hinted earlier that they'd broken up a couple weeks ago. Meaning she was available and ready to have Henry help heal whatever wounds her bruised heart and ego might be suffering. She was the exact kind of distraction he needed to help push Benny Sorensen out of his mind for at least one night. Only…

Once he had Valerie hanging on to every word he uttered, he'd needed space. Which was why he was up at the bar, drinking. Alone. Something that was doing little to improve his mood.

He turned to look at the woman again. Tall and blond and looking in need of a good solid meal, she watched him eagerly from hooded blue eyes. Blue eyes that weren't nearly as bright or sharp as another pair that he kept thinking about.

But she was here. And not mooning after some saintly doofus doctor.

Still… "I'll be along in a minute. Just want to catch the final score," he said and nodded up to the baseball game.

"Who's up?" Valerie asked and sidled onto the bar stool next to him.

"You follow baseball?"

"My dad was a huge Dodgers fan, so I know a little bit about it. Who's your team?"

He smiled wryly. "Giants."

"Probably best not to have you and my dad in the same room during the playoffs."

A woman who knew baseball. Normally that might have heightened his interest in the blonde.

She sipped her pink drink and eyed him over the rim. "If you're not interested in joining everyone, perhaps you'd be interested in watching the rest of the game somewhere more…private? I seem to recall seeing a sixty-inch television at that apartment of yours."

The invitation was clear, and he had to give her props for her forwardness. This woman obviously knew what she wanted and wasn't afraid to just put it out there.

But right now, the prospect of spending another night having meaningless sex with someone he barely knew, let alone knew if he liked, held no appeal.

He remembered what he'd told Benny last night. About men finding sex with any woman great and a beautiful woman fantastic. Words he thought he believed at the time. But now, with the opportunity presenting itself to have what should be fantastic sex with a beautiful woman, he wasn't so sure anymore.

What sounded infinitely more appealing was making love to a woman who challenged and intrigued him, who made him want to peel away the stuff at the surface and discover what made her tick. What made her smile, laugh, and maybe sigh in breathless pleasure.

Someone like…Benny.

Ludicrous.

What I should do is take Valerie home right now and let her take my mind off everything, especially Benny.

He took another drink of his beer and considered her offer for another moment. But it was no use. He'd only be comparing the two women the entire time. "Sorry, Valerie. Maybe another time."

She pouted for a minute, her bottom lip out, but when he didn't follow up, she changed tactics and smiled. "If you change your mind, you know where I'll be."

She turned and walked slowly away, moving her hips like she knew he was watching her. Which he was.

What was wrong with him? He'd never passed up sex with a beautiful woman before.

The problem was that maybe Benny had opened the door to the possibility of relationships that had real meaning, with her talk of happily-ever-after and family and all that.

Maybe it wasn't Benny that he was necessarily drawn to. It was what women like her represented. But the thing was, he'd decided long ago that women like her didn't really exist. That relationships like she wanted and what he'd seen surrounding him at her family dinner didn't exist.

So, fine. Whatever. Maybe it did.

For some lucky men. But if he'd learned anything in his life, it was that Henry wasn't so lucky.

He'd survived his thirty-four years without a broken heart

because he hadn't allowed himself the luxury of investing in a relationship that lasted longer than a baseball season.

It was safer. Easier. Less painful.

He wasn't necessarily writing off the Valeries of the world. But maybe, for now, he needed a little more time to himself to figure out exactly what he wanted.

And what he was willing to risk.

Chapter Fourteen

Benny had managed to swallow enough wasabi-drowned sushi to convince Luke that she'd enjoyed her meal nearly as much as he had. Even if her stomach was now at odds with its contents and she was trying to appease the uprising by downing lots of water.

"…the people of Sudan were so welcoming and the work so rewarding, I couldn't help but sign on another year. You really would enjoy it, too…" Luke was going on after she'd pressed him for details about his work through Doctors Without Borders. He hadn't stopped talking for a good five-minute stretch at least, so enthralled with his topic.

This was what Henry had encouraged. An open ear, letting Luke do all the talking because men liked nothing more than to hear themselves speak about themselves—provided one showed sufficient interest. Her nodding and smiling must have been all the encouragement Luke had needed to warm to his subject and then some.

Even if Benny was a little bored.

"You haven't touched the sashimi," he said and pointed

to three pieces of obviously raw fish that she'd been hoping to avoid. At least with the rice and cucumbers in the sushi roll, she could almost forget she was eating raw fish. But the limp, slimy pieces would offer no such distraction.

"Come on. You've got to at least try one. Here." He reached across and, with his chopsticks, clamped one of the pieces and held it up to her mouth. "This is the salmon, and I promise you won't be disappointed."

Really? What choice did she have here?

Reluctantly, she opened her mouth, trying not to feel self-conscious at the fact that Luke Seeley was feeding her, looking into her mouth right now.

She hoped she didn't have any food stuck on her tongue or teeth.

He pulled the chopsticks back, leaving a fat, slimy piece of cold fish in her mouth. He smiled encouragingly at her. "And?"

Unlike many things that tasted better than they actually looked, this wasn't one of them. It had looked like a thick pink slug—and eating it was even worse. Like eating an extra-salty fish-flavored slug.

She wouldn't lose it. No, she could do this. Just swallow with as minimal amount of chewing as possible.

But it was so chewy.

She forced as smile and nodded. "Mmm. You're right. Delicious."

Okay, time for water. Lots of water, which she quickly chugged down while Luke picked up one of the other pieces and shoved it in his mouth. "Mmm. Did you see Dr. Paulson yesterday?"

An image of the older doctor came to mind. Particularly the fact that his usual salt-and-pepper hair had been dyed a dark brown that looked somewhat unsettling with his pale skin. "I'm afraid so."

"He stopped me to talk about a concern he had for one of his patients, and I had the hardest time not chuckling outright. What is he thinking?"

She lowered her voice conspiratorially. "I understand from some of the nurses that he just finalized his third divorce, so my bet is he's already looking to find wife number four."

"Really?" He looked perplexed. "I don't get men like that. Not respecting the sanctity of marriage. You don't just marry someone based on attraction alone, but mutual respect. Common interests. Take my parents. Married forty-four years. Both on the greens bright and early five days a week. They took up Spanish and then Italian and are now both fairly fluent. They do everything together—it's great. They're like two peas in a pod."

See. There were men who believed in marriage and commitment and family. She'd try and ignore the part about his parents' golfing.

Almost. Every. Day.

Her parents enjoyed doing things together, of course, but they also had other interests. Other hobbies. It was that variety and independence that made it so much more fun to come home at the end of the day—or so her mother said.

But, hey, he was into family. That was good. She just hoped that he wouldn't expect her to golf with him as frequently. Okay, if at all.

"How about you? Tell me about your family."

For a few minutes she regaled him with stories, finding encouragement in his smiles and nods. She leaned forward again, happy to bask in the glow of that smile. She noticed that his eyes dipped a time or two down to her cleavage, and although ordinarily she might have objected had anyone ever suggest that one should lower herself to such physical and wanton displays, she leaned a little more forward. If you got 'em, flaunt 'em, as her aunt Bessie would say.

His eyes seemed brighter now as he smiled at her.

Good. This is good. Aside from the sushi and sashimi deal, things were improving.

The server stopped and left the check, which Benny tried to pay half of—something that Chip had usually taken her up on—but Luke refused and dropped some cash in the bill folder. Another reminder of why he was so perfect. Humanitarian, gentleman, great with kids, and hot as heck.

Everything she could ever want in a man.

For a brief moment, dark caramel eyes flashed in her mind, a lazy grin that melted her more than she'd like as he told her to move closer so he could teach her the fine art of kissing. The unabashed desire in the depths of those eyes as he stared at her just before they came to their senses and broke apart.

"You ready?" Luke asked. He'd come to his feet and stood next to her, his hand out and ready to help her up.

She nodded and pushed away the memories of the previous night and accepted his hand.

Nice.

Sweet.

This was what she wanted.

"I feel like I've been dominating the conversation here," Luke said a few minutes later as they stepped off the elevator at Benny's condo and made their way down the hall. "You'll have to forgive me. Sometimes when I get on a subject I'm passionate about, I just lose myself."

"No, it's been so interesting, all of it. I had no idea that the rules of the PGA could be so complex."

It was amazing how far a few well-placed words like "really?" and "mmm-hmm" could take a person. She hadn't dared venture much more in the conversation, not at the risk of displaying her real ignorance of the game of golf.

They arrived at her door, and she fished awkwardly for her keys in the tiny purse that Henry insisted she use instead of her larger leather satchel. It looked less high maintenance, he'd told her. She'd bowed to his wisdom, even if she did have a heck of a time fitting everything in it.

"There," she said in triumph and brought them out before sliding her key in the lock and turning it. The door opened, and she turned again to face Luke, unable to put off the most nerve-racking moment of the whole date.

The good-bye—and kiss if she were lucky.

She glanced up briefly to see his hazel eyes watching her, but she dropped her gaze again, suddenly feeling all of about thirteen years old.

"I was hoping," he said slowly and waited for her to look up again at him, which she did, reminding herself to take in deep breaths, "since I had to take a rain check last weekend, you might have an opening in your schedule for me on Saturday? I have a commitment to some friends for golf, but I'd love nothing more than for you to consider joining us. Then after, maybe we could just spend a little more time getting to know each other. Catch dinner and a movie or something."

"Saturday?" she asked, trying to buy time. That had happened much faster than she expected, and her mind reeled as she tried to remember if Henry had covered this. Was she supposed to accept another date at this point or throw in a rejection? "I think—I think I might be available...I can let you know."

"You do that, but be prepared. I am not taking no for an answer this time. I might just have to camp out outside your door until you give in."

"Is that right?" She bit back a laugh. Luke Seeley was insisting on a second date—with her.

Former chubby tomboy Benny Sorensen.

His smile faded, though, and it was hard to miss the way his eyes had dropped to her mouth.

He was going to kiss her.

The air was suddenly stifling, and she drew in a deep breath. Then his mouth was lowering to hers, and he was standing so close to her that she fought a tiny sense of suffocation.

This was it. This was the moment she'd been dreading and anticipating, a moment she wanted to be perfect.

The jarring slam of a door startled them both, and she nearly jumped out of her red heels.

"Sorry about that," a chipper male voice said from down the hall. Too chipper.

It was Henry.

Seriously? What kind of timing was that? What, was he just waiting at the door for the important moment so he could ruin it for her? But why would he do that?

He smiled in apology as he neared them, a white bag in his hands. "I was just throwing this in the garbage chute. Don't mind me."

Only, it was kind of hard not to, as he walked past them and down to the end of the hall and into the small utility room, where he proceeded to make such a ruckus—stuffing whatever the heck was in that bag in the chute and then slamming the chute door so loudly she almost could feel the vibration—that they could only stand and wait for him to finish.

He appeared again, looking so darn casual in khakis and a white T-shirt so thin that she swore she could see his pecs outlined underneath.

"I'm Henry, by the way," he said and stopped to hold out his hand.

Benny had to give Luke points for taking Henry's hand without hesitation the way he did, knowing the guy had just been dealing with the trash. "Luke Seeley. You look familiar. Have we met before?"

Henry shot a sly look at her before meeting Luke's gaze again. "Don't think so. Well, sorry again for intruding. I'll let you two get back to whatever you were doing…"

She narrowed her eyes at his retreating back. This was far too contrived for it to be an accident. At his door, Henry took one last glance at her and waved his hand in a salute before heading inside.

Leaving her and Luke alone again.

"Where were we?" Luke asked, a small smile playing on his lips. "Oh, that's right. I was about to kiss you."

He'd said it, and she could only wait for him, even if she was strung so tightly from waiting—and now wondering whether Henry could somehow be spying on them from his peephole—that she could have spun like a top.

But she didn't have to wait as long this time, and Luke's smooth soft lips were on hers, soft and yet firm. She closed her eyes, forcing herself to relax for the moment, to remember that she wasn't half bad at this kissing thing after all.

This is nice.

His mouth parted and he deepened the kiss; the touch of his tongue darting into her mouth, however, didn't give her the same heart-stopping feeling as another kiss. Rather, for a horrible moment, Benny remembered this same mouth chewing and swallowing piece after piece of raw fish—was that a hint of wasabi she could taste? Or the freshwater eel he'd gone on about?

Luke's hands were now at her hips, bringing her fully against him.

Stop, Benny. This is what you want, and he is doing an incredible job of this kissing thing.

And he was. He was a pretty good kisser, and after another moment, she stopped thinking about raw fish and another set of lips that had left her breathless and focused on the pleasant feelings Luke's kiss was arousing.

Maybe not as skin tingling, but right up there in the top three on her short list of kisses, for sure. Without the usual anxiety about her performance, she was finding that she rather enjoyed this kissing stuff.

Finally, he ended it, resting his forehead against hers. "I think we had better stop here." She nodded and watched as he stepped back, a smile tugging on his mouth. "I'll see you tomorrow, Dr. Sorensen."

Benny slipped inside and shut the door, aware of the sound of the elevator a minute later as it took him down to the main floor.

The coast clear, she dropped her purse onto the counter and did a spontaneous dance, enjoying the heady feeling of success.

Not only had she had a wonderful evening with the future father of her kids and delivered a pretty great kiss once she threw out all the other nonsensical thoughts, but she had procured the even more important second date.

Ten seconds later, there was a knock on the door.

Had he forgotten something?

She bounded to the door and peeked out of the peephole.

Henry leaned against the doorjamb, a smug smile on his face.

She swung the door open, her hands on her hips, and stared at him, remembering the suspicious timing of his trash trip just moments before.

"So how did it go?" he drawled.

"Tell me you didn't know that Luke and I were out here earlier. That you hadn't planned on interrupting us like that."

He looked the picture of innocence as he raised his brows. "I had no idea you were out here, not until my door had already shut behind me. Why? Did I interrupt something?"

She still wasn't sure if she was buying it, but then again, what motive would he have to try and sabotage her and Luke's first kiss? She'd give him the benefit of the doubt. "You happened to interrupt us at the very moment we were about to kiss."

He burst out into laughter. "That is lousy timing. I trust that he managed to get things back on track, though. I mean, from the way your lipstick is smeared and your mouth is a bit puffy, you either were soundly kissed or are having an allergic reaction to something."

She smiled, unable to stay mad, feeling more certain it was all unfortunate timing. "It was better than I expected. Thank you again for the, uh, practice session last night. It made the whole experience more than I could have hoped."

He nodded, and she wasn't sure, but she thought she saw a flash of something other than amusement in his eyes. "Well, you look absolutely amazing. Stand back for me, I want the full effect. I don't think I've seen you with the entire makeup treatment before," he said more thoughtfully. "Is that what my stylist recommended?"

"It is." Only he was giving her the same perplexed look she'd seen before. On Daisy. "What? What's wrong?" Her hands went to her face, self-conscious. Maybe she'd applied it wrong, had been doing the whole thing wrong all week.

"Nothing. You look beautiful." He said it with such utter sincerity that she dropped her hands, knowing he was being honest. "I'm just not used to it is all. You look…different. But beautiful."

"Thank you. Wow. I have to stop saying that to you. That's the last one you get." But she was smiling again, feeling infinitely happier than she had in a long time. Things were on track, and Henry Ellison, eternal bachelor and playboy, thought she was…beautiful.

"I'll let you go. I just wanted to see how things went,"

Henry said and backed toward the door.

She was suddenly overwhelmed with the need to have him stay. To keep her company. She hadn't quite realized before now how much she appreciated and enjoyed having him over, whether in conversation or just watching something on TV. "Are you sure you can't stay? I can put on an episode of *Property Brothers*, open a bottle of cheap wine?"

"Nah. I have an early meeting. Another time."

She nodded, tamping down her disappointment. "Oh. Before I forget. Luke asked me out Saturday. I hope that my saying yes didn't mess anything up. I know you said make him work for it, but I thought I'd have more time to prepare before he asked again, so…I just kind of said yes."

"You scored the next date before the first was over? I'd say that's a victory. He's on the hook. Just go with what feels natural. We're still on for golf Sunday? Or should I wait to make sure you aren't having a…late night with the good doctor," he said and smiled salaciously.

"Don't try and wiggle out of another coaching session with me. I can promise you that no matter how well things go between Luke and I, I will not be sleeping with him. At least not on the second date."

"Really? And is there some magical formula for when you will sleep with a man? Is three the magic number?" he asked teasingly.

"Wouldn't you like to know."

He wasn't far from the mark, though. Magical *was* what she was looking for. Because before she was ready to take that big step of sleeping with Luke or anyone, she wanted to be sure there were real feelings there. She wanted it to mean something to them both. And to be more precise, that couldn't happen until at least date number four.

Or so the book she'd read a few years ago had said.

"Okay, then. I'll leave you to it. 'Night again. Don't let the bedbugs bite and all that." He had a slight smile on his lips as he said this, the same smile that she'd seen on him dozens if not hundreds of times. Only the sudden beating of her heart and the way she had to catch her breath for a moment was something entirely different. And unsettling.

It had to be the effects of the sushi. Or of kissing two entirely different men twenty-four hours apart.

She forced a nice, neutral smile to her own lips. "'Night, Henry."

Chapter Fifteen

"You may not be the most talented chef, but you do make a mean omelet. Even if it is seven o'clock at night," Morgan said and ate the last bit of her spinach and goat cheese omelet.

"Thank you. I don't do a lot of dishes, but eggs are my specialty."

"Does that have anything to do with the fact that it's probably the only meal you know how to prepare? You know, on those mornings when you're trying to impress the latest goddess."

"You wound me," Henry said, touching over his heart. Even though his sister had hit the nail on the head with that assessment. Omelets of all varieties, eggs Benedict, scrambled, sunny side up…you name it and he could cook it.

"I think you'll survive. Ella, did you want any more scrambled eggs?" Morgan asked her daughter.

"I don't know. Do you have Lucky Charms, Uncle Henry? Like you did last time?"

Morgan lifted up a brow. "I thought I left you a bag of cereal for her to eat."

Of course she had. A no-sugar-added, high-grains concoction that looked like something he should feed a canary, not a little girl. "I must have missed that," he said vaguely.

"What is a goddess?" Ella asked and looked at him with curiosity. "Is that someone you pray to?"

"You could say that," Henry said and bit back a laugh as his sister shot him a warning glance.

"Never mind, Ella. And no, you're not going to have any Lucky Charms. You can have more eggs if you're still hungry."

"No, thanks. But can I watch some TV? Uncle Henry has a billion more channels than we do."

"I suppose," she said, and they watched as Ella scooted from her chair, went to the couch and expertly turned on the TV and began flipping through channels.

"So how are things going with you, Morgan? You seem to have a pretty full schedule these days."

"Better than even I expected. In fact, my publisher approached me just a couple of days ago and asked me if I'd be interested in writing two more books. A pretty generous advance was mentioned as well."

He could see that despite the modest delivery, she was excited about the news. As she should be. "That sounds terrific. Congratulations. What did you tell them? Yes, I take it."

"I haven't yet answered. It is a great opportunity, really. But it would mean I'd probably have to cut back a little on my speaking engagements. You know, if I'm to write the kind of word count I'd need to get these finished in the next two years."

"Sounds like a win-win to me. You get a healthy advance and you get to spend more time around here with Ella. Instead of having to travel to thirty different cities in a few months."

Like Henry, Morgan had wanted independence and separation from the Brighton family and wealth and had chosen to keep her own vast inheritance untouched. She planned on leaving the entire sum to Ella once she was a little older and without all the baggage that the money had for Morgan and Henry.

Not that Morgan was hurting for money, since Henry knew she was making quite a bit in her recent ventures, not to mention the generous child support payments her NHL superstar ex-husband sent her every month.

"I suppose." She picked up her glass of white wine and took a sip. "I just get a little worried if I take myself off the circuit whether I'd be undercutting any gains I've achieved so far. I like getting out there and engaging with readers. With an audience."

Because it's on a superficial level. Nothing actually intimate. Or real. But he couldn't tell her that. "No one said you couldn't. But you would be able to be more selective. I'm sure Ella will be thrilled. I know she misses you."

"Ella is doing just fine," Morgan said a little too quickly, a definite edge to her tone.

He'd have to step carefully. "She is doing fine. Better than fine, I'm sure. I just want to make sure you're not throwing yourself too much into your work that you're forgetting about the other more important things, important moments. Ella is only young once, and you and I know what it can be like to be left in the care of other people while our mother busied herself with work. Missing everything important in our lives."

Her eyes were hard now as she answered. "I know very well what it was like living with an absent mother, Henry. More than you might know. I am nothing like her. And besides, who are you to talk? Outside of your work, what kind of personal life do you have? Other than the brief interludes you have with" — she glanced over to Ella — "the goddesses."

"Uncle Henry has Benny," Ella chirped from the couch, her gaze still on the cartoon playing on the TV, but obviously still in tune with their conversation. How did kids do that? "She's really nice and helped get the candy from my nose and read me bedtime stories when I couldn't sleep and we picked out clothes for her at the mall, then she bought me a corn dog."

His sister looked surprised...and amused. "Who's Benny?"

"No one," he said too hastily. "I mean, we ran into her at the pediatrician's office after the whole...Skittle fiasco," he said quickly diverting his eyes. "She was the attending physician. We've become friends is all, not surprising since she lives next door. That's it."

"But you two went shopping together." She brought her wine to her mouth to cover a smile. "That's a little...unusual. Yet you're just friends?"

"Long story, but yes. She actually is completely hung up on some doctor at her practice and—"

"You mean Dr. Seeley," she interrupted, her eyes wide. "Oh, he is pretty cute."

He paused. "Yes, thanks for that clarification. Anyhow, she needed some tips, some suggestions, really, on what she might do to help draw his attention her way."

"And since you are a proverbial...connoisseur of women," she said again after a quick glance to Ella, "who else to be her coach, is that it?"

"Something like that," he said. He needed a change in topics and quickly. He wasn't comfortable talking about Benny like this, not sure if he was violating some confidence. "How's your own dating life coming? Seeing anyone?"

"No, I'm not. I don't really have the time right now. But getting back to your new friend—Benny, was it?—tell me. What's she like? Maybe I've seen her around."

"Benny is super nice and pretty and tells Uncle Henry when he's being dumb."

"Ella, we don't talk about anyone like that and we don't use the word 'dumb,'" Morgan said in disapproval before turning back to Henry with her eyes shining a little more. "I think I like her more already. Someone resistant to your charms?"

Unfortunately, that was a truth that was niggling under his skin a lot more recently. It wasn't like he'd set out to seduce Benny Sorensen or anything, but the time they'd spent together had been more interesting than he'd thought possible. And in spending so much time with her, getting to know her, he'd found that he not only liked hanging out with her, but that he'd opened up to her more than any other woman.

So the fact that she didn't seem to have the slightest attraction to him was a point of contention.

Although that kiss...that had been good. Something he was thinking about too much. And her response? The way her legs had wrapped around him and she'd pulled him into her, wanting more? Hot.

Which might have been why, when he heard Benny and Luke Seeley get off the elevator and head down the hall to her place the other night, he'd had a hard time staying away from his door, trying to hear and see whatever he could with his face pressed to the peephole. To see if she would kiss Luke just as responsively, so entirely, as she'd kissed him.

And although he'd denied it later, Henry sure as hell had intended to put a wrench in Luke's plan to kiss Benny good night. The thought of Luke's lips on Benny's had churned a strange emotion in him, and he had been unable to *not* do something. The garbage, he thought, had been a good idea, something he was certain would wreck whatever mood had been set.

Unfortunately, that had not been the case, when seconds after he'd returned to his place, he could hear Luke's words, then the silence that followed. He knew what was happening even if he couldn't necessarily see it.

And it had killed him.

He'd thought about that feeling, his anger and frustration, trying to make sense of it, and could only come to one conclusion.

Plain and simple, he didn't want anyone kissing Benny Sorensen but him.

But that was ridiculous. Stupid. He couldn't have feelings for this woman. Feelings that would eventually turn to pain when the inevitable happened and things ended. When, as was human nature, one or both partners grew tired of the other and started looking elsewhere.

Then the heartache set in. The disappointment. The bitterness.

He's seen it before in the years leading up to his dad's passing.

Sad was how Henry would have described him.

Suddenly he realized that his sister was staring at him with a wide smile, waiting for some response. What had she asked?

Right. What was Benny like, this woman resistant to his charms.

"Benny Sorensen is…I don't know, a pain in the ass sometimes. Did I tell you what she tried to pull with the home owners' association?" He detailed her complaints, starting with the moment she first stepped into his party in her pajamas and asked him to keep the music down.

"Good for her. You are so used to people—women especially—just giving in to whatever whim you have. It's about time someone withstood your persuasion. So that's why you did this, then? This makeover? So she'd drop her complaints against you."

His sister knew him better than he thought. He nodded

in agreement.

"Only I think you got more than you bargained for. You seem a little…different."

He laughed. She was really reaching here. "I'm different, huh. I assure you, I'm the same person I have always been, Morgan."

"No. Not really. You're a little more…sincere? No, that's not the word. Well, like tonight. You having us here? Don't get me wrong, I'm glad you called, but it isn't like you to be this big family man. I—I like it."

"Glad I have your approval." He stood and grabbed his plate and put his hand out to take hers, not sure if he was altogether pleased to hear her assessment.

He was no different than before.

"I've got mine," she said coming to her feet. "You do dishes, too?"

"Actually, I have a lady who comes in every morning to clean up. I just place everything in the sink."

Morgan laughed. "Of course you do. You know, it isn't very hard to operate the dishwasher. Here, I'll even show you."

Ten minutes later, the table was cleared off and Morgan and Ella were getting the movie ready while he made popcorn—microwave, of course—when someone knocked on the door. Morgan bounded from the couch and headed over with a sly smile his way before he could stop her.

For good reason. He didn't get many visitors. Save for one, lately.

With twenty seconds to go on the microwave—the most tenuous of them all, unless you liked scorched, smelly popcorn aroma—he watched as Morgan opened the door.

• • •

Benny didn't know what had brought her to Henry's. They had no plans, and with Operation Luke successfully underway with tomorrow's impending date, there was no reason for her to stop by Henry's place.

But she hadn't seen him since Wednesday night, when he made his hasty exit rather than hang out and discuss the finer details of her date or watch their favorite show. Then last night she'd listened for him, but by the time she finally turned in after ten, he still hadn't come home. It was something of a surprise when she pulled into the parking garage tonight—a Friday night, no less—and found his car in its space. Even on his side of the line.

Sitting at her place, she'd fought the urge to come over. She normally couldn't stand the guy and now she wanted to see him and talk to him and just…be with him. It was kind of pathetic. She'd become one of Henry Ellison's groupies.

So she'd resolved to let him come and say hi first.

That had only lasted until two minutes ago, when she decided she was being silly. They were friends now. Why not stop and see if he wanted to chat? And she did have a couple of questions to ask him about golf, since tomorrow she was supposed to be teeing off with Luke, acting like she actually knew what she was doing. She still hadn't figured out what she was going to do there.

What she hadn't counted on when she pulled on her slippers and navy polka-dot pajamas and headed over was that he would have a guest.

Not just any guest, either.

A gorgeous, towering blonde with honey highlights and lovely dark eyes, who was watching Benny with curiosity.

What had she been thinking? Best just to cut her losses and make a quick escape, especially since the silence seemed to go on as the woman waited for Benny to say something.

"Hi, can I help you?" she finally asked when Benny's

tongue remained twisted.

Big-girl panties. Pull. Up.

Benny smiled brightly. "Sorry. I was going to ask Henry a quick question, but I didn't realize he had company. I'll just stop by another time."

"No. Please. Don't go. He's just in the kitchen. Come in."

Benny stared at the floor like it was lit with burning coals. No way was she going in there to stand next to this gorgeous creature when she looked like this—least of all when it was obvious the two wanted to be alon—

"Hi, Benny!" A small pixie face appeared at the woman's side, and Benny looked at her in confusion for a minute. "Ella? What are you doing here?"

"So *you're* the mysterious Benny. I'm Morgan. Henry's sister."

At that moment, Henry reached the door holding a bag of popcorn in his hand. The buttery smell was almost as good as the sight of him standing there in a relaxed jeans that hung from slim hips, a formfitting black tee, and an easy grin. Yum.

Whoa. Where did that come from?

Friends, Benny. You're only friends. Henry Ellison is and will always be way out of your league. No matter what she was wearing or how she styled her hair.

Still…she wished she'd gone with something less embarrassing than her pajamas.

"Sorry to just stop by unannounced. As I was telling your sister, I'll catch you later."

"Why? Come in. We're about to watch a movie."

"You can sit by me," Ella said and grabbed her hand.

"I'll stay for a minute," Benny said as Ella led her over to the couch.

Only as the movie started and Ella nestled into her, Benny was having a harder time remembering why she needed to leave. Especially when Morgan would break in to give some commentary about society's expectations of girls compared to boys, and Henry played devil's advocate and agreed with the norms just to yank his sister's chain before giving Benny a quick wink and a playful smile that had her stomach fluttering unnaturally.

Soon enough, the movie was over and Ella was half asleep in Morgan's arms while they said their good nights. "It was really nice meeting you, Benny," his sister said before turning an odd smile in her brother's direction.

"I should be going, too," she said, making a point to look at the time on her cell phone. Only it was eight thirty, and she couldn't very well say it was time she hit the hay too.

"No, you should stay. You were going to ask Henry something until we dragged you into our movie. I'll talk to you later, Henry." She waved and shut the door firmly before Benny could make further objections.

"Nice pj's. I'm glad to see you haven't permanently retired the dinosaur slippers."

"How long have you been waiting to give that sparkling commentary?" she asked, but she smiled as she turned to find him nearly on top of her. "Besides, the slippers were a gift from my nieces and nephew. They won't be going anywhere."

He went to the kitchen island and poured himself a glass of wine. He started to pour one for her, but she stopped him. "None for me. Want to make sure I wake up looking my best tomorrow. The swollen-bags-under-the-eyes thing is so retro."

"Clinic hours again?"

That's right. He'd left before she could share the details of her upcoming date. "No, actually. Luke's picking me up at noon. We're going golfing. Then he just wants to—get this—spend the rest of the day with me. Impressive, right?"

"Um. Sure, up until you whack him in the head or fail to make it past the first hole. You do remember that you still can't golf, don't you?"

He grabbed his glass and took a seat on the couch. She did still need some tips, so she took a seat on the leather chair next to the couch. "Of course I do. But I got a few swings in, and I'm pretty sure that I have the hang of it now. I can totally envision myself making contact with the ball now."

"Golf isn't just about hitting the ball and sending it careening wherever you want. You're actually supposed to get it *in* the hole."

"I know how it works. I'll be fine. I can wing it. I just need a little help from you on the actual rules. The jargon. Like what's 'love' and all that."

"Well, the first thing you should know is that 'love' is a tennis term. Not golf. What about clubs? Did you actually buy some or are you planning on renting them?"

She hadn't considered that. "Do you think I might borrow the set from last weekend?"

"Of course. Fortunately for you, I forgot to return them to Morgan, so they're still in the closet." He stood and headed to the coat closet and hauled them out.

"Speaking of Morgan, I got the impression she was studying me the whole time. Did you happen to tell her anything about our…arrangement?"

He cringed. "I'm afraid so. Not that I had intended to, but Ella was really helpful with providing details about our shopping excursion, and Morgan naturally wanted to know why." He lifted a club up. "Here. Just to get you started, don't worry about all the other clubs in the bag. For now, worry about using these three."

She thought about revisiting his revelation, but what was the point? Morgan wasn't going to blab it all around, and Benny supposed she couldn't expect Henry to lie to her. Something she was feeling more guilty about when she thought about how she'd been less than truthful with her own sister.

Rising to her feet, she joined him and listened as he explained the different clubs, with names like driver, iron, wedge, and putter and a few other descriptions of why she'd ever need any of the others.

And although she'd usually dismissed golf as boring, she found the abbreviated lesson actually...fascinating. Managing to hit the ball was just one aspect, of course, but Henry's explanation of how using a different size or weight or angle head could affect the trajectory of each swing gave her something to think about.

"You're going to show me how all this works Sunday morning, right?" she asked.

"I have us down for tee time at nine. And I'm packing a helmet."

She rolled her eyes. "I am not going to hit you again, Henry. Jeez, I'm not that much of a klutz."

"My head begs to differ."

"Well, that time was different. I was...distracted."

He raised a brow. "By what?"

Crap. Had she just admitted that? Well, there was no way she was going to elaborate how just having him standing behind her, his breath in her hair, the heady scent of him surrounding her, had left her a little unbalanced.

"I can't remember." She dropped the club back in the bag, unsure how she'd handle herself if Henry decided to give her another up-close-and-personal lesson on swinging. Not when she'd spent the past two nights thinking about what it had been like to kiss him. Even *after* she'd kissed Luke Seeley, when the only thing running through her mind should have been kissing him again. Not Henry.

"Try not to get too distracted again tomorrow. By the way, if the two of you are looking for something to do, I'm having a get-together tomorrow night. And before you say it, I'll keep the music down to a respectable level."

"Thanks, maybe we will. I should go. I'm sure you have other plans. I really hadn't meant to be here so long."

"No worries. Actually, I think I'm going to stay in tonight. Get my own beauty rest."

Henry Ellison was staying in? And on a Friday night, no less.

For some reason, she felt a tiny sense of relief at knowing he wouldn't be out and about, hooking up with the latest flavor of the week. He'd be here, just down the hall.

She grabbed the golf clubs and slung the bag over her shoulder. "Okay. I'll see you Sunday."

"See you." She was out the door and halfway down the hall when Henry called out, "And remember. Keep your eye on your target, follow through on your swing, and for heaven's sake, whatever happens, don't let yourself get distracted." He touched the top of his head where she'd whacked him and grinned.

She lifted her hand in a weak wave.

Distracted? It seemed these days the only time that happened was when she was in the presence of one man. Luke should be safe.

Chapter Sixteen

"How did things go on your date with the esteemed Dr. Seeley?" Henry asked her early Sunday morning as they whizzed down the freeway at a healthy clip. Benny had tried to coerce him into letting her drive, but considering she looked still half asleep, he wasn't about to risk it. "And by how did things go, I mean did you manage to avoid clobbering him with a golf club?"

"You're never going to let me forget that, are you?"

"Not a chance."

"No, I didn't hit him. In fact, we had a great time. I impressed everyone."

He lifted his brows in surprise. "You did?"

"Yep. Right up to the moment I was lining my hips up the way you showed me, raising the driver for an impeccable delivery, and my right ankle completely went out on me and I fell gracefully on my butt. Unfortunately, the ankle was just too tender to try and walk on, and I resigned myself to sitting and watching the game from the cool shade of the golf cart."

He laughed and shook his head at her ingenuity—or

desperation. "And saved yourself, yet again, from displaying your total ineptitude at playing golf. Kudos. What will you think of the next time? A fake bee sting? Passing out from heatstroke?"

"Not necessary. Somewhere between the seventh and the eighth hole, Luke joined me on the golf cart and we watched the other players take their shots. 'You don't really have a clue how to play golf, do you,' he asked me. And not like he was angry or anything, but like he was trying not to laugh. So I came clean."

"The truth. How novel," he said drolly.

"I even told him about you. At least about how you've been helping me with my golf game up until I'd whacked you in the head. He told me to thank you for that." She grinned, her eyes flashing with humor.

"Tell him I appreciate the gratitude. So it sounds like you two had a nice date, then."

"Oh, that was nothing. After the game, he drove us up the canyon and we hiked to this spot with an amazing view of the entire valley and had a picnic, right there. Later, over wine, we watched the sun set and then just lay under the stars."

The man was good. Too good. Setting up the scene like that, the ambience. Very manipulative. He thought about Benny lying on the blanket with the calculating Luke Seeley creeping nearby, maybe starting with a little hand-holding and then stepping it up. Maybe brushing the hair off her face as a way to make eye contact before dropping his greedy mouth down for a kiss, his hands mauling Benny's body, feeling her softness, her curves, her—

"Uh. Henry, you might want to ease off the gas there. You're pushing ninety-five."

He glanced down to see she was right and lowered their speed. His fingers were taut as they gripped the wheel, and he loosened them, flexing them. "Sounds like you two really hit it off."

She sighed and looked out the passenger window. "It was perfect."

His heart felt like it was seizing. Did that mean—had she—no. She wouldn't, she'd as much as told him so. But he had to know. He cleared his throat, trying to sound cavalier. "Did you two take it to the next level?"

She laughed and shook her head at him. "No. Luke is a gentleman. You might think all dates culminate in a tumble in the hay, but for other more cerebral people, like Luke and me, a meeting of the minds is even more rewarding than a meeting of the bodies."

Now he snickered. "I highly doubt that. And if you really believe that, then you have never had anyone actually make love to you. Because that, my dear, is the reason for everything."

"Everything? Seriously, you believe that? You don't think two people can have a rewarding relationship without sex?"

"No."

"Have you ever had a relationship with a woman that didn't end with her in your bed? And I don't mean your sister."

"Yeah." He grinned and met her gaze for a moment. "You."

Not that he hadn't had visions of that happening a time or two.

Or a hundred.

"You're frightening sometimes," she said. "But why am I not surprised?"

"You know, if Luke's discovered that you don't know how to play golf, why are we still going through with this?"

"Because Luke likes golf. If we're going to have any kind of relationship, I think it's important that I be able to enjoy the same things he does. Or at least understand them a little better."

"And what if you don't end up liking it? Does that mean you two won't be compatible? Or will you just continue to act like you do?" He sounded a lot more annoyed than he intended.

"Wow. You're in a mood."

"No, I'm just trying to understand."

"Understand what?"

"What makes you so sure that Luke Seeley is *the one*? I mean, before you'd said two words to him, you were already picking out the names of your kids. What do you know about him other than he plays golf, served some humanitarian stint for a couple of years, and is a doctor?"

"First, the fact that we both are in the medical profession says a lot about his character already. That we have common interests and goals and worked hard to get where we are. Second, I know that he feels just as strongly as I do about family and marriage. His parents have been married more than forty years, and he, like me, wants to emulate that."

"So if a person comes from a broken family, maybe raised by a single parent, you're saying they wouldn't be compatible with someone whose family is intact, for lack of a better word."

"No, you're twisting my words. I'm just saying that he *believes* that a good marriage can exist. That there is such a thing as happily-ever-after. Unlike *some* people, who think a meaningful relationship is two people who make it to lunch the next day."

"You don't think I believe in marriage?"

"Well, do you? I seem to recall you expressing your cynicism before that such a thing was akin to a fairy tale."

"I never said anything about a fairy tale." However, he couldn't deny that up until recently, he'd been convinced that that stuff only existed in Hallmark movies. Or in commercials that aired over the holidays to make everyone feel incompetent and wistful over something that wasn't real.

Only, having spent time with Benny, he was actually starting to believe that such things were real. That maybe a man and a woman—or two women or two men or whatever fate chose—could find a special spark with another person and that they could be happy to spend the rest of their lives happy to experience the ups and downs of life together.

Not that he was going to try and explain that to Benny. "Let's just say that you've made me believe a lot more things are possible."

She grew quiet, so he risked a glance at her. She was looking at him with an odd shine in her eyes. He turned his attention back to the road in time to catch their exit, and they rode in silence the last few minutes to the club.

· · ·

"See where you want it to go. Now…tap it. Very gently. If you hit it too hard, it's going to sail right past."

The ball was six feet from the hole. It might have taken too many swings to count to get her there, but she was, and was so close to getting it in she was wired.

Benny took in a breath and lifted the club and brought it lightly down. The ball moved gracefully one then two then the final three feet and for a minute looked like it was going to miss, but it looped in the curve of the hole and, for a long second, hung there before it finally dropped in.

"Woo-hoo!!" Benny cried and moved her hands in front of her in her trademark dance. Henry lifted his brows, a smile on his face as he watched her in amusement. But she didn't care.

Wow. *Is this what it's like once you master actually hitting the ball with the club?* This invigorating feeling as they finished another hole?

"Grab your ball, tiger," Henry said. "We've got to get to the next hole before the mob waiting behind us takes matters into their own hands."

The disco beat of "We Are Family" trilled from her phone, and she pulled it from her back pocket, already knowing who it was. "Hey, Daisy."

"Wow. Don't you sound chipper. What are you doing?"

"Golfing."

"Again? I thought after you nearly maimed Henry last weekend you gave up on that. Who are you with?"

"Henry."

Daisy laughed. "He's a brave man. Well, I was going to ask if you wanted to come and hang out here and drive over to the parents' for dinner, but I can see you're already busy. You should bring him tonight. Henry, I mean. The kids loved playing Twister with him, and it would be worth it just to see Cruz and Dominic going all psycho on him again. They're really ridiculous sometimes."

"I'll think about it. He might have other plans."

"Ask. Because if you're not interested, then I might try my own wiles on him. Before you tell me how much of a womanizer he is and that his attention span is the lifetime of a mosquito, let me remind you it's been nearly a year since Leo left me and even longer than that since I've had any kind of action. Sometimes a girl needs to get out and remember she is a girl and just have some fun."

Benny's grip on the phone tightened. Daisy and Henry? Daisy was certainly beautiful enough to hold someone like Henry's attention. But the two of them? Henry holding Daisy, kissing her and doing untold things to her...*no*. The thought made her want to claw her eyes out. Actually, everyone's eyes out.

But she managed instead to only say, "We'll see."

"Oh, and while I'm remembering, have you talked to

Payton about arranging for the tables and chairs for the party next week?"

Benny groaned, having totally forgotten. Party planning was not her thing, but fortunately for her, her new sister-in-law had a knack for it. But Payton hadn't wanted to step on any toes, being new to the family, and had been holding off until Benny could work out some of the details with her so she didn't feel that Payton had taken over. Not that Benny would.

"You haven't," Daisy said, clearly annoyed. "You know Mom and I are doing all of the food planning and Kate and Dominic are working on the present. This is the only thing you have to do. So give her a call this week, since we can't very well talk about it tonight, not if we want this to be a surprise party for Dad."

"I know, I know. I promise I will. But look, I have to go, we need to move to the next hole."

"Is that your sister?" he asked her as she returned the phone to her pocket and slipped the strap of the golf bag Henry was holding for her over her shoulder.

"Yes. Why?" she asked sharply, far more sharply than necessary. Had she heard a tone in his voice? Interest in Daisy?

"No reason," he said, looking at her strangely as they walked across the grass running beside the club's pond. A pond that had already taken four of Benny's balls.

"Yes, sorry. She just wanted to make sure I was coming to the family dinner tonight and to give me a guilt trip about forgetting to do something for my dad's big surprise party next week."

"A surprise party? How old is he going to be?"

"Fifty-nine."

He looked puzzled. "Am I missing something? I could see a big shindig for sixty, but why fifty-nine?"

"Last fall he had major heart surgery, and up until then, things were kind of scary. And now that he has this clean bill of health, we wanted to do something big to celebrate his life."

He nodded. "That's…nice."

She remembered that Henry had lost his own dad at a young age, and she worried she'd put her foot in her mouth. Sometimes she forgot how lucky she was. "I'm sorry, Henry. Going on about my family and dad and obligations. I probably sound ungrateful."

"Not at all. Your dad seems to be an amazing man. I'm glad he's in good health now, and I think this party is going to make him feel even more blessed to be around."

They reached the start of the next hole, and Henry stood for a moment, practicing his swing. Like before, she couldn't help but appreciate the strong form he presented, so sure and smooth, as he whipped the iron through the air. Or the cute butt that she was free to stare at while his attention was diverted.

But it was more than that. She just liked looking at him. Being with him. Talking about her day as they cozied up on the couch. Laughing with him or at him or some combination of the two.

Which was completely…terrifying.

Because if she were honest with herself, she knew that her feelings for Henry had intensified somewhere in the past few weeks. That the way she was looking at him and thinking about him were far from platonic.

She was falling for him.

How was that possible? She had been in love with Luke for months.

She considered Daisy's suggestion about inviting him to dinner. The prospect of hanging out with him and the rest of her family was enticing. "I know this is silly, and you probably have a million things to do after this, but if you are free…

you're welcome to come to dinner again tonight."

"And risk brain injury from your brothers?" He grinned at her, though, as he pulled a golf ball from his pocket. He bent over to push it and a tee into the grass, and when he straightened, he looked more thoughtful. "I don't know. I don't exactly have a reason to impose."

"Believe me, my mom loves to feed everyone, and she'll be overjoyed to have you. Daisy and the kids, too." Her brothers? Well, they'd just have to get over it.

He hesitated another moment, and her stomach sank. What had she been thinking? Of course she might be having feelings for him, but this was Henry Ellison. Playboy extraordinaire. Why would he want to hang out with her and her family?

"If you consider a rematch at Twister, then maybe I will."

Immediately, her spirits buoyed, and she returned his grin. "Not a chance."

Although she'd be lying if the thought of the two of them tangled up again didn't have some appeal.

Chapter Seventeen

"You Sorensens are really a competitive bunch," Henry said, following Benny after a backbreaking game of badminton—a game that he thought was supposed to be more...tame. Gentrified.

"We just like to keep things interesting. It was better than beating each other up."

"I thought that was what we were doing."

"Not even close."

She took a seat on a bench tucked away at the back of the flower garden. It was hard not to stare at the pretty pink flushness of her face, now highlighted by the fading summer sun, the way several more pieces of hair had fallen around her face to frame it just so. The way he wanted to pull her in his arms and tilt her chin up and kiss that full mouth, feel the warmth of this woman who had made him laugh more than he'd laughed with anyone.

Maybe sitting in such a private location out of sight of the rest of the Sorensens wasn't such a good idea.

He cleared his throat and took a seat next to her before

handing her one of the two plates he'd been carrying. Chocoflan was what Daisy had called it. Benny took it, her eyes widening even more as she coveted the dessert that had a thick, gooey chocolate cake on the bottom and a rich caramel-covered flan on top. She took the first bite and closed her eyes over the richness.

Damn. Now he wanted to know what that mouth would taste like even more.

Best to keep his gaze from hers. Instead, he looked back toward the house. From their position, they could see inside the house, where the kids were playing a mean game of Apples to Apples with their mom and grandparents at the dining table, Dominic and Kate were at the kitchen window laughing and doing the dishes together, having lost the bet made in the heat of the game, and Cruz and Payton were whispering and laughing together out on the deck, their arms around each other as they rocked in a porch swing.

He supposed this was what it meant to have a family. This happy, warm contentment of just being in one another's presence one minute, even if an hour before they'd been shouting threats of pain and torture as they egged one another on. Of knowing that they had somewhere they fit, where they belonged.

There was a strange tugging sensation around his heart. The scene was something out of a Norman Rockwell painting. Something he'd never really believed existed outside the painter's mind.

"I'm glad I came. This was fun."

"Me, too." She took another bite of the rich dessert and kept her gaze on the house. "You know, when I was growing up, I used to come out here at night and sit with my dessert, too. Watching everyone inside. Of course, back then Daisy wasn't playing board games with her kids or our parents. She was usually where Cruz and Payton are now, whispering and laughing with some jock. She was never at a loss for a boyfriend." Benny said this wistfully. Maybe even a little begrudgingly.

"How about you? You didn't have any high school boyfriends over? No one you liked?"

"When I was fourteen, the only boy I liked was too in love with another girl to see me as anything but a kid." She smiled a little sadly.

"Then he was an idiot."

"No, quite the contrary. He was heading to college on a full scholarship," she said, missing his point. How could anyone not appreciate this woman? But she was lost in her own memory now as she continued. "Scottie was the lifeguard at the community pool and I'd been kind of stalking him all summer. I knew his schedule and always made sure to be sitting in whatever vicinity he was, usually reading Tolkien while sneaking glances at his near-godlike physique from behind my sunglasses. One afternoon Daisy and a couple of her friends decided to come by. He took one look at her and was as instantly in love with her as I'd been with him. Daisy has that effect on people."

"Did you ever tell her?"

"Tell her what?"

"Tell her that you were in love with Scottie the lifeguard. She's your sister. She might not have dated him if she knew what it was costing you."

"No, of course not. I mean, he was this gorgeous creature and I was—I was…me. Still a tomboy with twenty pounds of baby fat. No one was going to look at me."

She said that with such certainty that it angered him as much as it made him want to hug her. "Ridiculous. I think you sold yourself—no, I think you *still* sell yourself short, Benny. I don't know what you were like back then, but there are some things that time and age don't change. Like the fact that you're easily the most stubborn but also strong and determined and fiercely loyal woman I've ever met. That you're not only smart and intelligent but have a sharp wit that makes me laugh and wonder what you're going to say next. And when you look at me sometimes, with those large, expressive eyes, I am utterly convinced you're the most beautiful woman on the entire planet."

She swallowed and looked at him, almost as if waiting for a punch line.

He only smiled, shaking his head. "Any man would be lucky to be with you. Don't ever believe otherwise."

And he'd never meant anything more. From the long, graceful arch of her neck to her expressive face, the dark lashes that framed the most beautiful set of blue eyes he'd ever seen. But he knew beneath the soft, demure picture she painted now, Benny Sorensen was a tough, independent and strong woman who had a lot to offer some lucky guy.

It pained him to think of that lucky guy being Luke Seeley.

No. If he were honest with himself, it pained him to think about that lucky guy being anyone other than…him.

Unable to help himself, Henry reached out and ran his finger across Benny's full bottom lip. "If a guy can't recognize how special you are, then you don't want them." Without taking his gaze from hers, he lowered his mouth until he was inches away from that delectable mouth. He could smell chocolate and caramel on her breath.

He wanted her to know what he was about to do.

He cupped the side of her head in his hand and moved slowly until he was kissing that bottom lip, sucking on it and then parting her mouth open with his. Tasting her. Feeling the softness and strength of her. There was the sound of a fork clattering against the bench as she released her hold on her plate, then her hand was gripping his shoulder as she leaned into him. Embracing him. Tasting him as well.

It was almost like this was where she belonged.

In his arms. Her mouth opened to his, demanding as good as she got.

Almost.

• • •

Benny knew that she should stop him. That she wasn't supposed to want kisses from Henry. But what she knew was entirely different from what her body wanted.

She wanted to kiss him more than anything. The moment he'd smiled wickedly before letting a birdie fly her way she'd been hit with a sudden wave of desire. She'd wanted to bolt over the net and toss him to the ground right then and kiss him senseless for challenging her like that. And it hadn't let up.

And now *he* was kissing *her*, his tongue tangling with hers as the heat grew around them almost like they were in a fireball of energy and she could shut everything out but the taste of him. The feeling of his mouth, his lips, his hand on her head, and his other hand resting—no, gripping—her right hip as he held her closer.

It was like before, but now she could hear the subtle chirps of the crickets and smell her mom's lavender surrounding them and Henry's sure and haunting scent.

She never wanted this to end. She wanted to hold him like this, kiss him like this…forever.

But something outside their cocoon was happening, and she felt Henry freeze and start to pull away, but she resisted, trying to pull his mouth back to hers.

"Henry," Jenna called out, echoed by Natalie a moment later.

Benny froze. Her nieces were looking for him.

Oh. Lord.

She was making out with Henry in her mom's garden as her nieces scoured the backyard with their laser-beam eyes looking for them.

If they saw them kissing, the girls would shriek the news to everyone. And it would be impossible to convince anyone that Henry was just a friend.

Henry came abruptly to his feet, his face turned away from her.

A sudden fear reached her heart. Was he regretting what had just happened? Had she misjudged him, misjudged the moment when it seemed everything had faded away and it was just him, and they'd kissed—

No. Wait. She was almost sure that it had been Henry who'd initiated it. Right?

Well, she didn't have time to analyze right now. She had to minimize damage. Picking up her plate, she crossed the lawn, the grass soft and warm under her bare feet. "We're right here, girls. But I think we are going to have to call it a night. We both have early days."

There was no way she could risk any scrutiny from any of her family who might see her undoubtedly flushed skin and guess the truth.

Not when she didn't know what any of it meant.

. . .

They'd driven home in silence, which was fine with her. The wind whipped her hair, and she savored the rush of the air against her face, trying to clear her thoughts. She caught him watching her a few times, his expression impossible to read. Maybe he was giving her some time to process. That's it. Not that he was…regretting anything.

It was only as they stepped onto the elevator that Henry finally spoke. "About earlier. That kiss. I'm sorry. That was entirely inappropriate."

Her stomach felt like it was dropping through the floor, and they hadn't even started their ascent. He was sorry?

She couldn't say anything, only stood there frozen. Nodding. Like she understood.

"I think we'd just had such a great day and there was this sudden rush of adrenaline as I saw you sitting there, your face flushed and bright. I couldn't resist. It just felt like the most natural thing to reach down and kiss you. Only…" He paused and raked a hand through his hair, trying to find words as the elevator grunted and started to climb.

"Henry, you don't have to explain anything. I get it. You're used to planting that mouth on anything with breasts, and I was no exception." Even though she'd said this through a forced smile, intending it to be a joke, she'd sounded more bitter than she'd intended, but it couldn't be helped.

"No. It's not like that. You're not like anyone else. That's why my kissing you was most definitely the wrong thing to do. In the past couple of weeks you and I have become friends. Really good friends, and I don't think I could ever say that before about a woman. It's been really, really nice and not something I want to risk losing. Not with my track record."

Right. Why was she such an idiot? She knew this. He'd so much as told her so himself. Men either wanted to sleep with you or they didn't. She'd been permanently friend zoned. And it hurt a hell of a lot more than she'd thought possible.

The elevator was just cresting seven. Three more flights. Time to get this conversation over with and run back to her place to lick her wounds.

For now, be positive. Don't let him see how much his apology stung.

"Henry, don't be ridiculous." She delivered a megawatt smile, her face feeling like it would crack under the pressure. "It was a nice kiss—no. A great kiss. But you don't have to worry about me. I know we're friends. Luke is the whole reason I've been doing all of this, and thanks to your help, I'm finally getting what I want. Really. Don't give it a second thought."

His shoulders sagged in obvious relief. He faked a punch to her right arm. "You're a great woman, Benny Sorensen. You're going to make some lucky bastard the happiest man in the world."

The doors were opening, and she rushed forward, needing to distance herself from him as fast as she could. "Well, thanks for the lesson today. But I'm pretty wiped out, and if I'm going to look human again tomorrow, I should probably get to bed."

"Okay. I'll catch you later." He didn't argue with her or try to coerce her into an episode of *The Good Wife* like he'd done in the past.

She made it to her place before any tears could fall, thank God.

It wouldn't be fair for her to make Henry feel guilty over her misguided feelings. She should know by now that men like Henry were completely out of her league.

Unlike Luke and the other men who've shown her interest in the past couple of weeks thanks to the shiny new package they'd concocted, Henry wasn't fooled by the makeup, the new clothes, or the haircut.

Henry knew the real Benny.

And as she'd feared, he knew she just wasn't good enough.

Chapter Eighteen

Henry was in a foul mood. He knew it as he nodded and ignored the well wishes when he left the gym earlier that morning, when he snapped at the parking lot attendant as he'd pulled into the lot at work, when Marion, his assistant, mused about why he'd looked like something the cat dragged in.

Two cups of coffee later, his mood still hadn't improved, and he knew why. Because he was furious. Annoyed. Frustrated. At one person.

Himself.

What had he been thinking getting so close to a woman like Benny when he should have realized how dangerous she was? Dangerous in how absolutely perfect she was, and it was inevitable that he'd start having feelings for her.

Because just as much as he wanted her, wanted the happiness that would come with being with her, wanted that kiss to go on forever, he'd known deep down that things would never work out.

People like Henry didn't have a happily-ever-after. People

like him were destined to be alone.

He felt like he'd spent his entire life alone. Not wanted and abandoned by his mother, abandoned in death by his heartbroken father.

So just for another moment, he'd pretended that what he and Benny had could be real. That it could be forever.

Only as soon it was over, the reality of the situation came crashing down. He could never have Benny Sorensen. Not the way she wanted. Not forever.

So although it had been a little late, he'd had to be honest with her last night in the elevator. Had to put the brakes on things before he was too far gone. Before he did something stupid like fall completely in love with her. Before he could be too invested only to have her realize things wouldn't work out and leave him. Like everyone inevitably did.

He had to admit, however, that seeing how quick Benny had been to agree with him that their kiss had been a mistake had been a bit of a bruise to his ego. She could have at least had the courtesy to look a little disappointed.

But then, why would she? She finally had Luke eating out of her hand. Dr. Luke Seeley, who was everything she could ever want in a man. Ambitious, hardworking, selfless, loving, from a good family, and apparently, if all signs were correct, on his way to falling in love with her.

Yes. Benny was definitely going to be better off.

All the same, knowing this stuff and coming to terms with it were completely different things, and Henry'd spent the entire night torturing himself with these thoughts until he finally rolled out of bed and headed to the gym to work off his stress.

He was cradling his baseball in his hands, still recalling the details of yesterday's afternoon with Benny, when he realized someone was talking to him.

He looked up to see Becks standing at the door with a

bemused expression on her face.

"Henry? You doing all right?"

Lord. How long had she been standing there trying to get his attention? "Just fine. Sorry. Had a rough night's sleep."

"I could probably come back when you're feeling a little more...animated," she said, and walked across the office before sinking into the seat opposite him, "but since I have some big news I thought you should know straight away, I'll take what I can get."

He'd been about to toss the ball to his other hand, but her statement stopped him. "News?"

"I just got off the phone with AirPro Athletics. They were impressed by your presentation the other day, not to mention your assurances that you understood and shared their vision of family and community. We've got the account."

She was looking at him expectantly, and he supposed he should express some modicum of enthusiasm. "That's great. Just what we wanted. I told you it wouldn't be a problem."

"That's it? That's all I'm going to get?" She smiled, though, shaking her head. "Whoever she is, she's really messing with your head."

He sat up straighter. "She is? I assure you, that's not what's going on here. I told you. I just didn't get much sleep last night. This news is...great. Unbelievable. I'll be sure to meet with the team right away to give them the good news."

She came to her feet. "You do that, Henry. You might also just want to take a day or two off. Get some real relaxation in. What with landing this account and earning that nomination, not to mention managing to go three full weeks without so much as a byline from any of the tabloids, you've earned it."

"I'll keep that in mind. Thanks, Becks."

Only he didn't feel like celebrating now any more than he had before Becks walked in that door. In fact, his mind was somewhere else. With someone else.

He wondered if she'd already taken the steps she'd need to move on with the good Dr. Seeley. He just hoped he'd be able to keep up the pretense that imagining her with anyone else wasn't like a knife to the chest.

She deserved to be happy. Even if it wasn't with him.

• • •

"You know, my parents are going to be in town next weekend. They really would like to meet you," Luke said, wrapping his hands around her waist and facing her while the elevator slowly crept upward to the tenth floor.

It was Thursday night, and they'd just come from a movie where she'd eaten too much popcorn and drank too much soda, and she felt a little sick.

"Your parents?" Luke's parents had moved to a retirement community in the sunny southern climes of Tempe, Arizona, which was about ten hours' drive away from Salt Lake, so their trip up, she hoped, had nothing to do with meeting her.

"Don't look so worried," he said and laughed, tucking a stray hair from her face. "They'll love you."

"They're not coming all this way to meet me, though. Right?"

"Not that that would be so unbelievable, but no. There's actually an amateur golf tournament next weekend they already had planned on attending. Meeting you is just a happy coincidence."

"In that case…I can't wait."

She tilted her head up to catch his kiss, a move that, after Saturday and two more dinner dates under their belt, was feeling much more natural. He was a good kisser, and she closed her eyes, enjoying the sweet moment.

She hadn't even been aware that the elevator doors had opened until the sound of someone clearing their throat brought her back to earth. They grinned at each other and turned to apologize to whoever had caught them in such an awkward moment.

Holy Hannah.

All her sweet, tingling feelings were swept away as she stared into Henry's brown eyes. "Sorry to interrupt," he said to her before turning his attention to Luke. "How's it going?"

Luke seemed to recognize him, and as they stepped off the elevator, he held his hand out to take Henry's. "Good, man. It's Henry, right? The golf instructor?"

"I suppose that's accurate enough."

Luke draped his arm casually over Benny's shoulders, unaware of the tension between the two. "Well, I appreciate you helping out. Actually, if you had a minute, I was wondering something about your club. I might be looking to move somewhere new, and I hear the course there is excellent. What's the USGA course rating?"

Benny worked to keep a slight smile on her face as the elevator door shut behind them and Henry answered the question without any sense of urgency. His demeanor was easy and casual. Not seeming to be affected in the least by coming upon the two of them kissing just a moment before.

And dang. He looked so freaking good, even if it hurt her heart a little bit to see him right now.

Since their last encounter on Sunday night, they hadn't seen each other—not even in passing. She'd kept to her regular schedule, one that usually involved her passing him once or twice in the parking garage or at the mailboxes.

But it was as if Henry was purposely avoiding her, which was a relief as much as it was a stab to the heart.

"Oh, by the way, Benny mentioned to me that you're a bit of a baseball fan and"—Luke paused and looked down at her with a grin—"I thought as a way of thanking you for your helping out with golf, that I'd pick up a few extra tickets for the Bees' game on Saturday."

Henry finally leaned forward and pressed the call button to the elevator. He was dressed to go out, clearly. Even though it was after ten. "That's pretty nice of you. But I don't know if I'm going to be free that day…"

"I know that it's not going to be anything like seeing the Giants," Luke added, "but I managed to get four front-row seats. You'll feel like you're on the field."

Four tickets? Like…a double date?

Not. Going. To. Happen.

"That's sweet of you, Luke," Benny said and leaned her head against Luke's shoulder, "but it sounds like Henry's already got plans. We don't want him to feel obligated to take us up on your offer. You know, I can check with my brother Dominic and his wife, Kate. You haven't had a chance to meet them yet, but I'm sure they'd love to—"

"I didn't say I wasn't available," Henry said a bit loudly, and she pulled her gaze from Luke's to Henry. "In fact, front-row tickets…that's nearly impossible to say no to."

What was Henry thinking? This whole week he'd worked to avoid her, and now he wanted to be part of this double-date nightmare?

She narrowed her eyes at him.

Henry smiled, nodding. "Yeah. I think I can make it work."

"Great," Luke continued. "I'll leave the tickets with Benny tomorrow, if you and your date want to just meet us there."

"I look forward to it."

Benny had no words, and fortunately the elevator arrived and Henry was stepping on it making further conversation unnecessary.

It was hard to miss the smugness in that grin as it shut a moment later.

Well, fine.

They were friends, weren't they? Maybe Henry was just trying to regain that platonic footage they'd had up until Sunday's fateful kiss. If he was okay with seeing her with someone else, she could be just as okay. No, better than okay. She would be great.

Everything would be just…great.

. . .

Henry had to be insane.

To put himself through this torture of watching the happy lovebirds teasing and laughing with each other as they returned from the ballpark's snack bar, looking to the world like they were completely head over heels in love with each other.

Wasn't it enough to have that gut-kicking moment the other night, when the elevator doors opened to reveal Benny and Saint Luke in a passionate lip-lock, unaware of anyone or anything but each other? It had made him want to pull Luke off her in a blinding moment of fury and slam his fist in his gut in the same way it felt someone had slugged Henry.

He should have just politely declined the invitation—Benny had given him the opening. But no, she had to mention her brother and inviting him and his wife for a little family excursion with the new beau.

Sweet. Disgustingly so.

And suddenly the thought of Luke being welcomed into the embrace of Benny's family had been too much and he'd spoken before he'd really considered what he was doing.

"Here you go," Luke said and passed down Henry's date's nachos, followed by a hot dog with the works. The guy had insisted on picking up the tab, of course.

Luke waited for Benny to take her seat before sliding in

the one next to hers. He draped his arm around her shoulder, looking far too cozy and content as he leaned over to lay a quick kiss on her mouth.

Yeah. This was complete torture.

Made worse by the fact that seeing Benny all dolled up like that struck a chord with him.

Not that she didn't look stunning. She did. Gorgeous, even, in a long sleeveless dress, a deep blue color that matched her eyes. But her usual natural makeup palette—a touch of color to those full lips and a swipe or two of mascara—was abandoned for this more airbrushed, magazine-perfect face with carefully sculpted cheekbones and dramatic eyes and lips.

She didn't look like...Benny. Not the Benny he knew. More like she was dressing up just to appease Luke.

Wasn't that what he'd been telling her to do from the beginning? To make herself into someone else, someone that Luke would want?

Henry was beginning to question the wisdom of his advice. Of everything.

Why should Benny have to dress up as anything other than who she was when she was so perfectly intriguing and wonderful as she was? Why couldn't she see that?

"Thanks again for the tickets," Henry said. "I insist on repaying you. How about joining Lela and me for dinner tonight? My treat."

What on earth had he just asked? As if this afternoon wasn't torturous enough, he wanted to add a meal?

"Ah, man. That's nice of you," Luke said. "But I actually already made reservations for that new Market Place restaurant. It's an anniversary of sorts." He squeezed Benny's shoulder.

For crying out loud. They had only been seeing each other for two weeks. What on earth could they have to celebrate?

Wait. Had he said Market Place?

"I've heard that place is good. Isn't their specialty... seafood?" Henry asked, looking directly at Benny.

"It is. Brought in fresh daily," Luke said enthusiastically. "Their sushi is phenomenal. I was there a few weeks ago and have been meaning to take Benny ever since."

"Do you even like sushi?" Henry asked Benny, having a distinct memory of her gagging when he'd offered her a bite of his California roll he'd picked up last week.

"It's great," she said and gave him a piercing look that told him to drop it.

"Uh-huh."

Luke glanced down at her, not reading the obvious lie she'd just spoken. "Yeah. We had it our first date. She loved it. I'm this close to becoming vegan, but I just can't give up my sashimi."

"You going to let me have a bite of that?" Lela asked from Henry's side, probably not liking her sidelined role in the conversation.

He looked down at the loaded hot dog still in his hand. Without hesitating, the woman leaned over, opening her mouth in a bold way, and took a bite from the end.

A move that any other time probably would have been a welcome and appreciated act by him and any other hot-blooded guy. But right then, it felt just...uncomfortable. He risked a glance past the woman to find — sure enough — Benny watching the entire thing.

She met his gaze and raised her brows as if to say, *Really?*

Well, it wasn't like he'd asked the woman to do it, had he?

Lela, however, was now licking the mustard off her top lip, and he forced himself to look away.

And he'd thought coming along to the stupid date had been a bad idea. Asking Lela, a woman that he knew would annoy the hell out of Benny, might have been even worse.

Why had he chosen her instead of any other nameless woman he'd gone out with in the past week?

Someone might say it was a form of punishment, some way at getting back at the woman who so evidently preferred Luke to him. But that was ridiculous. He had made it clear they should only be friends. That she *should* be with Luke.

Benny rolled her eyes now and grabbed Luke's hand, lacing her fingers with his. It was hard to miss the softening on Luke's face as he smiled back at her before lifting her hand and pressing a kiss to it.

Another punch to the stomach.

"There's no way I can eat all these on my own," Lela said and bit into one of the nachos. "Here." Before he could say anything, she was pushing a cheesy chip his way, and he barely had time to open his mouth. Her finger reached out and dabbed at his mouth. "Sorry. You missed some."

It was a trick from the same book he'd once tried to teach Benny. And he had to admit, it was kind of…annoying. From the look of open disgust he saw on Benny's face a second later when he turned to see if she'd caught the moment, which she had, of course, she appeared to agree.

Although it didn't stop her from picking up her churro and feeding a bite to Luke. Benny one-upped them all when she leaned over and removed the cinnamon sugar from his lips.

With a kiss.

For some reason, the superficiality of the whole thing suddenly made him furious. At the game, at Benny for playing it, and at men like him who thought women had to play. It was too much.

Benny shouldn't have to sell herself out for anyone.

He waited until she excused herself to use the restroom, waylaying her outside the door before she could go in. The image of her kissing that sugar off Luke's lips permanently emblazoned in his brain.

"What are you doing out there?" he asked, his tone harsher than he'd expected. He took a breath in and out, trying to explain. "Feeding him and kissing him like that? It's a little desperate, don't you think?"

"Really? You're going to accuse *me* of desperation after you asked out Deep Throat out there. I almost threw up right then."

He acted like he hadn't heard her, unable to fully understand the anger and jealousy roiling in his gut. "And what's with all the makeup? I thought you abhorred the whole glamazon thing. And now you're dressing like someone else entirely?"

Her face went a deep shade of red. "Are you kidding?" she practically shouted. A few people passing them paused and looked over, and she lowered her voice. "Everything I'm doing—how I dress, how I act—is because you *told* me to. And now you're judging me?"

Of course he'd told her all of that. He'd been an idiot and hadn't realized then the utter perfection that was Benny Sorensen.

He raked a hand through his hair, trying to understand what he wanted to say. "Okay, so maybe I did. But I was wrong. Luke should be able to appreciate how great you are without all that."

Luke should be able to see past it to the inner strength and beauty that was Benny.

She put her hands to her head as if to calm herself down and then returned them to her sides, her hands now balled in fists. "I don't understand where this is coming from. This was what we were working for. And now that Luke and I are finally getting to know each other, you're springing this on me? Whatever *this* is."

He laughed in derision. "Getting to know each other? Is

that what you're doing? Because as I recall, up until Saturday, he was convinced you loved—and were quite adept at—playing golf. And sushi—how long are you going to pretend you like that? Up until the wedding? Maybe after the first child is born? I hardly think what you two are doing is being honest with each other."

"That's the most sanctimonious bunch of BS I've ever heard. What would you know about honesty? Coming from a man who was lapping up the same crap from Lela a few minutes ago, your words lack any real meaning. *That's* the type of woman you want to spend the rest of your life with?"

"I'm not the one looking for happily-ever-after, one person forever, yada, yada. That's you. I've been honest from the start about my expectations in a relationship. I'm just looking for fun. What's wrong with going out with someone who likes to have fun? Who doesn't look at every motive with cynicism like you do? Who doesn't judge people or try to hold them up to the lofty standards you expect? We're humans. Not cyborgs."

Okay, so maybe he'd gone too far with that last part, especially after seeing the way she'd flinched.

"You know what your problem is, Henry? You pat yourself on the back for being so honest. *I'm Henry, I don't do commitment,*" she said, dropping her tone to imitate him. "You're not honest, though. You're just a coward. You are too afraid to try and have anything real with someone because you're worried they'll see that, deep down, you have no substance. That you're just a kid who never grew up. A woman, a relationship—they're just toys to you, something you play with until the next shiny thing comes along. Isn't that what you said all people were like? Looking for the best and brightest and newest? Well, I've got news for you, Henry. Real people aren't like that. They have more substance, more maturity to find something good, something special, and make it work. Geez. I was such a moron to ever listen to you."

Silence fell between them, her words weighing heavier on him than he'd have liked.

What had been his point in confronting her like this?

Because this? This conversation hadn't been what he'd intended.

"Is everything okay here?" They both looked over, startled, to see a security guard next to them.

Henry smiled, even though it pained him to do so. "Everything's fine."

The guy was looking at Benny now, waiting for her agreement. "Yes, we're finished," she said, leveling her gaze on Henry. "Nothing to worry about."

The guy nodded, and with a warning glance Henry's way, walked away.

Benny took a deep breath in. "Henry, I'm going to use the restroom, and when I get back to the seats, I'd...I'd really like it if you and your date could be gone."

He nodded. "Certainly. You two enjoy yourselves. I just want to ask one thing. If you're never honest with Luke about what you truly want, how is he going to really know you? Stop trying. You shouldn't have to."

Before they could start another argument and continue saying things they could never take back, he walked away.

He remembered her words, though. About his cowardice. His superficiality. And his own comments that hadn't been framed as eloquently as he would have liked.

Maybe...maybe it already was too late.

Chapter Nineteen

Benny sat back on her sister's couch the next day and listened to Daisy argue with the girls upstairs that they'd had just as long of a snuggle time as their brother, Paul, and to stop getting out of bed or there would be no TV time in the morning. It was a familiar argument and despite the tears and sadness that had hung over her all day, she smiled at the antics.

Benny had arrived at Daisy's about an hour before, not long after her sister had called to demand an explanation for why Benny had skipped family dinner. Daisy hadn't bought the story she'd given their mom about coming down with the stomach flu and insisted Benny come over that night to explain or she'd haul the three kids over to Benny's. It was as if ever since her sister had become a mom, she'd developed some radar that told her when something was wrong.

Even if Benny couldn't entirely understand what was wrong herself.

That explosion at the ballgame yesterday? To say it was unexpected was an understatement. That Henry had the gall to call her on her behavior had been infuriating. And what he'd said after had been…devastating.

So much so that after she'd returned to her seat and found that Henry had followed her advice and taken off with his date—something that she'd instantly regretted saying, along with a lot of others—she'd felt even worse. It hadn't been hard to beg off after the game, pleading she wasn't feeling well, even though she knew that, like Henry had accused, she wasn't being fully honest. But she'd needed time to regroup.

Or fall apart.

And that's what she'd done for the past twenty-four hours—fall apart and try to figure out how everything had gone wrong. Why she felt so horrible.

A few minutes later, Daisy was on couch next to her. Waiting. "So what happened? Did you and Luke get into some sort of argument?"

Benny smiled a little wistfully. "Luke and I? Hardly. We have nothing to argue about. Being with him is so…easy."

"Then what's wrong? Why have you been crying all day— and don't try to deny it, I can spot the signs."

Well, they'd actually be kind of hard to miss, what with Benny's eyes and face as puffy as the Pillsbury Dough Boy, which was precisely why she'd avoided her family and dinner tonight, to avoid these very questions.

Benny sighed. Trying to figure out exactly where to start things. Because it had started much earlier than yesterday. More like the moment she'd make that deal with the devil.

So she jumped back, relaying to Daisy exactly what she'd been up to the past few weeks with the makeover, the clothes, the golf lessons. Stopping short of detailing the feelings that had developed out of nowhere for the wrong guy.

"So as I understand this, you and Henry have been working together to make you into someone else? Like a real-life Henry Higgins and Eliza Doolittle?" Daisy asked.

"Something like that, I suppose," Benny said almost

sheepishly.

"I see," Daisy said, but she sounded confused while also—knowing Daisy—a little hurt. "Why did you think you couldn't tell me this?"

Benny shrugged. "I guess I was a little embarrassed. I mean, you've never had to worry about catching a guy's attention. They're naturally drawn to you. I've never known how to act or talk around guys. Not that they were ever looking. I mean, I've never really been much to look at."

"What are you talking about? Benny Sorensen, you make it sound like you were some sort of golem or something. You have always been so funny and strong and independent. *And* pretty."

Benny snorted. "Come on, Daisy. I was a lot of things, but pretty was never one of them."

"Are you freaking kidding me? You have those amazing blue eyes, lashes I'd give my right leg for, and you've never had to worry about stuffing your bra. You're funny and smart, not to mention that you just have this way of feeling so… certain about everything."

Benny looked into her sister's dark eyes, pretty and hypnotic, full lips that easily smiled and beguiled. "Great big boobs and great eyes. Just what every girl wants to hear. Daisy, you have to know that you are, and always have been, the beauty of the family. You never had to try with guys. They just wanted you. I, on the other hand, couldn't get one to take a second look at me."

Daisy shook her head, still disbelieving. "Like who? I don't remember you ever even being interested in a boy when we were growing up."

"Scottie."

Daisy's mouth opened and then closed as she thought another moment. "The lifeguard?"

Benny nodded. "That summer, didn't you think it was odd

that I dragged myself to the community pool nearly every day with my pile of library books? Me, the girl who hated wearing a swimsuit and usually shunned the sun? I was there because I hoped that maybe, just maybe, Scottie would look at me and see me as someone he might…like."

"Why didn't you ever tell me? I would never have dated him had I known you liked him."

"It didn't matter. He didn't want me."

"That's not fair. Benny, think about it. He and I were both eighteen. You were…what? Fourteen? I don't think Scottie would have dismissed you because you weren't his type, but because you were still a kid. You know, when we were dating, he always liked you. He thought you were funny and cute. Do you remember that time we took you with us to the Fourth of July fireworks show? We were all set to go and you were in lying on the couch reading a book. It was his idea to bring you along. And why? Because he liked you. Maybe not the way you wanted, but with time and age, that could have changed."

Benny hadn't known any of that. Especially about the Fourth. She'd been certain that Daisy had dragged her with them because she felt sorry for her. "He really thought I was cute? You're not just saying that to try and make me feel better?"

"You were cute. You *are* cute. There is nothing to make up. Which is bringing me to my second question. Why did you think you had to change at all? I mean, come on, Benny. You're the success here. Out of the two of us? You've always been so smart and independent, knowing what you wanted and then setting out to get it. You're a doctor, for crying out loud, and everyone is so proud of you, me included. But what can anyone say about me? I'm the failure of the family. I didn't get good grades in school and never really knew what I wanted to do when I grew up. Two months pregnant with Jenna, I dropped out of college before I even completed my degree to get married to Leo. Being pretty only goes so far. Now I'm divorced and, other than three of the most amazing kids on the planet, what do I have to show for myself? If anyone needs a makeover here, it's me."

Benny had never ever thought of her sister as a failure. But hearing Daisy say all of that, she could see her sister believed it. Daisy thought Benny was the success. It was like her world was being flipped upside down.

"Daisy, you are not a failure, and I'm so sorry that you could ever believe that. You are smart and warm and have the biggest heart of anyone I know. You also have your own talents. You started over with nothing, financially wiped out, and over the past year you have found a job you love, moved you and the kids out of our parents' home and into a place you're paying for on your very own, and your kids are bright and smart and happy. You are a success."

They looked at each other for a moment before Daisy reached forward and pulled Benny into a hug. "You are, too. Don't sell yourself short."

This time, the tears that filled Benny's eyes weren't because of her own pain, her own self-pity, but in realizing that she wasn't the only one who'd thought she wasn't good enough.

Who would have thought that Daisy could ever have been jealous of *her*. It seemed insane.

Tears wiped away, Daisy studied her again. "So…is it Henry you want?"

That had come out of nowhere. "What?"

"Don't play coy with me. I've seen you two together. We all have. It's clear you guys are crazy for each other. What you're doing with this Luke guy—perfect dream guy or not—is beyond me. Is that why you're upset? Did something happen with Henry?"

"You could say that." She dropped forward, covering her

face with her hands. "There may have been a few more things we practiced together."

Daisy sat openmouthed as Benny detailed the first kiss she and Henry had shared on her couch followed up with the totally unexpected but heart-stopping kiss out in the garden at their parents' on Sunday. Not to mention last night's horrible fight.

There was a moment of silence as Daisy continued to process.

"Are you going to say anything? Because I feel like a totally horrible person right now, having said those things to Henry. Half of them weren't even really true. Then there's the utter crap he said to me."

More silence as her sister studied the ceiling.

"What? What are you not saying?"

"I think both of you embellished things a bit, but I also think there was some truth in each of your comments."

Benny blinked. "Wait. Whose side are you on?"

"Yours. Always yours. It's just that…Henry does have a point. If you're not being yourself—not being the same outspoken, strong-minded person who I love and appreciate, then you *aren't* being honest. How can you know if you're right for each other if you can't tell Luke something as simple as the fact that you hate sushi?"

"I *will* be honest with him. Just like with the golf, in time I will…" She trailed off. It was hard to hold on to a position that you were beginning to doubt yourself. "Okay, but the thing is, Henry told me to do all this—be this person who licks her lips, bats her eyes, pretends avid interest in anything her date says—and it's a tad hypocritical now for him to chew me out for following his advice."

"Yes…Henry. That leads me to the other question. Why was he so outraged by it all? If he is 'just a friend' and not interested in you, why does he feel so strongly about seeing you feed a churro to your date?"

"I haven't the faintest idea."

"Don't you?" her sister asked, smiling. "Because I think that maybe Henry is feeling something stronger for you than friendship. But because of this distorted view you have of yourself and your own value, you've convinced yourself that Henry could never be interested in someone like you. The thing is, until you tell him the truth about how you truly feel, put it all out there, how will you really know?"

"Know how I feel?"

Her sister just smiled.

Was Benny that transparent? Because the truth had been hitting her over the head for the past couple of weeks, but she'd refused to accept it. She studied her hands. "That I love him."

"Yeah, you dope. That you love him. Have you seen him at all since last night?"

Benny shook her head. "No, I've been hiding out in my bedroom all day up until now."

"Chicken."

Benny laughed, even though the prospect of doing what her sister was proposing—telling Henry that she loved him—had her absolutely terrified.

She came to her feet, already feeling the tiniest bit hopeful.

"Heading home already?"

"I've got a lot of thinking to do. A few people to speak to."

One person she *needed* to speak to. Needed to tell how she really felt, now that she was ready to recognize it herself.

• • •

Henry had been stalking his front door, listening for the sound of the elevator all day with the hopes of catching a glimpse of

Benny.

He felt horrible for how things had gone last night, for things that were said. And he needed to know whether she finally came clean to Luke about everything. Let him truly see who she was.

Even if that prospect completely terrified Henry.

Because Luke was everything that Benny wanted. A true hero who was compassionate and honorable, not at all superficial or—how had she described Henry? With no substance. There was nothing stopping them from being crazy happy together.

And so what? So she'd be happy. Henry had been perfectly happy before Benny Sorensen came into his life, and he'd continue to be happy long after she rode off on that priggish white horse with Saint Luke.

He was happy, damn it.

Someone knocked on the door, bringing his pacing to a halt. He was certain that he hadn't heard the elevator. Henry sauntered to the door, curious.

It was Benny.

He opened the door, noticing her flushed face and her heavy breathing. Had she taken the stairs to the tenth floor?

"Hey," she said breathlessly.

That's it? Okay, he could be casual, too. "Good evening."

"Can I come in? I promise I won't yell at you or insult you," she said in a tone that was almost…upbeat.

"Of course."

He stepped aside to let her in and shut the door. Had he imagined the evening before? Or put too much weight on their words, spoken in anger? He was new at this 'just friends' stuff. Maybe blowups like that were par for the course.

"Is everything okay?" He studied her face, finally noticing the red-tinged, swollen eyes. She'd been crying? "What happened, did something happen with Luke?" he demanded, more abruptly than he'd intended.

"No," she said and smiled slightly. "Nothing like that. I, uh…well, I've been doing some soul-searching since our talk yesterday. And after a conversation with Daisy today, I've reached a few realizations."

He nodded, trying not to feel alarmed. "Do you want to have a seat?"

"No. I don't think I could sit right now. I'm too nervous. I just need to get this off my chest." She took a few steps closer, her gaze on the floor, as if gathering her thoughts. "The past few weeks have really surprised me. Not just because I liked my haircut or my new clothes, or the attention I suddenly was getting. It surprised me because I found myself actually enjoying one more unexpected thing…spending time with you." She looked up now, meeting his gaze. "I like hanging out with you."

She couldn't like at him like *that*. All soft and hopeful. It was playing havoc with his head. He swallowed but remained still as she went on.

"Whether it's watching television from my couch, getting golf instructions at the crack of dawn, or watching my brothers beat the crap out of you…I enjoy my time with you. You make me laugh, sometimes at myself, sometimes at you. Then last Sunday, when we kissed on the garden bench, I—I lied when I agreed with you about it being a mistake. Kissing you was one of the truest moments in my life. Because sometime in the past few weeks, I went and fell in love with you. Not with Luke, with you," she said, her voice trembling at the end as she continued to gaze at him, her blue eyes bright and hopeful. "And I think that you feel the same way."

Whatever Henry had expected her to say to him tonight, he hadn't expected this and he struggled to comprehend.

She loves me?

This crazy, complicated, and beautiful woman thought

she loved him. The unexpected joy and exhilaration he felt was immediate and surprising. But it didn't last long, as the shadow of doubt followed just as swiftly.

Benny only *thought* she loved him. But she'd also thought she loved Luke up until this moment.

Love was fleeting. It didn't last.

Especially where it concerned him. He just wasn't a lovable guy. Nor did he think he was capable of loving someone, especially someone like Benny, with the devotion they deserved.

But the last thing he'd wanted in all of this was to hurt her. To have to pretend that hearing her say she loved him hadn't been about the best thing in the world to hear.

He flexed his jaw, trying to think of what to say, what words he could utter that wouldn't completely crush the spirit of the woman before him.

"Benny. I…I've really enjoyed our time together as well. More than you could know. In the short amount of time we've known each other, you've become the best friend I've ever had. And that friendship is so important to me that I would hate more than anything to lose it. To lose you." His voice cracked at the end and he cleared his throat, trying again. "And it's for that reason, I can't return those words. Those feelings."

It ripped his heart out to say that, especially when her face, so bright and hopeful before, seemed to fall, her eyes pooling with tears that clung to her lashes.

"Henry. Don't do this," she said, shaking her head. "Don't push me away because you're afraid. I need you to look at what's in front of you. At what we can have. Yes, it's scary to let yourself feel those things, to love someone, to give yourself over to that feeling of not knowing what can happen, but loving each other can also be a miracle. It can be the most amazing thing we could share. You just need to let yourself fall."

"I—" he stopped, not trusting himself to say anything

more, nor did he think he could, as his throat seemed to be closing, shutting off air.

She studied him for one long, painful minute. Then, he saw it. The moment she gave up. When she knew.

He fought the urge to go to her, to hold her, to tell her what she needed to hear. But something stopped him, some kernel of doubt that told him that whatever pain he felt now would be nothing compared to the pain of losing her love later.

Instead, he watched as she lifted her chin almost defiantly, nodding slightly, and walked out the door, letting it close softly behind her.

No slamming, no yelling, just quiet acceptance.

Henry didn't know how long he stood there, staring at the door. Hoping that she'd come back and tell him that being friends would be enough. But, of course, the door remained closed. The place eerily silent.

A dark cloud seemed to be hovering over him. A dredging sense of sadness that he just couldn't shake. When he'd entered this bargain, he'd thought only to get Benny off his back and ensure he didn't do anything to risk getting that account at work. He hadn't expected to have these feelings for her.

He'd meant what he said. He'd never cared as much for any woman in his entire life. And somehow he'd managed to mess that up.

He glanced over at the monstrous black piano in the corner of the room. Benny had asked him once if he played, and he'd answered vaguely. There actually had been a time when he was a kid when he enjoyed playing the piano, losing himself in the music, the melody. He'd expressed his emotions through the songs he played. It was funny, because for so long he'd balked at the lessons his mother made him take, lessons he was certain had only been a way for her to get him out of her hair.

Which was why when she'd passed last fall, it had been surprising to find that of all the things that had been donated and passed through the estate, the piano was the one thing she'd directed in her will to go to him. He'd nearly sent it to the landfill. Even thought about taking a sledgehammer to it in epic fashion. But he'd kept it. For what reason, what purpose, he didn't know.

But right now, it seemed his fingers were itching to finally touch the keys. To express his warring emotions with music.

He pulled out the bench and slid behind the instrument. He didn't make any movement to touch the keys at first, simply staring at them. He knew the surface would be clean and polished thanks to the efforts of his maid.

Taking a deep breath, Henry settled his fingers over the keys, positioning them as the instinct to play started to kick in. Would it be like riding a bicycle? Would he feel what came next without having to think too much about it?

He pressed a few keys, the sound strange but welcoming. It took him only a few more strikes before he relaxed his shoulders and let his fingers move across the keys on their own. He closed his eyes.

Why had he waited so long?

Because he hadn't wanted to be reminded of those feelings from long ago. Those feelings of abandonment. Of feeling unloved. Unwanted.

Maybe, just like him, his mother hadn't been capable of loving someone. Not entirely. And maybe this piano had been, in her way, a peace offering to him. An apology of sorts.

He couldn't possibly know what had gone through that woman's mind, and maybe he was being fanciful, but his conclusion felt right.

Maybe there was room for a little forgiveness for his mother after all. And hopefully, one day, maybe Benny would feel the same toward him.

Chapter Twenty

Bright and early Monday morning, Benny sat in the corner chair in Luke's office, sipping her coffee. She'd been sitting there for twenty minutes already, and it was a test of her will not to stare obsessively at the clock as she waited for his arrival.

But she needed to get this off her chest before she could move on. Move on to pretending that her life was going to be okay now that Henry wouldn't be in it. Pretending until the pretense eventually became reality.

And she felt like she could breathe fully once again.

It wasn't until ten to eight that Luke finally appeared in the door. "Benny? Well, good morning, beautiful. This is a nice surprise." He walked in, accepting the cup of coffee that she held out for him and took his seat. "Are you feeling better?"

"I'm doing okay." Luke had actually called and checked in on her briefly last night, but she'd kept the call short, not trusting herself to get into things with him on the phone without bursting into tears. Besides, this needed to be done in person.

He seemed to suddenly recognize her fatigue as his face clouded over with concern. "You sure you're okay?"

He really was a great guy. Why hadn't she fallen in love with him?

She smiled. "Let's just say that whatever is bothering me isn't physical."

"Okay…so what seems to be the trouble?"

"It's just that—well…wow. This is harder than I thought." She leaned forward, trying to gather her thoughts. "Let's just say that over the past few weeks, I've learned a lot about myself. About who I am. About what I need to be happy."

Luke looked confused, but he nodded, waiting for her to go on.

"I don't know if you knew this, but when I started working at the clinic, I kind of had a bit of a crush on you." Luke grinned, but she couldn't let her embarrassment stop her. "But as you may recall, I struggled with how to talk with you or approach you or even be seen as anyone other than a klutz. I was sure the only way you were going to be interested in me is if I changed everything about me. So much so that I don't even know if what you like about me is because of who I am—or who I've pretended to be. Who I thought you wanted me to be."

"I don't think I understand." He shook his head in confusion. "I think you're wonderful."

He wasn't making this any easier on her. "Tell me something. When did you first consider asking me out? When did you first really look at me as someone you might be interested in?"

Luke scratched his head. "I don't know. Maybe when you brought me that first cup of coffee."

She nodded. "You realize that I'd been working here for about two months by that point. What was it about that particular moment that changed things for you? Was it because I'd cut my hair, layered on lipstick and makeup, bought some new clothes? Was that why I suddenly became more attractive to you? Finally caught your attention?"

His forehead creased in confusion. "No. I mean, I don't know about you changing your hair or any of that. It was just that…well, before, you always seemed to run away from me. I didn't think you even liked me, frankly. But that day, you actually spoke to me. And we talked. And after that you just seemed…more confident."

Benny hadn't necessarily expected Luke to admit he was so superficial as to only have seen her, really seen her, until after she'd had the makeover. She'd thought he'd be evasive or uncertain until she pointed it out to him. This, however, was unexpected. "When we talked? You mean when I pressed you to talk about your interests, about golf?"

He paused. "I don't remember what we talked about, but I was flattered that you actually sought me out. Finally had a conversation with me. Not that I hadn't noticed the way you were suddenly dressing differently, or that you were wearing your hair differently. But before, you were kind of…unapproachable. And then you suddenly weren't. And sure, I thought the changes were great. However, I've dated attractive women before; I don't always necessarily ask them out for second dates. Or ask them to meet my parents. We just seem to have so much in common, have the same interests."

"What would you think if I told you that I haven't been very up front with you? Maybe even a bit…misleading."

"I don't think I follow."

"Okay. Let's start with the sushi. I loathe it. The look, the smell, the taste and consistency. Most of the time, I prefer my seafood well cooked or slathered in mayo on a sandwich. And up until a few weeks ago I hadn't owned an eyelash curler, let alone used one. Then there's golf, a sport I only took up in th first place because I wanted to impress you."

He looked thunderstruck. "Why would you do all that?"

"I guess I wasn't convinced that you'd find me interesting enough or pretty enough just...being me. But over the past couple of days, as we've grown closer, I've come to realize that you aren't really getting to know the real me. That for so long I wasn't even sure if the real me was worth getting to know." She held up her hands as he looked like he was going to disagree. "I know, that sounds really pathetic. But it was true. It's only now that I'm finally able to recognize that maybe the old Benny wasn't so bad after all. The real Benny would have told you she hated sushi and told you she didn't know how to golf or think it was a very interesting sport."

"You think I wouldn't have liked you if you'd told me these things? That I'm so superficial that I'd have rejected you?" He actually looked affronted. Rightfully so. "That's crazy."

"It is crazy. Which is why I think that until I'm more comfortable in my own skin, confident in who I am, you and I should probably take a step back. Maybe just try being friends for a while."

He was staring beyond her shoulder, as if still processing what she'd said. He was going to need time. And she was okay with that. She needed it herself.

She came to her feet. "I am sorry for leading you on like this, Luke. I really am." And she was, even if she'd had the best intentions. "I hope that, maybe with time, you and I can become friends. Because you're a really, really great guy."

He nodded, finally meeting her gaze. "I'd like that," he said and smiled. Not a bright, all is forgiven smile, but it was slight and sincere all the same.

The weight she'd been feeling these past few days—likely the guilt for her deception—was suddenly gone and she felt the tiniest bit better. It was good to finally be honest with people again.

"Okay," she said, returning his smile. "I'll catch you later."

She stopped short a few feet outside his door, however, when she nearly ran into Roz. For a moment, the woman's eyes widened, and she looked slightly uncomfortable.

"Morning, Dr. Sorensen," she said stiffly.

"Morning, Roz," Benny returned. She had some suspicions as to whether the woman had overheard her conversation but it didn't bother her. It wasn't like her feelings for Luke had ever been a secret around the office. Or what she thought she'd felt for him anyway.

The woman didn't rush away as Benny expected, though, instead taking a moment to study Benny as if for the first time. Then just before it became awkward, Roz nodded briefly with something that almost seemed like…approval, and walked away.

Benny shook her head, not even trying to understand what happened but feeling a sense that she'd somehow finally gained Roz's approval.

She continued to her office, relieved to finally reach the sanctuary. She shut the door and sank back against it, processing her morning.

Hearing Luke describe how it was her finally having the confidence in herself to speak to him that first brought her more firmly onto his radar confirmed what Daisy had been saying. Benny had been selling herself short for too long.

She hadn't realized that maybe being herself was enough.

Not to say she was going to do a complete 360 and revert back to wearing scrubs on a daily basis or not giving a hoot about her appearance. But she could see now that by eschewing those things, she'd been hiding. That she had been the tiniest bit afraid that people would think she was trying to be something or someone she wasn't. That she was a fraud.

She'd been wrong. There wasn't anything wrong with wanting to look her best. With wanting to feel a little pretty. It made her feel good about herself, gave her confidence in ways she hadn't appreciated before.

So even though half the crap that Henry had dished out might have been completely moronic, half of the crap had actually also been...right.

Henry.

Her heart felt heavy when she conjured his face. His voice. His touch.

Tears swiftly swelled but she whipped her hands up to wipe them away.

Stop.

She couldn't break down again or she might not be able to hold herself together. It had taken every ounce of her strength to get out of bed this morning and push him and the memory of his rejection to the back of her mind.

But it didn't mean she didn't feel the pain.

The only solace she took from the evening was that she'd laid out her feelings, told him everything. She'd been honest with him. Even if he wasn't able to say the same things back.

She sniffled and took in a deep breath.

There was one more thing she had to do to fully move on. To protect herself from the pain she'd experience every time she saw Henry, whether alone or with another woman. She glanced at her watch. She had two minutes left to still do it.

Pulling her cellphone out of her pocket, she dialed the number she'd thought she wouldn't need again for a very long time.

Voicemail.

She took a breath. "Hi, Vivienne. It's Benny Sorensen. I need your help again. I'm putting my place back on the market."

• • •

It was nearly noon on Saturday when Henry stumbled from his apartment with a bag of garbage, the remnants of a large — albeit quiet — party he'd had last night to try and fill the void that had taken a permanent place in his life since Benny had walked out his door the week before.

It was like she'd disappeared off the face of the planet.

But she was safe, he knew, having texted her Tuesday when he still hadn't seen or heard from her only to be told in a short text she was staying at Daisy's for the week.

It still hadn't stopped him from cricking his neck every morning and every evening when he reached the parking garage, hoping for a glimpse of her or her car so he'd know she was back. He couldn't help stepping off the elevator and wondering if he'd spot her, maybe getting her mail or getting some things from her place. But…nothing.

So he'd tried to fill his time with dates and parties and evenings out with his friends, anything to take his mind off the fact that he missed her.

He missed Benny. He missed her smile, her brilliant blue eyes, her sharp wit and way of cutting through the bullshit, the way she made him laugh, the ways she smelled and tasted… the list was endless.

Hell. He drew his hand through his hair. This entire week hadn't gone anywhere near how it should have. With the letter from the home owners' association confirming that all complaints against him had been withdrawn and there was no risk in the near future of any eviction, he was in the clear with the tabloids — and with the clients of his new big account. Combined with the satisfaction of landing that account and the nomination for best ad campaign, he should be on cloud nine.

Not feeling so totally lost.

He shoved the garbage bag down the chute and headed out, only to be completely taken aback to find Benny just a few feet way, on her way out of her place.

When had she come home?

She looked as stunned to see him as he probably did at seeing her. Another woman was with her, someone he didn't recognize in a navy pantsuit and with a clipboard in her arms. A bit formal for a Saturday.

"Benny. Hey. You're back," he said, suddenly at a loss for anything clever or witty to say.

"Oh." Her eyes darted from him, looking nervous. "I was just leaving, actually."

She looked good. Tired, but good, if the shadows under her eyes were any indication.

"Hi, I'm Vivienne," the woman at Benny's side said too cheerfully, taking his hand in a firm shake. "Are you another resident?"

"Henry lives in the three-bedroom next door."

"Really," the woman said with a calculated gleam in her eye. "Why don't I leave you my card, then."

Her card?

He must have looked confused, because the woman laughed as she placed a card in his hand. He glanced down at it just as she clarified. "I'm a real estate agent. Dr. Sorensen has hired me to help get her place listed and on the market. You know, I have quite a number of clients who are interested in getting into this building, and they'd be positively rabid if they heard you were putting your place up on the market. How many square feet did you say you had?"

"I didn't." On the market? Benny was moving? He looked at her accusingly now. "I hadn't realized that Dr. Sorensen was moving out. In fact, since it looks like you two are finished, maybe I could have a minute with Dr. Sorensen."

This time Benny raised her eyes to meet his. "No. I'm afraid I have an appointment I have to make."

Really? She was going to play it this way? He looked at

her in accusation. Who was the coward now, he wanted to ask, but he bit back the accusation.

Although what exactly he hoped to say or tell her in privacy he didn't know. Nothing that hadn't already been said. Nothing that he *could* say.

The agent seemed to finally sense the tension in the air as she looked back and forth between them. "I can wait out here, if you two need—"

"That's not necessary," Benny assured her. "Henry, I really do have to go. I think we've said everything there is to say, don't you?"

"I suppose." Unless you counted the fact that he missed her and this distance was causing him all sorts of misgivings and doubts.

He just wanted her here. He wanted things the way they were. Her the way she was. And now, if she was actually putting this place up for sale, that wasn't going to happen. Things were really…over.

She nodded, almost looking disappointed at his response. "Why don't I walk you down," she said to her Realtor, already dismissing him.

"Okay. It was nice meeting you, Henry. Don't hesitate to call me if your real estate needs change," the woman said, nodding to her card still in his hand before following Benny back down the hall.

"Benny."

She stopped and turned, waiting for him to say something.

What was he doing? What was he going to say that would stop her from leaving? He didn't know, he just was having a hard time seeing her walk away again.

"You'll let me know if you need anything more, won't you? Maybe a hand with the move?"

"I think I've got it all covered, but thanks. Good-bye, Henry."

The words, so final, were a kick in the gut.

With that, she turned and continued the rest of the way to the elevator. He wanted to shout something more. He wanted to ask her—no, beg her—to stop. To please reconsider. To... not leave him.

But he'd realized long ago that he couldn't stop someone from leaving.

There were just some things he couldn't control. But he *could* limit the amount of power, of control, he gave people over his emotions.

By making it clear to Benny there could be nothing more between them than what they already had, he'd protected himself—and her—from the inevitable heartache that would follow.

His dad had suffered so much after leaving Henry's mom that he'd never recovered again.

Henry wouldn't make that same mistake. He couldn't. And someday, Benny would thank him.

Chapter Twenty-One

"No one is going inside empty-handed. You're all going to help me carry something," Daisy said after pulling into their parents' driveway just after one on Sunday, the following afternoon.

The doors were thrown open, and three kids hopped out with boundless energy and excitement that Benny couldn't help but envy.

It was the big day. The happy celebration of her father's life, a party for which everyone her father loved and cared for was arriving en masse to surprise him—including his brother and his family from Wisconsin. It was a day to be happy. Grateful.

Not like her heart had been pulverized and then shoved back into her chest, raw and aching.

But as Daisy had reminded her, it would get easier.

Benny was holding on to that promise. It was what pulled her through every morning this long week after laying her heart out and having Henry stomp on it.

Kate and Payton met them at the door and took some of

the pans from their arms.

"Any word on what Dad is up to?" she asked her sisters-in-law.

The two women looked at each other and grinned. "Cruz, Dominic, and your dad are all stuck in a boat in the middle of the lake, last we heard," Kate said. "Not intentionally. I think it's fair to say we have a couple more hours to get everything together before the guests start to arrive."

"Whose idea was it to go on this father-son fishing expedition anyway? None of them fish."

Payton looked sheepish. "I hadn't realized that when I booked the package. It had just seemed so perfect at the time, and I really wanted to make a good impression for Father's Day."

Benny couldn't help but smile at the image of the three men stuck elbow to elbow on a fishing boat in the middle of nowhere. "How did they get stranded, anyway?"

"Something about the engine. They radioed the outfitting company and they're sending someone to get it up and running—and gave us a heads-up as well in case we grew worried."

In the kitchen, they set all the platters down while shrieks from the kids running wildly in the backyard carried inside. Curious to see how things had progressed since the rental company was to have dropped off the tables and chairs and tents, Benny and Daisy went out to the backyard to check things out.

It was beautiful.

When Payton had first mentioned the possibility of transforming the backyard for the party rather than renting out the church hall, Benny had been pessimistic. She'd envisioned cardboard tables and red-checkered tableclothes, maybe a barbecue in the corner. Something that would have been more appropriate for a casual family dinner rather than the scale of the party they'd been planning.

Instead, the area looked more immense and elegant than she'd thought possible. Several round tables had white tableclothes and linens and pretty but simple floral arrangements for a centerpieces. White wood chairs — rather than the metal ones from the church — completed the look, as did two small canopies covering the oblong tables at one end of the yard for the food. The final touch to the scene was the large square floor laid down for dancing, a must for her mom, where the kids were already dancing and spinning around.

"Where is Mom?" she asked.

"She and your Aunt Glenda are picking up your uncle and his family from the airport. She is so excited to surprise your dad with their arrival that she wouldn't allow anyone else to do it for her," Payton said.

Their dad's last living brother, Jansen, lived in Wisconsin, and even though the flight time was negligible, neither brother was keen on flying and Benny guessed that it had been at least four years since they'd last seen each other. It had probably been even longer since she'd seen her uncle Jansen's sons, and she was looking forward to catching up with them.

"Well, if you ladies aren't doing anything…" Daisy said in a voice that warned Benny they were all about to be hooked into some chore or another. "Although the caterers will be here in a couple of hours with the main entrées, I still have a couple hundred fresh homemade tortillas that need to be rolled out and cooked for the carnitas. Anyone willing to help?"

"We're willing," Kate said, while Payton looked a little less certain.

"Excellent. And to help get us moving along, I thought margaritas might be in order. Benny makes a mean margarita."

At that, the three women turned their attention to her. From the concern shadowing the eyes of both her sisters-in-laws, she had a strong suspicion that Daisy had shared a little of Benny's grief from this past week. And it was only a matter of time before they pressed her for details, details that were going to be painful and humiliating.

She was definitely going to need a drink.

. . .

The sun was so merciless as it passed overhead at the zoo Sunday afternoon that even the snow cone he was finishing off for Ella couldn't cool him down. It was no small relief when they hit the sea lion exhibit and were able to walk into the cool, air-conditioned building.

Henry hadn't been to the zoo since his third-grade field trip and would have preferred to have never returned again had his sister not called him this morning and invited him along with her and Ella for an excursion. Morgan had claimed that Ella had asked for him to come, and although the prospect of massive crowds and hundred-plus-degree temperatures normally would earn an immediate no, he'd agreed. It beat sitting home and thinking about she who should not be named.

He and Morgan took a step back from the glass where Ella was pressed, waiting for the sea lion to return on its loop around the large tank, careful to keep her in their sights.

"You look tired. Another late night?" his sister asked him, not taking her eyes off Ella.

"Just the usual," he said, equally casual.

"Oh? With anyone I should know?"

Up to now, he hadn't had a real moment alone with his sister, and he'd been grateful, knowing that from the worried looks she gave him now that she would have a lot of questions. But ever aware of Ella's fondness for listening to every discussion and chiming in with her own questions and comments, she'd waited.

"Not that kind of night, sis. Just me and a few coworkers."

"I see." She was quiet again, and he knew the topic wasn't yet over. He waited. "You know, now that I've decided to take that book deal, I've been looking for a more permanent place for me and Ella. And the funniest thing happened yesterday. My Realtor called me about a few new listings, including some that popped up around your place. In fact, if I'm not mistaken, one of them was right next door to yours. Where Benny lives."

That was funny. Or perverse.

Best to act nonchalant. "Yeah. She's selling. But it's a one-bedroom. I hardly think it's something you would be interested in."

"No, and as much as I want to be somewhere closer to you now, I think the same building might be a bit much." She licked her strawberry ice cream cone and mulled something over. "But I am sorry to hear that Benny's moving out. I like her. Hate to see her go. How did that come about? I thought she bought that place just a few months ago."

This needling was torture when they both knew she was going to eventually get to it at some point. "Come on, Morgan. Ask me what you really want to know. You want to know if it had anything to do with the two of us."

"Okay. So the thought had crossed my mind, and taking into consideration your willingness to submit to scorching temperatures and masses of screeching kids for this little foray, not to mention the way the bags under your eyes are large enough for Ella to seek shade under, you can't blame me. I worry about you. So what gives?"

He chomped on a chunk of now melted ice and tossed the rest of the snow cone into a nearby garbage can. "The usual. She's looking for the declaration of love, the big commitment, happy-ever-after, the whole shebang. Stuff that I can't offer."

"Huh." She licked her cone again, barely stopping a drip

from reaching her hand.

He knew his sister. No way was she done. And the longer she stayed silent, the more jittery he was getting. Fine, he'd bite.

"You don't have anything to add? No helpful tips or an offer to analyze my dark demons and figure out why I'm such a tragic figure?"

She scrunched her nose. "Sheesh. You sound like my high school English teacher wanting to delve into that horribly depressing book…what was it? Oh. Ethan Frome. I can't remember. Did he die at the end? Or was he the one physically maimed forever?"

"I must have missed that one." He waved to Ella, who'd turned around with unadulterated delight after the sea lion passed right in front of her, looking almost like he'd smiled.

"Sorry, I've got nothing for you. Who am I to talk about happily-ever-after? But I've got Ella, and I think that's all I need."

That was a topic for debate, but since he wasn't in any position to critique her dating life without inviting the same, he stayed quiet.

It wasn't until they reached the polar bear exhibit that Morgan tried to broach the subject again. "It's actually too bad. Ella and I really liked Benny. And I could tell you did, too. I mean, don't get me wrong, neither of us know what a healthy, loving relationship looks like by any stretch of the imagination, but I'd venture to say what I saw between you two was closer to anything I could ever wish for. Maybe not exactly the gushy crap like in all those Disney shows you used to watch with me. But close. And the fact that she didn't hang on your every word earned her a few extra brownie points."

Yeah. Benny did tend to call him on his bullshit without blinking an eye. It had been a refreshing change, really.

"Did I mention that I met Ella's new teacher? She's pretty

cute, and I'm certain she's single. Maybe you might want to pick Ella up after school some time and check her out."

That was it? His sister had already moved on, not even a little more disappointed to see that the best woman he'd ever had the luck to spend time with had dumped his ass? Who this very moment might be still snuggled in bed with the humanitarian of the year—oh. Except that she was probably at her dad's big surprise party right now, celebrating the man's life. Maybe playing a game of Twister or badminton with her family.

Had she brought Luke with her? Was he, even now, in the middle of a scrimmage with her brothers, pretending they weren't out for blood?

The thought made him crazy sick with jealousy. And a little sad.

It should have been him.

He should be there.

He should be telling Benny she was beautiful, whether she was in scrubs and a ponytail or those silly slippers and her hoodie. Waiting for the next outrageous comment that would come from that lovely mouth.

Why had he ever told her that men liked women who hung on their every word, shared the same interests, even if they had to pretend?

Why had he thought she needed to be anyone else but herself?

She was perfect just as she was. Ponytail. No ponytail. Scrubs or no scrubs. Pj's or teddies or, preferably, nothing at all...

Ahead of them a little boy, no older than three, was balancing on the head of a statue of a bear. As expected, his foot gave out, and for a terrifying moment, he was sure the kid was going to crack his head open on the asphalt under him. But two arms reached out and grabbed the tyke before disaster could strike, and the man who Henry presumed was the kid's father easily slung the boy to his shoulders. The woman next to him wrapped her arm around him and smiled up at the two obvious loves of her life.

He watched as they mouthed the words *I love you* and continued in step to the next exhibit.

And more than anything else in the entire world he wished, right then, that he was that man. That Benny was that woman. That the two of them could smile at each other, each certain of the other's love.

That it would be forever.

Forever.

Something he had been so certain he couldn't offer to anyone. Or that someone could offer to him.

So he'd chosen to be alone, instead of embracing what he could have, for however long.

Chosen to never have another moment when Benny's hand rested perfectly in his, or she turned those clear, mischievous blue eyes to his and grinned, or said something so crazy and hilarious that he could only laugh and look forward to what she'd say next.

He'd said no. Said no to the *possibility* of forever. He'd said no, because what kind of guarantees were there in life of anything, least of all someone's continued love and affection?

Well, save for one exception.

Henry knew, without a doubt, that no matter what crazy thing that woman said or did, he would never stop loving her.

He loved Benny Sorensen. And he would love her until he could no longer draw breath. He wanted to wake up with her at his side every morning, and he wanted to end every night with her next to him—or under him or above him.

Wasn't that something worth risking any possible heartache on?

Because this past week had been hell. Pure hell. And if

this was his future, then what was the point of anything?

Only...he had really blown it. Pushing her away, making it clear that there could never be anything more than friendship between them. He'd been a complete schmuck. Too afraid to recognize what was right in front of his face. He was already head over heels in love with the woman. She'd been right. He was a coward.

But not anymore.

No matter if she—or her brothers, or even Luke—sent him packing, he had to let her know that she was the only one for him and he was certain he was the best man for her. He had to convince her that he loved her quick wit and sauciness, her refusal to bow out of an argument, that he didn't care if she wore ratty pajamas every day for the rest of her life, that he wanted her and only her.

"Hey, Morgan?" He looked back to where his sister was hand in hand with her wilting daughter. "You two ready to go? I have somewhere I need to be."

She didn't even blink. "Whenever you are."

• • •

Morgan smiled in bemusement as they pulled up in front of the house brightly decorated with balloons and party banners. The unmistakable sound of a mariachi band was coming from the backyard.

"Ella's still napping. Why don't you bound in and I'll go around the block a few times. Not that I wouldn't give anything to hear what you're about to say."

Henry climbed out, careful not to slam the door and risk waking his niece. He stood there for a minute, preparing himself to head inside to face whatever was going to come his way.

Benny was here. And the sooner he told her how he felt,

the sooner he could breathe a little easier. Or at least a little less painfully.

Entering the backyard from the side of the house, he followed the steps until he was on the lawn, looking out over a dozen tables overflowing with guests. The mood was happy and energetic as people laughed and visited with each other, some of them even dancing, and he tried to take heart in that energy, hoping that maybe it would make Benny more susceptible to what he was about to say.

He wandered around looking for a familiar face to ask the whereabouts of the woman he was here for. Hopefully they didn't want to bash his face in.

At one table a priest laughed with a group of older couples, all of them enjoying salt-rimmed margaritas. Something he could use about now after the oversweet, melted snow cone he'd had at the zoo. Benny's dad was the first person he spotted, seated next to another blond figure so similar in size and coloring he was left no doubt as to their relation. Henry didn't want to intrude there, though, so he moved on.

A small hand tugged on his, and Henry looked down to see Natalie, Benny's younger niece, staring up at him. Her hair was pinned up, and she was smiling at him like he was some kind of rock star. At least she was glad to see him.

"Hi, Natalie. I almost didn't recognize you, you look so grown-up. I was looking for your aunt Benny. Have you seen her?"

"She and Mama are in the kitchen."

"Thanks. Make sure you save a dance for me." That was, if he wasn't thrown out before then.

He climbed the stairs of the deck and slipped inside the house. Several more unfamiliar faces met his—from the logo on their aprons, he took them to be caterers. He squeezed past the crew working to fill bowls and trays with food at the dining table—only it was a larger and newer table than the one he'd seen on his last visit, and he recalled Benny telling him that Dominic had custom made it as a surprise.

The sound of laughter brought his attention to the kitchen. His heart felt like it was going to beat out of his chest as he saw her, standing with her sister placing candles across the surface of a cake.

Benny. The look of happiness and joy that radiated through her entire being was hard to miss as she threw her head back in laughter at whatever Daisy had said.

She was lovely.

Engrossed in conversation with her sister, she still hadn't noticed him, even as he drew close enough to reach out and touch her. Daisy caught sight of him, however, and instantly her eyes widened in surprise and then speculation as she glanced at her sister. They both waited for the moment when Benny finally looked up to see what had captured her sister's attention.

Their eyes met, and he saw a flicker of surprise as her eyes widened twice as big as Daisy's.

"Benny. Daisy."

Daisy stepped back. "I think I'll let you two have a minute—"

But Benny grabbed her sister's arm, keeping here there. "What are you doing here, Henry?"

"I'm here to see you, of course." He wouldn't be scared off by the sharp tone in her voice. He was due her frustration and anger.

Her eyes cut away from him to glance around the room. When she spoke, her voice was low and quiet so as not to be overheard. "I don't think this is the time or place."

"Maybe not. But there is something I need to say to you, and it can't wait. Not another day, another hour, even another minute." He took a step closer so that she was only a couple of feet away. "You called me a coward the other day. A coward who was afraid to try and have anything real with someone. That I had no substance. And you were right. I was a coward. I won't go into all the reasons that might have made me that way, afraid to be vulnerable—just know that I'm not afraid anymore. I know what I want, who I want."

She was so still, almost as if she was afraid to take a breath, and he smiled. "I want you. You, Benny Sorensen. A woman who loves with her entire being and who isn't weaker or more dependent because of it but is actually stronger. Who loves her family and friends, her job and her patients. You don't need to wear your hair a certain way or wear layers of makeup or sexy clothes to be attractive to anyone—although the dress you're wearing now is enough to give me a mild heart attack," he couldn't help adding. "You're lovely and perfect just the way you are, Benny, and I wouldn't have you change for anything, or anyone. Least of all me."

Benny had been slack-jawed during his speech, and now, as the room was so quiet—save for a few sniffles and the music thrumming through the windows and walls—she glanced down at the cake, not meeting his eyes.

He looked over at Daisy, who smiled and nodded at him, encouraging him to go on.

The words were there, in his heart and his mind, just waiting to be said. He swallowed and took a step forward, clearing his throat. When he was just inches from Benny, he tipped her face up with his hand. "What I'm trying to say is…I love you. I love and adore you and want to show you each and every day how happy you make me and how good our life is going to be as long as we're together. Whether we're here or following your passion on a golf course in Scotland"—he saw her mouth twitch into almost a smile—"or in Africa doing whatever you need to do to save the world, I'll be there to s. port you. And love you. Always loving you."

It was funny, now that he'd finally spoken the words,

he found it easier to say and believe in. Now he just hoped Benny believed the words he'd uttered.

Believed that she was *the one*, the only one, for him.

And that he was still the only one for her.

• • •

Benny had managed to get through most of the past couple of hours by pretending that Henry Ellison didn't exist and that the gnawing pain in her heart was merely indigestion from too much of Daisy's guacamole.

The last thing she'd ever expected was for Henry to be standing in her parents' kitchen while half a dozen pairs of ears listened to each and every word he spoke. Words so wonderful and perfect that she had to be dreaming.

Only…in her dreams she couldn't see and experience the warmth and humor in those deep brown eyes, or smell the heavenly and seductive scent of Henry's skin. She wanted nothing more than to kiss that slightly twisting grin right off his face, which with him just inches away would be so easy. But she had her own confession to make first.

"I shouldn't have said those things. Because if there's one thing I've learned in the past few weeks it's that you have so much to give, so much to share with people. You have a lot more layers under that easy grin and that pretty face than even you know. We both do."

He lifted his brow up. "Pretty face?"

"Don't pretend you don't know." But she smiled, unable to suppress the crazy joy and giddiness that were making her dizzy and breathless. She knew it was crazy to just let all her doubts slip away and accept that this was really happening, that what Henry said was true.

But she also knew that Henry wouldn't have said any of those things if they weren't true. He was and had always been honest with her from the start. Often brutally so. And if he was finally ready to accept what was in his heart, what she knew was in hers, then she wouldn't question it for even a minute.

Because that's what you do when you love someone.

You trust.

Her arm slipped so easily around his shoulders, and she couldn't stop the laughter that finally bubbled from her chest. Yes, she Benny Sorensen, ardent member of the cynics-'r'-us club, believed that she and Henry were going to have their happily-ever-after.

"Say it again."

He knew what she meant, and his arms wrapped around her waist, that sexy grin of his sliding in place. "I love you. Even when you are cracking nine irons against my skull, I'll still love you."

He didn't hesitate as he pressed his lips to hers. Lips that were sweet and tasted surprisingly like cherries as he crushed her against him.

Someone whooped next to her, and she realized it was Daisy, then another shout rang out that sounded an awful lot like her mother, and she smiled against his mouth.

"I love you, too, you know."

"I do. Now that we've gotten that out of the way," he said and took a step back, keeping his arm firmly wrapped around her waist, "let's get this cake lit. Because I saw a dance floor out there and it's calling your name."

"Oh, no." She shook her head and laughed, backing away from him playfully. "No, no, no. I don't dance, I told you. You already suffered one near concussion at my hands—do you want another one?"

He smiled smugly, and her heart tripped again in her chest. "I'll take my chances."

• • •

It was hours later, when the sun had finally sunk in a blazing halo of purples and pinks against the night sky and the twinkle lights that someone had spread around the backyard lit to life, when Henry finally got Benny out onto the dance floor.

Her mom and dad danced seamlessly under the night sky, as did Cruz and Payton, Dominic and Kate, Paul with Daisy, and Natalie and Jenna with each other. Even Morgan and Ella were dancing and having a great time.

As she'd promised Henry, her moves weren't quite as graceful or seamless, and she stepped on his foot at least eight times. But the moment in his arms was no less thrilling or fun when, despite her objections, he twirled her around until she couldn't catch her breath from laughing so hard.

Finally a slow song came on, and he pulled her close, his breath tickling the hair around her ear.

"I think dancing is one more thing we can add to that list of things you're going to need to work on with me."

His hand squeezed her waist, and he held her impossibly tighter. "There were actually a number of things I thought we might work on together," he said not so subtly.

She laughed and looked around her. "*Shh.* Someone might hear you."

He peered around. "I don't think anyone is even looking at us. In fact, maybe we could sneak away and start that tutorial sooner rather than later."

A thrill shot through her, and she melted farther into him. "Soon."

But for now she was just going to enjoy this moment. Here. Now.

With the man who loved her. Exactly as she was.

Epilogue

"You know, I think we should wait a week before we tell anyone," Benny said, running her fingers across Henry's belly, smiling as he sucked in and tried not to flinch. One thing she'd learned over the past couple of months was that Henry was surprisingly ticklish. Something that had come in handy a time or two.

He lifted her hand, holding it up so the early September sunlight pouring into his master bedroom glinted across the massive diamond that sat on her left ring finger. "What, are you saying this so you have time to swap this ring out for something better?"

She laughed. "Hardly. You—you did good," she said and smiled as she stared at the stone and the entire setting. Better than good.

When he'd actually gotten down on one knee last night and asked her to become his wife, she'd cried and laughed with absolute joy and happiness.

Life couldn't get better than this, she'd thought.

"Is it because you think they'll question our sanity in

getting engaged so soon?"

"Hardly. You remember the track record my family has when it comes to…hasty weddings," she said, Cruz and Payton's coming to mind with the win at less than a week. Real or not. Besides, as Henry had put it, once you know who you want to spend the rest of your life with, then there's no sense in waiting to get that life started. "No, I just wouldn't want to take anything away from Kate and Dominic's big news. I mean"—her voice rose several octaves higher—"having a baby! That's just simply amazing."

He dropped his arm so that both their hands rested, still entwined, over his heart. "You wouldn't be taking anything away. You know your family would want to share in this news with us. And maybe I can finally get your brothers to tone down the defense any time we play ball."

But he was smiling as he said this, especially since she had caught Henry throwing out a few moves of his own the last time, something that had earned a slight smile from even the ever-stoic Cruz. Henry was really enjoying having this new family as much as they were enjoying having a new punching bag.

The alarm, set for seven, went off, and Henry hit it with his free hand.

She breathed in a sigh. "I guess I should probably get in the shower. My day is going to be packed with all of those extra patients."

Patients that came from Luke's wide list, since, as of a month ago, he'd decided to go on another stint with Doctors Without Borders and needed to distribute those patients among the rest of the doctors in the practice. Not that she wouldn't miss him, even if it had been awkward in those initial couple of weeks after their talk, when he learned that Henry might have been more than just a golf instructor after all. But he'd taken it remarkably well and, in fact, had become a good friend.

"Would you like some company?" Henry asked and gave her a devilish grin.

"Not a chance. You'd only make me late," she said, although she made no move to get up from her cozy spot pressed up against Henry. "Besides, you have your own meeting to get to. Aren't you presenting the big campaign to the AirPro folks?"

"Not until after lunch. Which, if you recall, I'm having with my sister. Is it safe for me to tell at least her about our engagement?"

"Absolutely." Benny couldn't be more excited to make Morgan and Ella a permanent part of her family as well, having spent a lot of time with them both. And Paul, whether he'd admit it or not, was a tiny bit smitten with Ella, which was adorable. "Maybe she and Ella can come for dinner tonight, if they're free."

"I'll let her know."

They both were quiet, neither making any move to get up.

This was where she always wanted to be. She closed her eyes, savoring the moment. A couple seconds later, Henry was nuzzling her neck and she smiled.

He was really going to make it hard to get up and going.

"You sure you want to go take a shower right now?" he asked.

The swirling in her stomach said no. She hesitated, and Henry pressed his advantage home when he deepened his kiss, knowing just how she'd react.

"Maybe...maybe I might have just a little time after all."

"Babe, we have all the time in the world."

And with this man in her life, loving her so sweetly and honestly, she couldn't ask for anything more.

Acknowledgments

A huge thanks to the entire Entangled Publishing team, including Alycia Tornetta, Debbie Suzuki, Crystal Havens, Jessica Turner, Melanie Smith, Heather Riccio, Sara Brady, and so many others who provide their endless time and support to their authors.

Biggest hugs and kisses to my husband and kids who have gracefully accepted cereal as a substitute meal at least weekly.

And finally, to the readers, who are the reason I do this. Thank you.

About the Author

Ashlee Mallory is a *USA Today* Bestselling author of Contemporary Romance, Romantic Suspense, and Thrillers. A recovering attorney, she currently resides in Utah with her husband and two kids. She aspires to one day include running, hiking, and traveling to exotic destinations in her list of things she enjoys, but currently settles for enjoying a good book and a glass of wine from the comfort of her couch.

Ashlee loves to hear from readers. You can find her at any of the following links, so please feel free to drop her a line, or you can subscribe to her email list and keep updated with any news of upcoming releases, sales, and giveaways by clicking here: http://bit.ly/1lPwwE3

AshleeMallory.com

@ashleemallory

https://www.facebook.com/AshleeMalloryAuthor

https://www.goodreads.com/author/show/7912393.
Ashlee_Mallory

Find your Bliss with these great releases...

THE BAD BOY'S BABY
a *Hope Springs* novel by Cindi Madsen

Cam Brantley is the town's bad boy, a soldier, a protector, but *never* a dad. Until he returns home from military duty to discover the girl he had a one-night stand with, Emma, is now mom to a two-year-old girl with his eyes. Cam and Emma are both shocked to discover he truly wants his daughter in his life. But as the long-simmering heat between Cam and Emma reaches a boiling point, he'll have to work past his demons in order to be the man both girls need.

FROM FAKE TO FOREVER
a novel by Jennifer Shirk

Sandra Moyer's preschool is struggling, so she reluctantly agrees to let super-famous actor Ben Capshaw research a role there. Ben's always joking around, never serious, but there's something about the buttoned-up, beautiful Sandra and her young daughter that makes him want to take life more seriously. But Sandra won't trust him—what if it's all an act, research for the role? As the lines between make-believe and reality blur, Ben will have to decide if love is worth casting aside the role of his life for a new role...that could last a lifetime.

FALLING FOR HER ENEMY
a *Still Harbor* novel by Victoria James

Alex McAllister always dreamed of a life filled with family, but being abandoned at a young age left her wary of letting anyone in. Now that she's settled in Still Harbor, Alex is faced with the magnetic pull of Hayden Brooks, the handsome workaholic who claims he's the biological father of her adopted daughter. A paternity test is all that's standing between Alex and her dream, but Hayden's about to make the most shocking decision of his life, just in time for Christmas...